THE SNOW FELL THREE GRAVES DEEP

THE SNOW FELL THREE GRAVES DEEP

— VOICES FROM THE DONNER PARTY —

ALLAN WOLF

CANDLEWICK PRESS

Copyright © 2020 by Allan Wolf
Map illustrations copyright © 2020 by Sophie Kittredge

First edition 2020

Library of Congress Catalog Card Number pending
ISBN 978-0-7636-6324-7

20 21 22 23 24 25 LSC 10 9 8 7 6 5 4 3 2 1

Printed in Crawfordsville, IN, USA

This book was typeset in Caslon.

Candlewick Press
99 Dover Street
Somerville, Massachusetts 02144

www.candlewick.com

For Klaus

CONTENTS

PART FIVE
Closer to Heaven
January 17–February 28, 1847

PART SIX
Angels in the Snow
February 28–May 16, 1847

DONNER PARTY TRAIL 1846-1847

Columbia R.

Willamette R.

Oregon City

Continental Divide

ROCKY MOUNTAINS

SHOSHONE

ARAPAHO

Independence Rock

OREGON TERRITORY

Fort Hall

Vote to take Hastings Cutoff / Donner Party forms

Sublette Cutoff (new)

PAIUTE

Snyder killed / Reed banished

Great Salt Lake

Luke Halloran dies

South Pass

Humboldt (Mary's) R.

RUBY MTNS

Fort Bridger

MAIDU

Sacramento R.

Truckee Lake winter camps trapped

Old Hardcoop left behind

Salt Lake Desert

Eddie Breen accident

Lake Tahoe

Humboldt Sink

Circle Ruby Mtns

GOSIUTE

Cut road through Wasatch Mtns

Green R.

UTE

MIWOK

WASHOE

William Pike accident

WESTERN SHOSHONE

Sutter's Fort

San Francisco (Yerba Buena)

NISENAN

SIERRA NEVADA

Colorado R.

ALTA CALIFORNIA

MEXICO

PACIFIC OCEAN

Rio Grande

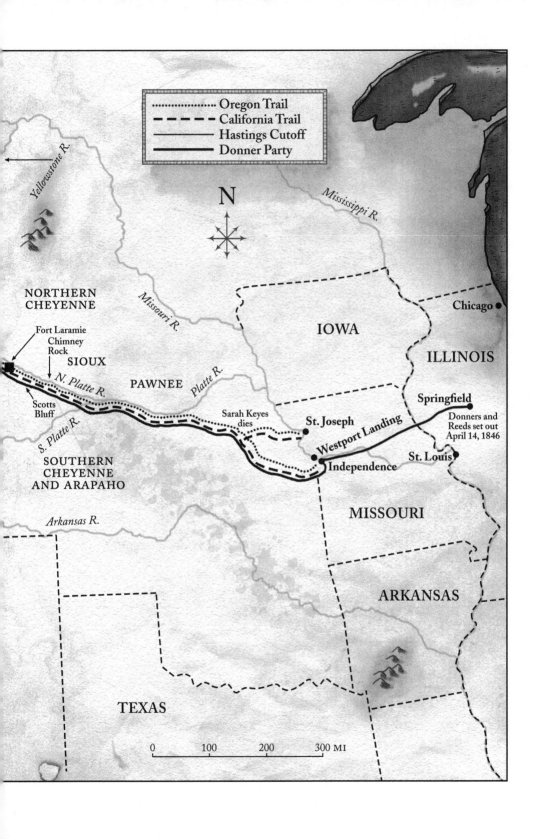

THE VOICES

— ❖ —

HUNGER: THE NARRATOR

PATTY REED: THE ANGEL

TAMZENE DONNER: THE SCHOLAR

JAMES REED: THE ARISTOCRAT

VIRGINIA REED: THE PRINCESS

LUDWIG KESEBERG: THE MADMAN

JEAN BAPTISTE TRUDEAU: THE ORPHAN

SALVADOR AND LUIS: THE SAVIOR AND THE SLAVE

PLUS

THE DIARY OF MR. PATRICK BREEN

&

SEVERAL OTHER RELEVANT DOCUMENTS

ADVERTISEMENT

Run March 26 and April 2, 1846
Sangamo Journal
Springfield, Illinois

WESTWARD, HO!
FOR OREGON AND CALIFORNIA!

Who wants to go to California without costing them anything? As many as eight young men, of good character, who can drive an ox team, will be accommodated by gentlemen who will leave this vicinity about the first of April. Come, boys! You can have as much land as you want without costing you any thing. The government of California gives large tracts of land to persons who have to move there. The first suitable persons who apply, will be engaged. The emigrants who intend moving to Oregon or California this spring, from the adjoining counties, would do well to be in this place about the first of next month. Are there not a number from Decatur, Macon county, going?

G. DONNER and others.   Springfield, March 18, 1846.

PROLOGUE

———◆———

HUNGER SPEAKS

None of this is my fault.

If you are looking to blame someone or something, then look somewhere else. Yes, I am Hunger. And in this story I am everywhere. I am in every stomach pang and every heartbeat. I am in every want. I am in every desire. Every dream and ambition. Even hope. For hope is born of Hunger. Even in the midst of the most sumptuous meal, I am there between bites. Hunger and abundance are constant companions. Two oxen connected by a common yoke.

But do not blame me for anything that happens in these pages. A single cell divides into two cells because it craves more. The unborn babe hungers unconsciously for consciousness. The soul hungers to become flesh—a wagon of blood and bone on which to ride. We cry so we might breathe. We open our eyes so we might see. We open a book so we might read. We read so we might know.

But do not blame me. I would not be speaking to you now if *you* did not hunger to know how the story unfolds. It is because of *you*, and your need, that I exist at all.

I have nothing invested. I am only Hunger. And Hunger has no choice. Just as the river has no choice but to flow and freeze. Just as the snow has no choice but to fall. And fall it will. But neither the river nor the snow have anything invested. They do not care. And neither do I.

Hunger does not make choices. Only humans can do that. So do not blame me. Do not blame Hunger. I am merely here to tell the tale.

PART ONE

—◆—

ALL IN THE GETTING STARTED

May 27–July 31, 1846
Big Blue River to Bridger's Fort

PATTY REED —•— *The Angel*
On the Oregon Trail

Dear God,
I know I ought not pray in the middle of a sermon,
but I reckon it's all right if a tiny prayer leaks out just a little.
This preacher man has got it all figured out.
I guess he must know you personally.
Now, God, you know that I was with Grandma Keyes when she died.
She gave me a lock of her hair and a pincushion.
And best of all, she gave me her tiny dolly named Angel.
"A dolly named Angel for an angel named Patty," she told me.
"I've had Angel since I was knee-high to a grasshopper," she said.
I said, "I should be crying, but I cain't make the tears."
"That's 'cause you're special, Patty Reed," she said.
"And *you* know I'm a-goin' to a better place than this.
So if you ever feel like cryin', you just look at little Angel instead.
And save your precious tears for more important things."
Then she up and died, but I guess, by now, you know that.

Amen

A hawk flies by overhead. Its shadow crosses the hatless heads of the funeral goers below. The fleeting shadow draws a line to a frock-coated preacher raising a Bible, eyes closed, face upward, as if speaking to the clouds.

Today our hearts hunger. A good woman is gone.
But as we weep we must rejoice in our faith
that the soul of Sarah Keyes now feasts with the Lord.

Listening to the preacher but catching few words is the man they call Old Hardcoop, standing by the open grave wringing his hat in his hands. A cutler by trade, he hired on, back in Independence, to work for a stone-faced German named Ludwig Keseberg. The small balding man in the blue satin waistcoat and dusty trousers is still winded from helping to dig the grave. Not his job, but he tries to be useful.

The deceased, a Mrs. Keyes, was a neighbor of George Donner from Springfield, Illinois. Old Hardcoop had never laid eyes on her, confined as she was to a feather bed in the Reed family wagon. Mrs. Keyes was practical enough to die while the wagon train was already in a forced camp, halted on the swollen banks of the Big Blue River so the travelers could build a raft to ferry their wagons across.

The men were already felling and hollowing trees for the raft, so it was easy enough to split the boards for a cottonwood coffin to hold Mrs. Keyes's feather-light remains. An Englishman named Denton has shaped a tombstone and chiseled into it the following:

Mrs. Sarah Keyes
Died May 29, 1846
Aged 70

The entire camp has ceased its labors out of respect. Closest to the waiting grave is the nearest kin, the Reeds. In life Mrs. Keyes had been the grand matron of the Reed family. Her son-in-law, the tall Mr. James Reed, comforts his sobbing wife, Margret. Next to them, holding hands, stand Eliza and Baylis Williams, the Reeds' household help. Eliza, an excellent cook, is deaf, and her brother Baylis, an albino, is nearly blind.

In front of Mr. and Mrs. Reed fidget their four children. The two Reed boys are busy teasing the little family dog, Cash. The girls, eight-year-old Patty and twelve-year-old Virginia, are standing with their arms folded tightly across their white pinafores. With Grandma Keyes gone, Virginia fears she will be expected to look after the whole brood herself. Her face casts out daggers in all directions.

For Sarah Keyes has gone to Jesus.
And Jesus is the bread of life.

Thirteen-year-old, redheaded Eddie Breen has fallen asleep on his feet. His redheaded mother, Mrs. Breen, holding a baby in one arm, flicks Eddie's ear with her free hand. When he wakes with a gasp, the five other redheaded Breen boys snicker. Redheaded Mr. Breen shushes them all. Mr. Breen is a man of God and wants to hear the sermon. Eddie nods off again.

Coughing slightly, standing next to Mr. Breen, is Jacob Donner, sickly and stick thin. And on Jacob's arm is his morose wife, Elizabeth—known to most as Aunt Betsy. Jacob Donner is the younger brother to George Donner, who, as I said, was a neighbor to the Reeds back in Springfield. The Donner brothers have a dozen children between them of various shapes and sizes. Standing dry-eyed and easy beside George Donner is his wife, Tamzene, barely five feet tall, barely ninety pounds. Mrs. Tamzene Donner, a retired schoolteacher and amateur botanist, is full of great ambition. She has a deep, insatiable hunger for knowledge. And she is as large in personality as she is small in body.

In the vernacular of the day, Mrs. Tamzene Donner is ten pounds of shot in a five-pound cannon.

PATTY REED —◆— *The Angel*
On the Oregon Trail, the Big Blue River

Dear God,
Thank you for the flavorful food and the real nice funeral.
It was a bit wordy but the singing was good.
Grandma Keyes would have liked the food part real fine.
Just so you know, I'm taking care of Tommy now
while Ma has her hands full with cooking and sick headaches.
I told Tommy that Grandma Keyes was in the ground.
I said, "Her body is in the dirt but the rest of her is in here."
I pointed, and Tommy says, "You mean Gramma's in your belly?"
"No, I mean *here*," says I. And, real careful, I pointed to my bosom.
I mean I pointed to the place where my bosom will one day be.
Then I pointed to Tommy's bosom. "In your heart, silly," says I.
Goodbye for now, God. I got chores to do.
And I know that you got chores, too.
But take good care of Grandma Keyes.

Amen

⚊ HUNGER ⚊

It takes two whole days to ferry each wagon over the rapid current of the Big Blue River. The men chop two large cottonwoods and hollow them out like canoes. Then they attach both canoes with crosspieces to fashion a double hull capable of carrying one wagon at a time. A guide rope is run from bank to bank, and oxen are used for the pulling, along with men who stand in the frigid water to their armpits. It is precarious work, and at first the men swamp one side or the other on the load-up or dismount. But after a dozen crossings they begin taking wagons over fully loaded, even carrying women and children. The animals are all swum over, and one bellowing ox is lost to the Big Blue's current. Even a river, you see, can have an appetite.

An ox is slow but cheaper than a mule or horse. An ox is slow but can eat just about anything. An ox is slow but it is strong. When an ox gives out, you can switch with a spare. And an ox is what they call "rations on the hoof," which means, in a pinch, you can eat it.

LUDWIG KESEBERG —◆— *The Madman*
On the Oregon Trail, going west

My full name is Johann Ludwig Christian Keseberg.
My dear wife, Philippine, calls me Ludwig, but to the Americans,
who are suspicious of anything foreign, I am Lewis.
I keep to myself and my family. And if the others think me strange,
that is because they treat me like a stranger.

Philippine and I married in Prussia. In the city of Berleburg.
I was born there. It was supposed to be my home.
But my father was Berleburg's Lutheran minister,
and Philippine was Catholic—and, oh, such a scandal that was.
We married for love, and those whom I loved have cursed me for it.
We had twin daughters, Mathilda and Ada.
But Father was a bitter man. He would not accept my new family.
And so we left to America. But our troubles followed across the water.
Not two months after we arrived, our little Mathilda died,
making her twin, Ada, a source of both comfort and pain.
Fits of anger would possess me. I would lash out at anything . . .

anyone.

Now Philippine is pregnant again.
We are on our way west hoping finally to escape our bad luck,
but the wagons are going too slow.
Arguments. Brawls. Cursing. Fistfights. Two men even draw knives.
It seems the greatest danger we will face on this journey . . .
is ourselves.

Tamzene Donner —◆— *The Scholar*
On the Oregon Trail, going west

Rise and shine, folks! Rise and shine!
I left my rooster back in Illinois!
Rise and shine! Rise and shine!
And if you can't shine,
well, at least you can rise!

That's my husband. As subcaptain, his job is to wake up the camp
and to get his little contingent all hitched and on the road.

I married George Donner when I was thirty-seven.
I was his third wife; he my second husband, and a kind friend.
My first husband, Tully, and I had been married three blissful years.
   And then . . .
our little son died in September. Our baby girl died in November.
And then . . . in December . . . Tully slipped away himself.
He died on the twenty-fourth, a cruel and bitter Christmas gift from
   God.
I was not there when he died. The doctor says Tully called to me.
He reached out his hand for me, but I was not there.

I nearly died myself from the grief of it.
I vowed I would never give my heart so completely,
and I've kept that vow to this very day.

Virginia Reed —◆— *The Princess*
On the Oregon Trail, going west

The first couple days after we crossed the Big Blue,
the weather was cloudy, cold, and windy. June felt like November.
It was too cold to ride my pony, Billy, so I huddled in the family wagon.
Through every bump and jostle Ma snuggled the younger children,
the way she used to snuggle me, back when I had her all to myself.
Jimmy. Tommy. Patty. Patty's doll, and me. We all sat and listened
to the wind whip across the canvas. It was a lonely sound.
"Grandma's pallet is so empty." Patty wept a little.
When Patty wept, Tommy cried, and *that* made Jimmy wail.
Then Ma started in. Then I started in, too. A regular weeping bee.
Now Ma laughs all o' sudden. She tickles the boys, and she says,
"We are weighing this wagon down with our sorrows.
Our hearts are so heavy, I'm surprised we haven't broken an axle!"
The children laugh, and so do I. "Not only that," she goes on,
"I think the wind has died down and the sun has come out."
And she was right. As if Ma just wishing had made it so.

The sun finally reemerges about the time the wagon train reaches the Platte River, the second week in June. The rain-soaked cold retreats across the plains, seeming to take with it the company's sorrow over the death of Sarah Keyes.

Abundant water and forage are essential to their success. An endless supply of water runs to their right. An endless supply of grass grows to their left. It seems as if the great herds that travel with them—the oxen, saddle horses, pack mules, milk cows, and beef cattle—might literally eat their way to the Pacific Ocean.

You see, dear reader, how our heroes are driven by hunger.

A New York newspaper calls it "manifest destiny." The twenty-eight United States are bursting through their frontier borders. No matter that the land is already occupied by generations of Pawnee, Arapaho, Cheyenne, and Shoshone. No matter that Northern California is already part of Mexico. The white man's maps are blank. The West is an empty gut that demands to be filled.

JAMES REED —◆— *The Aristocrat*
On the Oregon Trail, following the Platte River

I am a wealthy man. And I'm not ashamed to crow about it.
At the end of the day, James Reed gets the job done.
I'm not afraid to get my hands dirty, but that's what hired hands are for.
As for me, I'd rather be hunting. And there's plenty hunting here.
The wilds of Nebraska are a perfect hunter's paradise.
Grouse in the grass, geese in the sky, herds of buffalo to the horizon.
Yesterday I brought down the largest bull elk I've seen in all my life.
But my elk was soon forgotten when two old trappers one-upped me
by killing a buffalo each. They were treated like heroes in camp.
Two perfect stars. And I hungered to have my day.
So today I asked to join in the hunt—two shining stars and one sucker.
They laughed about it and said, "Okay, Mr. Reed. Bring yer pretty knife,
and you can do the butcherin' . . . after we're done droppin' 'em."
My only ambition was to remove the stars from their brows
and to erase the sniggering smiles from their tobacco-stained faces.
I had armed myself with two pistols, powder and lead to reload.
I'll have you know that I am no slouch in the saddle, and what is more,
I happened to be riding Glaucus, the finest and fastest horse on the plains.

My daughter, Virginia, who has been riding since she could walk,
rode up on her pony and said, "Wait for me, Pa!"
I bent down and whispered, "Not now, my princess. These two fellows,
they think your papa is green, and I'm about to take them to school."

Virginia Reed —◆— *The Princess*
On the Oregon Trail, following the Platte River

"Wait for me, Pa! I want to come along."
Each day Pa and I would ride out together,
he on Glaucus and I on little Billy,
and we would scout out the water and grass up ahead.
But this particular morning he left me behind
like he used to do back home.
I've seen Pa ride away so many times, I've memorized his back.

Suddenly a voice makes me jump near out of my saddle.
"Why so glum, Virginia? Your face is longer than your pony's."
It is Eddie Breen, all red hair and freckles and a big toothy grin.
"Lord help me, Edward, you are always sneaking up on me!" I said.
I liked to call him Edward instead of Eddie like everybody else.
"I was watching you," he said. "And your daddy, I mean.
Glaucus has got to be the fastest horse I ever did see."
Edward spoke with an Irish accent that sounded like music.
Pa has the same accent, though he tries to undo it.

"Glaucus is no faster than Billy," I said.
"Ah, would that be a challenge, m'lady?" Edward grinned.
"First one to the parlor wagon is winner," I said.
"Keep an eye out for gopher holes. You can count us off."
Billy's head turned toward our family wagon in the distance.
"One!" Edward shouted.
"Two!"
"Th—"
And before he could say "three," I was off like lightning.
"Hey, you cheated!" Edward shouted behind me.
Me and Billy were like a single animal in flight.
"Don't you know nothing, Edward Breen?" I shouted back.
"Way out here there ain't no rules!"

PATTY REED —◆— *The Angel*
On the Oregon Trail, following the Platte River

Dear God,
Please keep a lookout for Virginia's good stiff-brim bonnet.
She lost it somewhere out on the prairie,
and, as you know, whatever you lose on the prairie
you lose forever.
Pa went off with the hunters
and I'd appreciate if you would
guide Glaucus around any gopher holes.
Glaucus is a smart horse and very brave.
And it would be a shame to lose
Grandma Keyes and our best horse
within the same month.
Let Glaucus run fast. Let Pa's bullets fly true.
And God, we would *all* like some nice buffalo steaks.
Miss Eliza discovered buffalo poo patties
(once dried) can be burned for fuel,
and buffalo poo flavors the food "better'n hickory coals."
Did you know that dried buffalo poo tasted of hickory?
Well, I guess you *did*! Since you *are* God and all.
Anyway, keep your eyes peeled for Virginia's bonnet.

Amen

TAMZENE DONNER —◆— *The Scholar*
On the Oregon Trail, following the Platte River

150 pounds flour, 50 pounds sugar
75 pounds meat for each, 30 pounds cornmeal
Of all the items I packed into our wagons
40 pounds bacon, 20 pounds beans
in preparation for this amazing trip west,
20 pounds coffee, 5 pounds tea
½ pound saleratus, 10 pounds rice
Of everything, there is nothing more valuable than . . . the sunbonnet.
I've outfitted all five of my girls in bonnets and linsey dresses.
Elitha and Leanna, my stepdaughters, are thirteen and eleven,
so they're in charge of Frances, Georgia, and Eliza.
I've sent them all off to gather buffalo chips.
(With chalk and slate, I have calculated the wagons at two and a quarter
    miles per hour,
so there is very little danger of even a toddler being left behind.)
Meanwhile, I've taken a moment for a bit of botanizing.
The prairie between the Blue and the Platte was beautiful beyond words.
I've collected many specimens and pressed them into my book:
the creeping hollyhock, lupine and tulips, primrose, larkspur,
and a couple blooms that I've never seen the likes of!
These moments to read and botanize are rare and far between.
Mostly, I cook and tend "the Littles"—as we call the three younger girls.
Churn the butter. Tend the girls. Gather wood or chips for the fire.
    Cook again.
They eat. I cook. They eat. I cook. They eat. And eat. And eat!

JAMES REED —•— *The Aristocrat*
On the Oregon Trail, following the Platte River

My two hunting companions could not believe their eyes!
I had brought down two big buffalo bulls,
and then had a little calf square in my sights,
but the shot went wide and my bullet just grazed it.
It was a flesh wound on the little fellow's shoulder.
The calf stopped and froze, more startled than hurt.
I started to reload, but then the creature came over to me
and stood there bawling like it thought Glaucus was its mother!
I couldn't bring myself to shoot it after that.
And damned if that calf didn't just follow me
all the way back to camp—where I was welcomed as a hero!
Not only had I provided buffalo steaks for all,
I had brought the children a pet calf as well.
Our star hunters acknowledged I shined brighter that day
for I had brought down two buffalo and herded a third.
And, yes, I bragged a bit. But what of it?
What use is a sunrise without a little cock-a-doodle-doo?
Nobody but Keseberg seemed to mind,
and even *he* quieted down once the meat was sizzling in the fire.
Everyone's your friend . . .
so long as their bellies are full.

You see by now how healthy Hunger can be.

The first half of June, the emigrants hunt their way through the abundant game. James Reed, George Donner, and even Ludwig Keseberg all bring in buffalo, ducks, and pheasant for dinner. Each morning a bugler sounds reveille. At their fires the women fill the air with the scents of coffee and bacon. George Donner mounts his gray mare and rides throughout the camp shouting, "Chain up, boys! Chain up!" By 7:00 a.m. they are on the move.

Midday, they stop for the "nooning," and a lunch of cold meat and cornmeal is served. The draft animals graze and drink. Some of the hired men are double tired from guard duty the previous night, and sleep beneath the wagons.

The nooning naps last no more than an hour, and then the journey recommences. By 4:30 or 5:00, the pioneers stop for the night. The wagons are drawn into a circle to form a corral for the animals. Family tents and campfires are set outside the circle.

The first woman to arrive and set up her fire will take care to pass on her embers to the next. And from camp to camp the fire is passed around. Dinner is cooked and eaten. The dishes are washed. Babies put down. Diapers hung. And the younger folks gather round the fires. Talk. Gossip. Flirt. Sing a song or two. After dark the men and older boys sit outside the perimeter to guard the herd.

The next day will be a repeat of the last. And so on. Fifteen miles in a day is considered a good pace.

In time our pioneers ford the shallows of the Platte's south fork and cross a barren patch—nearly a day without water. Then they quench their thirst at the Platte's north fork, which will become their new road for a while. They pass the famous Chimney Rock, a sandstone pillar, towering three hundred feet above the surrounding flat land. The soil becomes sandy. The landscape is punctuated by rock outcroppings and cactus. As June comes to a close they begin to encounter the occasional ox or cow, gone lame and left behind to die.

JAMES REED ━◆━ *The Aristocrat*
On the Oregon Trail, at Fort Laramie

A man named Lansford Hastings,
has written a book that claims the existence
of a shortcut—which I cannot get out of my mind.
As a stroke of luck, after we reached Fort Laramie
I met an old acquaintance, James Clyman,
whom I fought side by side with in the Black Hawk War.
Clyman had just come east over the shortcut
with none other than Lansford Hastings himself!

But Clyman says, "I advise against the Hastings Cutoff, Reed.
It is true, of course, that *I* made it through,
but you don't have the same experience
and you've got wagons and women and children.
All *I* had to care for was a horse and a pack mule.
Take the regular wagon track and never leave it.
It is barely possible to get through if you follow it,
and may be *im*possible if you don't!"

Now an ordinary man would listen to that
and hear the word "impossible."
But James Reed is no ordinary man!
The words *I* heard were: "I . . . made . . . it . . . through."
And if Clyman could make it through,
I figure James Reed can make it through, too!
There is a nigher route, and it is of no use
to take a roundabout course.

I feel it in my gut.

PATTY REED —◆— *The Angel*
On the Oregon Trail, along the North Platte River

Dear God,
Thank you for the sweet lemonade.
And thank you for letting us rest our feet awhile.
And thank you for the pretty hills
that shine all around us like gold.
Thank you for the glorious Fourth of July
and for letting the United States of America
reach the good old age of seventy years—
the same as Grandma Keyes. I drank to her memory
and I gave my dolly, Angel, a tiny tipple, too.
Thank you for the fiddle, flute, and dog drum.
And a special thanks to the dog
from which the drum was made.
On July 3 that dog was barking all night to wake the dead.
By July 4 that dog was dead himself
and his skin was stretched tight over the drum.
I got no earthly idea what became of the rest of him.
I suppose he's barking up there in heaven with you.
Up there in heaven I guess a noisy dog's bark
sounds like twittering birds on a soft breeze.
Here on the trail that dog drove all of us crazy.
Anyway, thank you for the dog.

Amen

JAMES REED —◆— *The Aristocrat*
On the Oregon Trail, along the North Platte River

At the evening camp meeting, a lone rider, a Mr. Bonnie,
who had come from California, delivered an important open letter.
Bonnie had been sent from Fort Bridger to share the letter's contents
with every emigrant he encountered, and he had some good news.
The letter advised of a cutoff from the usual California road
that would shorten the journey by three hundred miles!
What's more, the writer of the letter said he was waiting at Fort Bridger
to show the way and *personally* escort any wagons through.
The letter was signed *Lansford W. Hastings*—the very man
who had written *The Emigrants' Guide to Oregon and California.*
I had the book in the back of my wagon, and so did George Donner.
George Donner's eye met mine, and we both smiled.

VIRGINIA REED —◆— *The Princess*
On the Oregon Trail, Independence Rock

I had heard talk of Independence Rock all the previous year.
And we expected to find it so tall as to hardly see its top,
but from the distance we was at, it looked tame and uninteresting.

Eddie Breen and I set out on our ponies to have a nigher look.
"Have you noticed," I ask Edward, "how the closer you get to grown,
the more you learn that the real truth is never as exciting as a fancy lie?"

"I got no idea what you're talking about," he says.

"Like that story Milt Elliott told us round the campfire,
'bout the Nebraska farmer who left his horse in the cornfield.
A swarm o' grasshoppers blows in and descends on the corn,
and the farmer goes off for help. But when the farmer gets back,
not an hour later, his entire corn crop is gone and his horse is gone, too.
And the grasshoppers are drinking corn liquor 'n playing horseshoes!"

"Yup, that's a stretcher, all right," says Eddie. "And funny, too!"

"It's funny. But it ain't the real truth," I say. "The truth is simple:
a huge swarm of grasshoppers ate up all the corn."

"The simple truth ain't near as funny," Edward says.

"Well, everything I've heard about Independence Rock was a fancy lie,
'cause I'm looking at it now and it ain't much," I say.
Then a thought occurs to me out of the blue.
"Do you think Hastings Cutoff is just a fancy lie?" I say.
"Not according to me da," Eddie says.
"And *your* father says it's for real as well.
Don't you believe what your da says is true?"

"I sure don't believe what Pa says about *you*," I blurt out.

"What do you mean? What does he say about *me*?"

I imitate Pa, using the Irish accent he tries to hide:
"'That Eddie Breen, he has got the fastest horse on the plains.
Why the Breen boy's horse is even faster than Glaucus! And that's fast!
But there ain't *no way* that Breen boy,
on his lame-foot near-dead sorry old nag,
can beat Virginia Reed's Billy in a race
from here to that uninteresting humbug of a rock.'"

Edward jumps at the challenge, like I knew he would.
"This time *you* count us off," he says.

I count: "One . . . two . . ." And I set off before I reach "three."

"Hey, you cheat!" yells Eddie behind me.
But I am already gone. Mc and Billy light out across the grass.
We splash across the Sweetwater River, cold in the hot sun.

And that's how I lost my *second* bonnet.

Upon Independence Rock

With gunpowder, tar, and buffalo grease
They enter their names to the registry
Of those going west and away without cease
Toward a future of promise and mystery
Full of gunpowder, tar, and buffalo grease

With gunpowder, tar, and buffalo grease
Recording the roster for heaven to see
Writing lines to a pioneer litany
On a primitive emigrant altarpiece
Made of gunpowder, tar, and buffalo grease

PATTY REED —◆— *The Angel*
On the Oregon Trail, Independence Rock

Dear God,
Tommy and I are agreed
that Independence Rock is a wonderful wonder.
I think it looks like the hump of a giant buffalo
that's been buried under the ground.
Tommy says it looks like
a very large mountain of buffalo poo.
About halfway up the rock
is a little pine tree growing all by itself.
Tommy says, "Hey, Patty, how'd that tree get up there?"
And I says, "God put that tree there, of course."
And he says, "I bet God put that little tree up there
so the little tree could be closer to heaven."
Ma says we're not supposed to wonder
why God—I mean why *You*—do anything
'cause only You and the angels know the answer.
But I reckon Tommy's answer was pretty close to true.

Amen

Ludwig Keseberg —◆— *The Madman*
On the Oregon Trail, Devil's Gate

We set up camp at a place called the Devil's Gate,
a narrow passage with sheer granite cliffs, maybe four hundred feet high.
And this is where I first heard the beautiful voice of my son.

With the help of Mrs. Donner and Mrs. Reed, Philippine brought forth
in the nighttime, by candlelight inside our family wagon.
"Come in and meet your son," Mrs. Donner said.
I climbed into the wagon.
"Johann Ludwig Christian Keseberg," Philippine said,
"let me introduce Johann Ludwig Christian Keseberg *Junior.*"

"Hallo, Ludwig Jr.," I said. "Welcome to the new world."

Mrs. Donner lingered awhile.
I had always felt especially comfortable around Mrs. Donner.
She was a poetic soul.
And she harbored a heavy sadness somewhere deep inside her heart.
We never spoke of it, but I sensed she saw it in me as well.

The Devil's Gate seemed to glow magically in the moonlight.
A far-off fiddle's music mingled with my new son's tiny coos.
"Through that gate," I told Mrs. Donner, "awaits *die Zukunft,*
the future,
a whole horizon of possibilities and second chances."

JAMES REED —◆— *The Aristocrat*
On the Oregon Trail, Parting of the Ways

On July 19, we finally reached the Parting of the Ways,
where the road plainly forks and you choose your fate.
To the right is the tried-and-true trail to Fort Hall.
To the left is the trail to Fort Bridger and the cutoff.
We camped on the Little Sandy River and a meeting was called.
A time to argue left or right and to finalize our crews.

The Parting of the Ways
On the Oregon Trail, Parting of the Ways

The left fork is the road to take.

          We say you're making a mistake.

          The right fork is the better road.

We say you're wrong. That road is slow.

The left-hand fork will lead the way
to Hastings Cutoff past Salt Lake,
a shorter road, a quicker trip.
The left-hand fork's the one we'll take.

          The right-hand fork is tried and true.

          Hastings and his claims are fake.

          The shortcut isn't worth the risk.

          The right-hand fork's the one we'll take.

We've made our point.
We've raised our voice.

          We've heard enough.

          We've had our say.

Left hand!

          Right hand!

Make a choice!   Make a choice!

Shake hands . . .

          . . . and go

two separate ways.   two separate ways.

JAMES REED —◆— *The Aristocrat*
On the Oregon Trail, Parting of the Ways

Then a vote was called:
>"All those for the right fork, raise your hand."

And another:
>"All those for the left fork, hold 'em high."

And suddenly We became Us and Them.

George Donner and his brother Jacob raised hands for the Cutoff.
And the Eddys, and the Murphys, the Fosters and the Pikes,
the Breens and Mr. Dolan (all of 'em Catholics),
the Wolfingers, Joe Reinhardt, and the Kesebergs (all Germans).
We had with us a dozen or so teamsters and hands, Sam Shoemaker,
Milt Elliott, Old Hardcoop, Charlie Stanton, and a bachelor or two.
All in all we counted nineteen wagons and a good many guns.
This wasn't half of what I'd hoped for, but it would do.
So long as we had proper leadership.

A captain was needed for our newly formed train.
And so another election commenced to see who it might be.
I knew I was the best man for the job. And all the others knew it, too.
But I also knew I would not likely be chosen.
I knew I wasn't well loved by some. But I'd rather be right than loved.

So, of course, I was not surprised when George Donner
was nominated and elected captain of our wagons.
Let history call our group "the Donner Party." I care not.
>The people may *elect* the man that they like,
>but they *follow* the man that can lead.

⬗ Hunger ⬗

We make our choices. It is that simple, really. Choose the left-hand fork, and follow the path that winds through pools of rancid water. Perhaps the oxen may drink it. Perhaps two or three oxen may die.

Choose the right-hand fork, and maybe the oxen will live to die another day. But the right fork may lead to a den of rattlesnakes. The lucky oxen may panic and run over a child. One never knows.

What if beyond the poison water there exists a pot of gold? Or a greener pasture? Or a shorter way to California?

Every explorer wants to see what is waiting around the next bend. Just like every gambler wants to see (*must* see) the face of the deck's next card. Curiosity is just a variety of hunger. Hunger is just a variety of hope. Take note of that fact, dear reader. It will come in handy later on.

JAMES REED —◆— *The Aristocrat*
The road to Fort Bridger

Not long after the Parting of the Ways,
as we followed the trail along Dry Sandy Creek,
we had stopped to noon at a spot by the river
with grass and standing pools.
The oxen foraged as usual, but after drinking they got sick.
Grandma Keyes used to tease me no end,
telling me, "You love your dang bulls more than my daughter!"
It is true, I've got a big heart when it comes to the animals.
Not just the draft animals and horses, but the pigs and chickens,
and the cattle and dogs. I call each one by name
and never fail to pat some critter on the head and share a word with it.
Any one of my draft animals is of more use to me than most men.
So you might imagine how I felt when my two best oxen,
Bally and George, started to bellow and shift on their feet,
then finally knee-buckled, one after the other, and died.
Bally was brindled and bald-faced (hence the name),
and George was a big Durham steer, smarter than most men.
Bally and George had worked as a pair at my mill for years.
"Better look at *this*, Mr. Reed," said Milt, who was kneeling by a puddle.
I could smell it myself. The water was stagnant and brackish.
Milt stood up with his hands on his face and spoke quietly.

"This water is poison."

PATTY REED —•— *The Angel*
The road to Fort Bridger

Dear God,

When Grandma Keyes died, there was a lot of praying.

But nobody has prayed not a word for ol' Bally and George.

So don't forget to open up the pearly gates once they arrive.

I assume Bally and George were Methodists like the rest of us,

but they could have been Presbyterians or Papists for all I know.

It's hard to cipher a bull's religious inclinations from looks alone.

Just ignore the brand and suffer the oxen to come unto Jesus

so that Grandma Keyes will now have some company,

aside from just You and Jesus.

Tonight Mr. Breen didn't play his fiddle at all.

The cattle dying has made the whole camp sad and quiet,

but Eddie Breen stopped by the fire.

The Breens don't sit much with us Reeds and Donners,

on accounta the Breens being Papists and foreigners.

But Eddie just plopped down easy as you please

and told Pa how sorry he was about ol' Bally and George,

and Pa said, "Thank you, son." And that was that and nobody died.

Except for ol' Bally and George, of course,

but they were already dead, as you no doubt know.

Amen

James Reed ⇢⟡⟣ *The Aristocrat*
At Fort Bridger

I still felt the sting of losing Bally and George
as our wagons arrived the next day at Fort Bridger,
a miserable and wretched jumble of ramshackle huts.
There weren't even pickets up for defense.
But the owners of the fort itself are two honest and industrious men.
Jim Bridger and Louis Vasquez are two diamonds in this rough wilderness.
They seem to me and George Donner to be men of quality and courage.
They praise our decision to travel the Hastings Cutoff.
They report the new route is perfectly practicable for wagons.
They tell us it is a savings of three hundred fifty miles and a better route.
A fine level road with plenty of water and grass.
As it happens, Hastings himself is guiding an advance party,
so we have the added advantage of following directly in their wheel ruts.
"You can camp in the medder by the fort," says Bridger.
"And we're happy to sell or trade out oxen or horses!"
Later at the trading post's corral I chose a yoke of oxen
to replace poor old Bally and George.
George Donner had his eye on a pair of huge Galloway bulls
standing at the back of the corral. Galloways have a good thick coat
that recommends them for the colder weather.
"How much for the Galloways?" asks Mr. Donner.
"Oh, them," says Bridger. "You don't want them animals."
"Why not?" says Donner. "They look to be in good order."
"Oh, they *are* the best yoke of the whole bunch," says Vasquez.
"Problem is, they won't take orders from nobody but the boy."

"The boy?" Donner says. "What boy is that?"
And as if in answer to the question,
a tall, lanky kid steps from behind one of the big bulls.
He walks over to us with long, energetic strides.
He is wearing buckskin britches and a calico shirt.

He has a worn-out hat on his head, a goad stick in his hand,
and a big hunting knife, like my own, in his belt.

"Sorry, but these animals, they ain't for sale," the boy says.
Then he grins really wide and says,
"Buck and Bright, they's the only family I got left."

BAPTISTE TRUDEAU —◆— *The Orphan*
At Fort Bridger

Buck and Bright really *are* the only family I got left.
My father, he is dead. And my mother, she ran off.
Father claimed she was Mexican, if you can believe him.
Father never was one to bother with the truth of a story,
but he sure did know a lot about training bulls to the yoke.
Father didn't care much for breeding, so he left that mostly to me
while he disappeared trapping for months at a time.
By the time I was fourteen I had taken care of the livestock
from Bent's Fort on the Arkansas to Bridger's right here.
I learned how to stretch beaver pelts on hoops to dry
and prepare the bundles for transport to St. Louis.
I learned to shoot and to cook and to ride and to stay alive.
Most important, I learned how to transform a steer into a working ox.
I was still down at Bent's Fort when I met Buck and Bright.
They were cute wobble-legged calves back then.
I got them used to handling and all the verbal commands.
I trained them to the yoke my very own self from day one.
We grew up together, you might say, and then Daddy got himself killed.
The one thing I have of him is a fine wool blanket.
I went north to Fort Bridger where I met John Frémont
and none other than Kit Carson himself, and I joined them headed west.
I had to leave Buck and Bright behind at the fort.
But Buck and Bright wouldn't take commands from no other drover.
They wouldn't work around the fort at all, and yet they kept on eating.
And at close to eighteen hundred pounds each, you can bet they ate a lot.
By the time I returned to the fort, Jim Bridger
wanted to turn them both into T-bone steaks and mule saddles!

"Sorry," I say to the two men, "but these animals ain't for sale."
I tell them, "Lansford Hastings came through a week ago

with about fifty wagons all wanting to buy Buck and Bright.
I got plenty o' offers." I go on. "I turned 'em all down."

The elder of the two men, he sizes me up and says,
"How old are you, son?" I can tell he's hatching a plan.

"I'm near twenty years old," I lie.

"You're lying," he says. "Bridger says you're sixteen."

"I may be sixteen," I say, "but I'm more a mountain man than you suckers.
I can speak to the Crow and the Snakes and the Sioux.
And I know more 'bout oxen than most men twice my age."

"Oh, is that right?" says the younger man.

"I know enough to keep my yokes from drinking poison," I say.

"Why you no-account mongrel!" he says. "How dare you—"
The younger man's face turns red, and he comes at me.

But the older man steps between us with a smile and says,
"You got to admit, Reed; the boy is right." Then he turns to me
and he says, "I tell you what, uh . . . What's your name, son?"

"Baptiste," I say. "Jean Baptiste Trudeau. Most just calls me Baptiste."

"I tell you what, Baptiste. Those are the two finest bulls I've ever seen.
My name is George Donner,
and it would be my honor if they pulled one of my wagons.
Plus, I'm short one teamster ever since Miller left us a while back.
I'll provide you bed and board along the way. You keep your oxen.
And fifty dollars in gold coins once we reach California."

"George," says the man named Reed. "Are you sure about this?"
The man named George Donner laughs.
"You said yourself, James, we need more hands.
This boy's got *two* hands. *And* he can handle the cattle."
Reed just spits and walks away.

Then George Donner turns to me with a big grin.
"Reed comes off like a horse's ass," he says, "because that's what he is.
But when push comes to shove, there's no better man."
And he puts out a leather hand, callused from the plow.
I turn to Buck and Bright, and they low real loud in unison!
I turn back to the man's big white smile and smile back.

"You got a deal, then," I say. And I shake the man's hand.
"All right, then, Baptiste," he says to me. "It's good to have you."
Then he looks over at my oxen, who have twisted their yoke
so they're facing in opposite directions.
"You too, Buck and Bright," Donner says with a laugh.
"Welcome to the Donner Party!"

TAMZENE DONNER —◆— *The Scholar*
At Fort Bridger

And just like that, George Donner has picked up another stray.

Baptiste resembles my darling Tully. And at sixteen years old,
this boy is the very age that my own son would be . . .
had he lived past his second year. Oh, my darling boy.
In my mind I can see him vividly, sitting on my desk as I write,
a baby grabbing my inkwell with his chubby perfect hands.
Then one day suddenly my boy was gone. And my desk was empty.
Now, almost sixteen years to the day that my own son was born,
this new boy stands in front of me breathing and healthy and alive.
He has come to the meadow to join us at our family fire.
It's as if he is meant to be here. To fill an aching vacancy.
My three younger girls climb up Baptiste like a tree.
I whisper to my husband, "Another stray, George?"

"You girls have me outnumbered six to one," George says.
"I just figured it was time to balance things out."

We both laugh out loud at that. The girls are breathless with giggles
as Baptiste rolls them up one by one in that blanket of his.
A lively jig from Mr. Breen's fiddle dances across the meadow.
Here the grass is good, and pure cold water runs nearby
in a pretty little creek alive with fish and lined by cottonwood trees.
In the morning we will set out over the Hastings Cutoff.
"According to Reed's and my calculations," George says,
"we should arrive in seven weeks if all goes well."

"Seven weeks to paradise," I say as George pulls me close.
"If we don't experience something far worse than we have yet,
I shall say the trouble is all in the getting started."

LETTER TO GERSHAM KEYES
Springfield, Illinois

From James Frazier Reed
Fort Bridger, 100 Miles from Great Salt Lake
July 31, 1846

Dear Sir,

I have fine times in hunting grouse, antelope, or mountain goat, which are plenty. Milt Elliott, James Smith, and Walter Herron, the young men who drive for me, are careful, first rate drivers—which gives me time for hunting. We are beyond the range of buffalo.

We have arrived here at Fort Bridger safe with the loss of two yoke of my best oxen. They were poisoned by drinking water in a little creek called Dry Sandy. I have replenished my stock thanks to Messrs. Vasquez & Bridger, two very excellent and accommodating gentlemen, who are the proprietors of this trading post. The new road, or Hastings' Cut-off, leaves the usual Fort Hall road here, and is said to be a saving of 350 or 400 miles in going to California, and a better route.

We are now only 100 miles from the Great Salt Lake by the new route—in all 250 miles from California; while the old route is 650 or 700 miles—making a great saving in favor of jaded oxen and dust. The rest of the Californians went the long route—feeling afraid of Hasting's Cut-off. Mr. Bridger informs me that the route we design to take is a fine level road with plenty of water and grass.

The independent trappers, who swarm here during the passing of the emigrants, are as great a set of sharks as ever disgraced humanity, with few exceptions. Let the emigrants avoid trading with them. Vasquez & Bridger are the only fair traders in these parts.

Your Brother,
James Reed

PART TWO

—◆—

NIGHER AND FASTER: HASTINGS CUTOFF

July 31–September 26, 1846
Bridger's Fort to Mary's River

Our travelers spend five days camped in that lovely little meadow by Fort Bridger. Mr. Keseberg begins to complain, and then Mr. Breen and some of the others, that too much precious time is being wasted. These complaints are common, for although George Donner is their elected leader, they are in the wilderness now. In the wilderness, the rules are different. The obstacles are deadly. Failure carries a heavy cost.

For weeks, warnings have been passing from wagon to wagon about Lansford Hastings and his new cutoff: the trail is too new; the trail is too narrow; the trail is too difficult. Some had said Hastings himself was not to be trusted; that Hastings was a power-hungry Munchausen bent on revolutionizing California with emigrants who would then take the land from Mexico. Whoever got there first might become the leaders of a new territory, a new state, maybe even a new country.

Reed and the Donner brothers have been hearing just as many favorable opinions about the shortcut. Some say the new route is as passable as the established road—and half the distance. What's more, hadn't James Bridger himself, along with Louis Vasquez, personally told Reed that Hastings Cutoff is perfectly navigable by wagons? Did they not say, to his face, that the route would be a saving of three hundred fifty miles? Did they not say that the journey would take seven easy weeks' travel, with the exception of one forty-mile stretch without water or grass?

So on July 31 the Donner Party sets out on the new Hastings Cutoff. With freshly washed clothes, mended wagon wheels, and well-rested oxen, every man, woman, and child feels up to the task at hand. And they've added to their numbers a small family, the McCutchens: William, Amanda, and baby Harriet. And of course young Baptiste Trudeau with his oxen, Buck and Bright. They think with luck they might even catch up with Hastings's advance wagons.

Jim Bridger and Louis Vasquez, ever the gracious hosts, escort the Donner Party for the first couple miles, before they say their goodbyes. Reed's cook, Eliza, presents Jim Bridger with a fat laying hen in a small wooden cage.

"I noticed you had no chickens at the fort," Eliza shouts. "I reckoned you could use one! The children have named her Daisy! And she's a good layer! Compliments of the Reed family!"

"For all your kindness and help," adds Mr. Reed.

Hands are offered all around. Daisy the chicken clucks forlornly from her cage as if she were saying goodbye as well.

The Donner Party pulls out, yoke chains ringing, bullwhips snapping.

Bridger and Vasquez watch until the last of the wagons disappears down the rough road, surrounded on all sides by stunted cedars, twisted by the wind into the shapes of demons. Jim Bridger, who has been holding Daisy the chicken all this time, now sets the cage gently on the ground and begins to collect tinder and small wood for a fire.

"They was real friendly folks," Bridger says.

"That they were," says Vasquez. "Although that James Reed was a bit ambitious for my taste. Still, he seems like a man who can get the job done. Once they add their muscle to Hastings's men, they might even be able to hack a road through."

"Reed's *wife* was nice, though," says Bridger. "Mr. and Mrs. Donner, too. I wish them well. I really do. I hope they all get where they're a-goin'."

"Oh, they will do just fine," says Vasquez, "long as they don't attempt to follow the creek down Weber Canyon." And he pulls a letter from inside his vest. A letter addressed in bold black letters in a refined hand: *Please deliver to Messrs. Donner and Reed.*

It had been two weeks since Edwin Bryant, the Donners' old traveling companion, had written the letter. Two weeks since he had entrusted it to the care of Louis Vasquez.

"I will be sure your letter ends up where it belongs," Vasquez had warmly assured Bryant. He was not lying, nor was he telling the truth. For years, Vasquez and Bridger had been telling travelers what they wanted to hear.

Jim Bridger brings his small fire to life, then pulls Daisy from her cage. He stretches the fat hen's neck out and breaks it with a violent practiced flick of the wrist. *CRACK!*

He plucks the hen. Then he guts it and singes the carcass in the flames. Within ten minutes, the Reeds' gift is cooking over the fire on a makeshift spit of willow sticks.

Vasquez kneels down, considering the paper in his hand. Then, carefully avoiding the sizzling bird, he tosses the undelivered letter into the fire.

"Smells good. It's been a long morning," says Vasquez. "I'm about to starve."

LETTER FROM FORT BRIDGER

Dear Messrs. Donner and Reed,

Yesterday I spoke with a Mr. Joseph Walker who is familiar with the course proposed by Mr. Hastings. Mr. Walker <u>speaks discouragingly of the new route</u>. Mr. Hudspeth, an advance scout to Mr. Hastings, has volunteered to guide us through this untried route as far as the shore of Salt Lake.

I am of the opinion that neither Messrs. Hudspeth nor Hastings has an intimate knowledge of this terra incognita. I therefore strongly advise you to <u>keep to the established trail</u>, via Fort Hall, as Mr. J. Clyman advised us some weeks ago.

My companions and I, bachelors all, risk this new route willingly, for we are mounted on mules, have no families, and can afford to hazard experiments and make explorations. I fear, however, with your wagons, oxen, women, and children, that you would be placing yourselves in uncalled for danger by following Hastings. It is not so late in the season. You should have ample time to keep to the established trail via Fort Hall and cross the mountains before winter snows set in.

I repeat, at any cost, <u>do not take the Hastings Cutoff</u>.

Respectfully,
Edwin Bryant
Bridger's Fort
July 18, 1847

Virginia Reed —◆— *The Princess*
Hastings Cutoff

Pa and I rode together less and less.
But Edward was always in the saddle and always up for adventure.
We rode out through several pretty little valleys
well watered with plenty of grass. The sun warmed my face
and reflected brightly off the snowy slopes to the south.
The sun cast shadows across Edward's muscular back.

"So far," said Edward, "Hastings Cutoff is a lark.
I don't see what all the fuss was about."

I said, "That's probably 'cause you're ridin'
a swaybacked, knock-kneed, out-to-pasture Nelly."

"She's faster, times ten, than your four-legged chicken," he said.
Then he said, "First one to the top o' that hill. My count."
Edward started the count. "One, two—"
And I'm off to my usual early start.
And we spur our horses and ride off up a hill,
dodging left and right around the scruffy sage bushes.
Then *CRACK!*
Suddenly his horse stumbled, tossing Edward to the ground.
I heard a thud. And then a loud *snap!*

"Eddie!" I shouted, and rode back to where he'd fallen.
His left leg had snapped between the ankle and knee.
A jagged bone jutted through torn fabric and flesh.
It gleamed in the sun, white bone and scarlet blood.

"Eddie!" I shouted again. But he didn't answer.
He didn't even move.

BAPTISTE TRUDEAU —◆— *The Orphan*
Hastings Cutoff

The Breen boy looked dead to me.
But then he opens his eyes wide and starts yelling!
Mrs. Donner and the boy's mother tried to stop the bleeding.
And Mr. Donner sent me back to Bridger's to fetch a doctor.
"Doctor?" I said. "There is no doctor; there is only Le Gross."
Le Gross is Fort Bridger's butcher and occasional dentist.
But I fetched him anyway, and Le Gross was happy to be wanted.

One quick look at the bone sticking out of the Breen boy's leg
and Le Gross shook his head. Then he unwrapped a leather bundle,
laying out his famous butcher knife, a whetstone, and
a short, gleaming meat saw. But I guess the Breen boy
was fond of his leg, 'cause he raised up a ruckus.
And Mr. Breen gave Le Gross five dollars for his trouble
and sent him on his way back to the fort.
Le Gross rode off on his mule looking a good bit dejected
as he said, "The saw was practically new!"

Virginia Reed ━◆━ *The Princess*
Hastings Cutoff

I must admit I am impressed with Edward's mettle
as well as Mrs. Breen's doctoring skills.
As the entire redheaded brood of Breen boys looks on with worry,
Mr. Breen and Milt Elliott tug at Edward's broken leg
until Mrs. Breen can work the bone back into place.
The new boy, Baptiste, brings in two long willow branches
that Mrs. Breen straps to either side of Edward's leg.

"That'll work for a splint," she says.
"Now I need an extra piece, here, to make a frame."

"What's the frame for?" says Edward.

"Oh, you'll find out soon enough," answers Mrs. Breen.
She positions and lashes a short length of willow sapling
across the bottom two ends of the splint.
Then she attaches a leather strap—one end around the crosspiece,
the other end around her son's ankle. Then, in the center
of this strap, midway between the crosspiece and ankle,
she ties another willow stick some eight inches long.

"This next part's goin' to hurt," warns Mrs. Breen.

"It already hurts!" says Edward.

And she begins to slowly rotate the stick around
its leather strap, thus stretching Edward's leg
continuously, in order to hold the broken bone in place.
As Mrs. Breen twists, Edward yells out in pain.

"Drink this, Eddie," says Ma, holding a tin cup to his lips.

"It's a toddy of laudanum and whiskey. Help you sleep."
Edward drinks and looks up at me. I feel my face redden.

"I'm sorry, Edward!" I blurt out.

"It's not your fault, Virginia. I hit a gopher hole was all."
And then the laudanum begins to show its potency:
"You know, Virginia . . . Virginiahhh . . . Virrrrr . . .
you knohhw." Edward tries to speak. "I woof hadda wuhn efff
ahh hunt holla . . . hehsh . . . "
Then he seems to just fall off to sleep.

With Edward now unconscious, Mrs. Breen pours whiskey
into the wound where the bone has torn through the flesh.
Then she applies a poultice of garlic and crushed dock leaves.
Next she covers the poultice with a clean pair of underdrawers!
(If only Edward doesn't die, I will tease him, no end,
about how he was saved by a lady's unmentionables!)
I have been standing nearby the whole time,
holding strips of cotton that Mrs. Breen now takes from me.
And after wrapping the bandages tightly around Edward's leg,
she squeezes my hand for just a second and she says,
"You did well, lass. You'd make a fine nurse, you know."

This is the first time Edward's mother
has even looked me in the eye, let alone spoken to me.
And at that moment the fear of the past few hours
comes crashing down on me and my eyes fill with tears.
"I thought he was dead," I tell Mrs. Breen.
And I begin to sob.

"I thought he was dead."

JAMES REED —◆— *The Aristocrat*
Hastings Cutoff

Aside from the Breen boy's broken leg,
Hastings Cutoff had given us very little trouble;
at least until we reached the Weber River,
where it flows into the opening of Weber Canyon.
The ruts of the previous wagons led clearly to the right,
following the river, which snaked from wall to wall.
Then the river and the trail both vanished around a bend.
It was here where George Donner noticed a piece of paper
attached to the forked branches of a sage bush.
"What is it?" I said.

"It's a note from Hastings himself," said Donner, reading.
"He says to stop following the advance wagons.
The road down the canyon is impassable, he says.
There's a more direct route that will cross the mountains,
and we can avoid this canyon altogether.
He advises us to go fetch him so he can explain an easier way."

NOTE FOUND AT HEAD OF WEBER CANYON
Hastings Cutoff

ATTENTION!
All Those Bound for California

Advance wagons are down weber cañon
DO NOT FOLLOW
Road very bad
Advise camp at this spot
send mesenger to me along cañon
I will guide you to better route.

Lansford Hastings

By now it is no surprise that James Reed is one of the three men chosen to pursue Hastings. Whether by fate, design, or ambition, Reed seems to be at the heart of everything the Donner Party does.

Charles Stanton. William Pike. And James Reed. Off these three men go, down a rough and rocky road that begins bad and gets worse with each step. The trail crosses the snaking Weber River over and over and over. The river itself is full of large boulders; the banks, clogged with thick brush and trees.

At one point, the trail leaves the river and climbs a rise where the three men discover the grisly evidence of a terrible accident. What looks to be an entire team of six oxen has apparently slid off the road and plunged about sixty feet to their deaths while still harnessed to the wagon they had been pulling. Flesh, bone, and wood all jumbled into one obscene amalgam.

Neither Reed, Stanton, nor Pike can imagine how the advance travelers had moved wagons over such an impassable road. But they now understand why Hastings's note had warned them against it.

As they proceed on, the canyon begins to narrow. The granite walls draw closer and closer with each successive mile until there is barely width for a wagon to pass.

"Look," says Stanton. "You can see, here, where they had to chisel away rock to accommodate the wheel hubs."

It is as if that canyon is a snake. And whatever the snake swallows—men, oxen, or wagons—will be funneled roughly through the serpentine digestive tract, only to be expelled out the other end.

At this point, both men and horses are exhausted. The former are slumped in their saddles. The latter are lathered with sweat. It is in this state that they finally encounter the advance wagons encamped near the shore of the Great Salt Lake. Scanning the camp, Reed is shocked by what he sees. This dusty makeshift city of travelers, three times the size of his own, looks like a defeated army retreating from a siege. Broken wheels, tongues, and axles are undergoing repairs. Tattered laundry is being hung out to dry. A grave is being dug. A cross fashioned.

As Reed and his companions take this all in, a tall, fine-looking man walks up and thrusts out his hand. Despite the heat and ubiquitous dust, the man looks relatively cool and clean. He has light-brown hair and a beard, neatly trimmed. He is dressed in elegant buckskin, handsomely embroidered and trimmed at the cuffs and collar with beaver fur. Reed takes note of the man's confidence and swagger. The handshake is firm.

"Welcome, gentlemen," the man says. "I see you found my little note. My name is Lansford Hastings."

James Reed —◆— *The Aristocrat*
Hastings Cutoff

There were only two fresh horses to be had
so Hastings and I left Stanton and Pike behind
to rest their mounts and catch up as they could.
Hastings was an amiable and charismatic man,
if somewhat diminished from the road.
As we rode along, I talked straight. I was not kind.
"I'll be honest with you, Hastings," I said.
"Your letter clearly indicated that you would act as our guide.
And I'm not sure which is more alarming:
that you left Fort Bridger without us,
or that you clearly don't know where you are going."

Hastings didn't seem ruffled in the least.
"Two reasonable questions, with two easy answers," he said.
"We left Bridger's without you because we had no idea you were coming.
And since my group was sixty wagons strong, it made sense to go ahead.
I knew any wagons to the rear would be left with an obvious road.
And as for the unfortunate turn down Weber Canyon," he chuckled,
"I can assure you that was not my idea. In fact I warned against it.
But detained at the fort, I left one of my men in charge.
I take full responsibility, but it was *not* my fault per se.
Had our advance wagons traveled the course I am about to show you,
we would have cut our way through the Wasatch in three days,
and we would *all* be crossing Salt Lake Desert as we speak!"

Hastings then seemed to lose his composure somewhat.
"Mr. Reed," he continued, "I rode back to the mouth of the canyon
in person to post that note to save you from a world of trouble.
You should be *thanking* me!"
I am speechless. Of course I do not thank him.
I said, "I will thank you to show me the path across the Wasatch."

"There is your path, Mr. Reed," Hastings said, pointing.
"Do you see that notch, three-quarters up the range?"

"I think so," I said vaguely.

"Take your time, Mr. Reed. Let's get this right.
Your wagons are stopped just beyond that notch.
Follow the defile westward along that indention of trees.
That distinct line is actually a series of small canyons.
It will take a few axes and a few days' labor, but
it will be quicker and less dangerous than the route we just took.
Once you reach the Salt Lake Valley, just follow our ruts."

"Hold on a minute," I said. "You talk as if you won't be guiding us."

"I *am* guiding you, Mr. Reed," he snapped. "But I cannot abandon
the forward wagons. *Your* wagons can *follow in our tracks!*"
Hastings stopped a moment and gathered himself.
"I apologize, Mr. Reed. As you saw, we buried a man today.
He was a good man. His life was an extravagant toll to pay
for the privilege of traveling such a hellish road."
Hastings became quiet and earnest. His eyes sparked.
"You have an opportunity, Mr. Reed,
to save your group from what we have suffered.
Walk down to those salt flats. Follow the base of the mountains.
Blaze your trail along the way to lay out your road.
Turn up toward that notch to reconnect to your wagons.
You can call that notch Reed's Gap, a mountain gateway that
every future California-bound traveler will pass through.
You can see for yourself, Reed, it is the straightest shot."

"Except that there is a *forest in the way!*" I yelled.
I had nearly fallen under Hastings's spell. He was *that* good.

"You are telling me that I must build a road.
Your letter said nothing about building roads."

But Hastings wasn't done. "Mr. Reed," he said.
"You have come all this way because you have a vision.
Hate me if you want, but why not see your vision through?
You won't be building a road, Mr. Reed;
you will be building the future."

We parted ways.

Hastings headed back to Salt Lake to catch the advance wagons.
I went on my way to blaze a trail through "Reed's Gap."
And so I had finally met the famous Lansford Hastings.
It crossed my mind how much Hastings was just like me.
So how can it be that I didn't much like him at all?

So Reed sets out alone to return to the waiting wagons. And as he goes, he blazes a path where he envisions the road should go. With each blow of his hatchet he exposes the white meat of the trees. Each blaze makes his vision more clear, his dream more real.

This solitude gives him time to think. To reorganize his reasoning. To unite the scattered fragments of his confidence into a new determination.

He has heard the girls teasing his daughter, saying Virginia has "set her cap" for the broken-legged Breen boy. "Well," Reed says, talking aloud to himself, "James Reed has set his cap for Reed's Gap! Let Keseberg and the others return if they must. Let them take the coward's way out. James Reed will move only forward."

He chops another blaze into the bark of a tree as he continues his one-man debate. "But you know for a fact, James Reed, there isn't a coward among them. No coward would have begun this journey in the first place, let alone get this far. You are a jackass, Reed. You know you cannot do this alone."

He goes on like that all day and into the night. He talks. He chops. He walks. He talks some more. He doesn't stop to hunt or eat. By the time he can smell the delicious aromas of the camp—the smoke, the bacon, the parched corn, and coffee—James Reed is ready to make his case.

The first face Reed sees as he drags into camp belongs to the scowling German . . . Ludwig Keseberg.

LUDWIG KESEBERG ⬥ *The Madman*
Hastings Cutoff

"Hastings promised to wait at Fort Bridger! He lied!
Hastings said he knew the route! Another lie!" I shout.
"He made us waste even more days sitting in camp!
Waiting for more lies!
Hastings lured us here by saying there was a shorter road.
And now he expects *us* to build the road for him.
I say we should go back to Fort Bridger. We're familiar with the land.
We can backtrack to the regular road in less than a week!"

"No," Reed answers back. "It may take a few days to cut a road,
but a few days now will save us weeks later on.
We've come this far. We can't lose our nerve just yet."

"I'm *not* losing my nerve!" I say to everyone.
"But neither will I be led by a liar and a fool."
At this last comment, I look Reed in the eye.

"Gentlemen," says George Donner, stepping between us.
"We won't resolve anything this way. We'll camp here one more night.
Everyone, please eat a good supper and rest awhile.
Then we'll gather, talk this through, and hold a proper vote."

Two Views, One Fate
Hastings Cutoff

Don't look back.
We must move on!

> Turn back now.
> It's not too late!

Don't look back.
Don't hesitate.

> Turn back now.
> The shortcut's gone!

The shortcut route will save us weeks.
A faster way. A smoother road.
From miles behind to miles beyond.
Don't look back.
Move on!

> The shortcut is a mystery.
> The road we left is tried and true.
> Hastings proved that he's a fake.
> Let's turn back now.
> It's not too late.

Don't look back.
Don't hesitate.

Don't look back.
We must move on!

> Turn back now.
> The shortcut's gone!

Ludwig Keseberg thinks backtracking is the right thing to do, but the idea of traveling alone with just his two wagons is out of the question. He is just one man, with a wife (still weak from her delivery), a three-year-old girl, a newborn, and the old man Hardcoop.

Everyone, in fact, is in the same situation. Whichever way they *do* go, they have to stick together. Their alliance is as necessary as it is uneasy.

The other thing that keeps them from backtracking is the very thing that brought them into this wilderness to begin with. Can you guess it by now?

Hunger.

Each mile thus far has been gained at a great cost. Unless death is imminent and certain, a retrograde march is unthinkable. And for now, death seems distant, like the howl of a wolf from deep in the canyon.

After all the debating. The arguing. The accusations and acrimony. After all is said and done. None of the emigrants turn back. Their hope had been to join forces with the advance parties. Now it seems clear that they may never catch up to Hastings. The nineteen Donner Party wagons are now alone at the very tail end of the year's entire emigrant exodus. There is nothing left to do but grab every ax, saw, and shovel they can find . . . and start cutting a road through the Wasatch Mountains.

Ludwig Keseberg —•— *The Madman*
Hastings Cutoff, Wasatch Mountains

chop chop chop
kaThunk chop chop
CRASH!

There is no *(gasp)* guide.

chop chop chop

There is no *(gasp)* road.

chop chop chop

There is no *(gasp)* Indian footpath.

chop chop chop

Not even a *(gasp)* rabbit trail.

chop chop chop

No rabbit would be so *(gasp)* stupid.

chop chop chop

Reed's Gap my eye!
The only gap I see is *(gasp)*

chop chop chop

the gap between Reed's ears!

chopchopchopchop
kaThunk

JAMES REED —◆— *The Aristocrat*
Hastings Cutoff, Wasatch Mountains

chop chop chop
kaThunk chop chop
chop kaThunk

Sickly Luke Halloran *(gasp)* has passed out
and had to be taken back to the wagons.

chop chop chop
kaThunk chop chop

Old Hardcoop has given out *(gasp)*
and the broken-legged Breen boy is still laid up.

chop chop chop
kaThunk chop chop

It's been two days since our camp
has moved at all.

chop chop chop
kaThunk chop chop

But today *(gasp)* we're in luck,
for out of nowhere we've been joined by
three additional wagons driven by a hardy
backwoods family from Illinois named Graves.

chop chop chop
kaThunk chop chop

Five or six fresh axes and mattocks!
And now we can see daylight *(gasp)*,
daylight ahead through the trees!

chopchopchopchop
chopchopchopchop
chop

VIRGINIA REED —◆— *The Princess*
Hastings Cutoff, Wasatch Mountains

chop chop chop
kaThunk chop chop
chop kaThunk

For two weeks me and all the other older girls
have been walking lunch and water to the road builders.
Mary Murphy, Elitha Donner, and me,
we're all three of us about the same age.
We gossip and talk along the way.

kaThunk

The sound of axes stops all at once
as three new wagons roll into camp
driven by the most ragtag travelers I have yet seen.
A dozen or so, men, women, girls and boys.

A full-bearded older man leads the first wagon.
A short, round older woman walks behind.
"That's the old man's wife," Elitha guesses.
The short, round woman holds a nursing infant to her breast
and clenches the stem of a clay pipe in her teeth.

A younger blank-faced fellow leads the second wagon.
Walking next to him is a younger version of the woman before.
The same plump figure; the same clay pipe.
"She's that younger man's wife . . . I hope!" says Elitha.
This younger woman clings to her man's arm so close you can't see
    daylight.
"She may as well be in his lap," Mary whispers.

Then the third wagon rolls up and all us girls just gasp,
for driving the oxen is *the handsomest* man we ever have seen.

"Girls, I think I may just set my cap for *that*," says Elitha.

"No you won't, Elitha," says Mary. "That man is ten years older than you."

"Besides," I say. "That's bound to be his wife walking behind."

And we all gasp again, for the woman in question
is even more beautiful than the man.

"That is the prettiest girl I ever have seen," whispers Mary.

"She looks like a queen," says Elitha.

As if she'd heard, the pretty girl turns and walks over to us.
She smiles and shows us a perfect set of white teeth.
And she says, "Hello, girls, my name is Mary Ann Graves."

"Is that man your husband or your beau?" asks Elitha
as she shakes Mary Ann Graves's hand up and down
frantically, like the handle of a water pump.

"Elitha!" I say, turning red.

"That's okay," says Mary Ann Graves.
"He's neither beau nor betrothed."

"Oh, well then . . ." says Elitha, smiling, "is he your brother?"

"Nope. That's John Snyder," says Mary Ann. "He works for Papa.
He's just *like* family. But watch out, he is quite the charmer."
She says this loudly enough that John Snyder can hear.

He shoots us all a look, pulls a face, and laughs.
Then he picks up an ax and . . .

> *chop chop chop*
> *kaThunk chop chop*
> *chop kaThunk*

We all giggle. Mary Ann Graves smiles.

> *chop chop chop*
> *chopchopchopchop*

And then we get back to work.

> *chop chop chop*
> *chopchopchopchop*
> *chopchopchopchop*
> *chopchopchopchop*
> *chopchopchopchopchop*

BAPTISTE TRUDEAU —◆— *The Orphan*
Hastings Cutoff, Wasatch Mountains

One last aspen. One final pine.
We hack and chop our way through the hills
until we reach a clearing where the men lie down exhausted.
By Mr. Donner's and Mr. Reed's estimates,
we have but one slim mile to reach the flatlands of Salt Lake.

To our right is a narrow canyon with an easy slope, but
it is so congested with trees that it makes us all quake.
To the left is a tall, steep bluff, mostly clear,
but the sheer slope is enough to make us all despair.
George Donner calls a meeting to weigh the options.
"The men are all spent," argues Mr. Keseberg.
"We cannot clear the final mile without rest."

"What about climbing the hill?" says John Snyder (Mr. Graves's man).
"Make the oxen do the work. What else are they good for?"

"That's insanity," says Reed. "Even if we triple-team,
the oxen won't likely ascend such a steep grade."

"With all due respect, Reed," says Mr. Donner, "I beg to differ.
With the proper team of oxen at the lead . . ." Then he looks at me.
". . . and the proper ox driver, we just might succeed."

Then Mr. Keseberg, Mr. Reed, Mr. Breen, and Mr. Eddy,
Wolfinger, McCutchen, and Graves
and all the rest . . . they all fall silent.

And then they, all of 'em, look at me.

BUCK AND BRIGHT
Hastings Cutoff, Wasatch Mountains

We shoulder the yoke.
We bow our heads.
Plod our hooves into the sod.
Dumbly, numbly pull the load.
Chains pull tight
from yoke to yoke,
from pair to pair.
We'll take the wagons there.

We press our cloven hooves into the hill.
We fill the air with dust clouds as we go.
We bow our heads.
Lumber slowly. Pull the load.
Chains pull taut
from yoke to yoke to yoke,
from pair to pair to pair.
We'll take your wagons there.

One wagon up, two wagons up,
three wagons up and twenty left to go.
We know no haste.
The slope will take as long
as time and gravity allow.
Meanwhile we bow. We step.
We bow. We step. We bow our heads.
Low and bellow. Pull the load.
Chains to chains pull taut
from yoke to yoke, from yoke to yoke,
from pair to pair to pair to pair.
We take your wagons there.

From sunrise to sunset they use every ox in the party. They also tie off ropes to the few existing trees, creating a crude pulley system. One by one, they tediously haul up each of the twenty-three wagons. Whenever an ox gives out, it is replaced with another. Buck and Bright, in the lead, never show any signs of fatigue. And all the while Baptiste is there at their shoulder, calling out "gee" and "haw."

Up and down the long train, the other men take turns coaxing the rest of the beasts. John Snyder, out of kindness, tries to hand Baptiste a big bullwhip, but the boy won't take it.

As friendly and well liked as Snyder is, Baptiste doesn't like the way he treats the oxen.

The descent into the Salt Lake Valley proves relatively easy. Our travelers follow a slow-moving river until it empties its waters into a swamp. Within an hour they have found a road of solid ground. And a little ways on from there, the Donner Party wagons intersect the tracks left by Hastings and the advance group. Thus they begin the first stretch of the journey along the flat white alkali trail around the southernmost edge of the Great Salt Lake. But just as they are leaving one nightmare behind, there is another waiting in the wings. Get used to that, dear reader. Get used to that.

TAMZENE DONNER —◆— *The Scholar*
Hastings Cutoff

Today we stopped to bury Mr. Halloran.
The journey's exertions proved too much
for his hemorrhaging lungs.
I was startled to find myself weeping over the grave.
What surprised me more was that I felt anything at all.
I thought I had buried my heart with Tully
and yet there I was grieving over a man I barely knew.
My heart was nearly breaking in two as we lowered the coffin.
But why? We'd known each other less than three weeks.
Before he died he told me how his life had become a blur,
the days flying past even as we lay stopped in the mountains.

"Mrs. Donner," he had whispered. "You have been kind.
You and your husband took me in when others cast me out.
You have tended to me as if I were your own kin."

"You've not been a burden, Mr. Halloran," I said.

"Still," he coughed, "I want you to have what's in my trunk.
You will find money there, and stocks, among my papers."

I tried to protest, but he sat up suddenly, clutching my arm.
He leaned closer until we were nearly nose to nose,
and he said, "I hope you find what you have lost, Tamzene."

Before I could ask his meaning, he lapsed into a trance.
He slumped forward, his head in my lap . . . and never spoke again.

PATTY REED —✦— *The Angel*
Hastings Cutoff

Dear God,
By now you have met Mr. Halloran.
He's the one coughing, I imagine.
We buried him in a grave made of salt.
Eliza Williams, our deaf cook, says he'll reach heaven
"as well preserved as a Virginia ham!"
We found a note today, posted on a signboard.
But the paper was mostly tore up by the birds.
Mr. Keseberg kicked the dirt and he said
some things I shan't repeat into your Godly ear.
Although since he mentioned your name more than a few times,
and since he was talking loud as Joshua's trumpet,
I reckon you probably heard.

Amen

BAPTISTE TRUDEAU —◆— *The Orphan*
Hastings Cutoff

Displayed on the board is a tattered notice.
Mr. Reed says, "It's a note from Hastings, but it's torn to shreds."

Then Mr. Keseberg starts kicking up dust and cussing.
And all the men start in all at once talking and arguing.
And Mrs. Donner bends down and starts picking up scraps of paper.
She says not a word, just goes about her business.
Then her three little girls join in, Frances, Georgia, and Eliza.
Then her two older girls, Elitha and Leanna.
Then Patty Reed with her little brother Tommy in tow.
The redheaded Breen boys, the Murphy youngsters,
and every other child in the train drops down to hands and knees,
running little fingers through the sand like it's a fun game.
They are all of 'em laughing and shrieking,
and whenever they find a scrap they run it over to Mrs. Donner,
who lays them all out flat to piece the message together.

I'm looking over Mrs. Donner's shoulder as the letters take shape.
And Mrs. Donner says, "Can you tell yet, Baptiste, what the words say?"
And—
Well, she can see by my face right away that I can't read.
She stops laughing and I feel my face get hot.
And she whispers low so that no one can hear.
"Why, Baptiste, you mustn't be ashamed," she says.
"I promise you this, by the time we reach California
you will be able to read this note and anything else!"

HASTINGS'S NOTE: SALT LAKE DESERT

Atten . . .
            . . . follow . . .
. . . 2 days . . .   . . . 2 nights . . .
. . . hard drving . . .
            . . . cross . . . desert . . .
        . . . reach water.
                Lan . . . d . . . stings

This may have been the hungriest place on earth. Or at least it was the thirstiest. And thirst is hunger's kissing cousin. The hellish landscape through which our travelers are about to pass was once a vast and ancient inland sea, one hundred miles wide, three hundred miles long, one thousand feet deep, filling a basin from the Wasatch all the way to the Sierra Nevada mountains that formed its western bank.

Rivers from every surrounding mountain poured their waters into this insatiable pit. But not a drop would ever make its way to the ocean. The water remained trapped for thousands of years until the swelling reversed itself and the waters began to recede, absorbed into the earth. Without the benefit of proper drainage, the toxicity increased as the shoreline shrank. The only thing left by the twenty-ninth of August, 1846, was the relatively elfin Great Salt Lake, whose stinking water contained so much salt, no fish could live in it.

For miles in every direction, the receding waters left behind a bright white wasteland, unrelentingly flat and inhospitable to anything that lives: plant, insect, animal, or man. Where days are deathly hot, nights are deathly cold. There are no old buffalo paths. There are no ancient foot trails. Simply put, the Great Salt Lake Desert is four thousand square miles of absolutely nothing. It is a veritable reservoir of emptiness.

Everyone in camp—man, woman, or child—is either hauling water or cutting grass for the long, barren trek ahead.

Every wagon has a ten-, fifteen-, or twenty-gallon water barrel attached to its side. These are fitted onto a shelf and held fast with a rope. To ease the oxen's burden, the barrels are typically kept empty, except for maybe a gallon to keep the staves from drying out. But with such a thirsty stretch ahead, the barrels will have to be filled, along with every available canteen and water bag.

Water is heavy. The calculations are serious: too little water and your animals die of thirst; too much water and your animals die of exhaustion. But with so level a road ahead, the travelers hope the oxen will have an easy pull. And the sheer desolation of the terrain frightens all in the party into taking as much water as possible.

In the distance to the south, Pilot Peak rises ten thousand feet above the flat horizon. At the base of that mountain, the pioneers know, waits a freshwater spring and browse for the oxen. Didn't Hastings tell them it was there? Didn't Bridger and Vasquez tell them this was true?

CROSSING THE GREAT SALT LAKE DESERT
Hastings Cutoff, Great Salt Lake Desert

Ludwig Keseberg: The Madman
Now with the added weight of the water
I've warned Old Hardcoop not to ride.
Oh, I've seen the old man time and again.
I've watched him cling to the wagon's side.
"If you kill those oxen you'll pay the price!"
I'll make him pay if the oxen die.

Buck
We shoulder the yoke.
We bow our heads.
Plod our hooves into the crust.
Dumbly, numbly pull the load.

Bright
Chains pull taut
from yoke to yoke,
from pair to pair.
We'll take the wagons there.

James Reed: The Aristocrat
It's true that Pilot Peak
looks farther than two days' travel.
But Bridger and Vasquez said it was so,
and Bridger and Vasquez are honest men . . .

Buck
We press our hooves into the crust.
We fill the air with salt dust as we go.
We bow our heads.
Lumber slowly. Pull the load.

Bright
Chains pull taut
from yoke to yoke to yoke,
from pair to pair to pair.
We'll take your wagons there.

Tamzene Donner: The Scholar

Only the three little girls will ride.
The rest of us walk and nothing more.
We walk. There is no wood to look for.
We walk. There are no chips to gather.
And walk. No specimens exist to botanize.
Walk. No animals. No plants. Walk.
Absolutely nothing.
My botany book is a blank white page.

Buck	**Bright**
One wagon goes, two wagons go,	We bow. We step. We bow our heads.
one and twenty left to go.	Low and bellow. Pull the load.
We know no haste. We slowly go.	Chains to chains pull taut.
We step. We bow. We bow. We step.	We take your wagons there.

James Reed: The Aristocrat

We walk and walk all the hot day.
We walk and walk all the cold night.
Now it is noon on the second day.
And yet Pilot Peak looks just as far away.
But Bridger and Vasquez said forty miles
to reach the water on the other side.
And Bridger and Vasquez are honest men.

Buck	**Bright**
We shoulder the yoke.	Chains pull taut
We bow our heads.	from yoke to yoke.
We feel the heat.	We feel the heat.
The sun beats down.	We'll take the wagons there.

Ludwig Keseberg: The Madman

My three-year-old Ada walks and won't complain.
My beloved Philippine holds my daughter's hand.
My beloved Philippine shelters my infant son from the sun.
"I see you clinging to that wagon, old man!
Let me catch you again and I'll shoot you dead!
See if *that* will lighten the oxen's load!"

Buck	Bright
We shoulder the yoke.	The sun beats down.
We bow our heads.	Our tongues are dry.

Baptiste Trudeau: The Orphan

I have never endured such sun and heat.
I have never seen a whiteness so blinding.
Now, in the distance, I see fifty giant wagons.
Pulled by hundreds of giant oxen.
I stop to ponder them. They stop, too.
I cup my hand to shade my eyes.
Fifty giant teamsters raise giant hands as well.
I wave my goad stick. Fifty giant goads wave back.
A trick of the desert. We are turned into ghosts
before we are even dead.

Buck	Bright
Step, pull. Step, pull.	From yoke to yoke,
Dumbly, numbly pull the load.	we'll take the wagons there.

Tamzene Donner: The Scholar

The margin fades forever and forever. Walking.
The horizon shimmers and clear as day I see
the familiar outlines of our farm in Carolina,
the fruit trees, the vegetable garden, walking
and (ah!) the crooked, creaking, broken gate.
And walking toward me—Tully.
Walking to me with a glass of lemonade
and shaved ice. I walk. And I stumble. Stuck.
Look down. And I've lost my shoe in the mud.

Buck	**Bright**
Step, pull. Step, pull.	From yoke to yoke, we trudge.
Dumbly, numbly stuck in mud.	We'll take the muddy wagons there.

Virginia Reed: The Princess

Our wagons have dropped to the rear of the line.
The Donners' wagons are a short ways ahead.
Milt and Pa are scraping thick mud from the wheels.
And Billy—"Pa! Billy!" I cry.
Billy is stepping into mud to his knees.
His coat is slick with sweat.
"Pa! It's Billy. What's wrong with Billy?"

Buck	**Bright**
We trip in mud. We step. We bow.	We need more water now.
We need to drink the water now.	Low and bellow. Pull the load.

Baptiste Trudeau: The Orphan

All the oxen bellow for water.
Even Buck and Bright are weak from the heat.
Our water is mostly gone.
I wet a rag and run it
over every ox's tongue.
Buck and Bright, at one ton each,
nurse the rag like calves on the teat.

Buck	Bright
We step. We stumble. Step and bow.	From yoke to yoke to yoke we trudge.
We need to drink the water now.	We take the heavy wagons there.

James Reed: The Aristocrat

Bridger was wrong. Vasquez was wrong. Hastings was wrong.
How could they not have known?
I will ride out alone toward Pilot Peak to find water.
I say my goodbyes to Margret and the children.
Virginia wants to follow, but Billy is too far gone.
Glaucus is nearly spent himself.
I instruct Milt and the others to move on
as far as possible before turning the animals out.
"We can't just leave Billy behind to die," Virginia cries.
"We're in a pickle, Princess," I say.
Then I turn and ride away.

Buck	Bright
We step. We stumble. Step and bow.	From yoke to yoke to yoke we trudge.

Virginia Reed: The Princess
I wipe the mud from Billy's hooves.
His fetlocks bleed from the sharp salt crust.
I cup my hand. Offer the last drops of water I have.
He will not drink.
The water drips through my fingers.
And Ma is suddenly there. She slaps my hand.
"How dare you waste that water!" she says.
"But he's dying, Ma."
"If we don't keep moving, we'll *all* be dying," Ma says.
"Now keep up with this wagon, or so help me Jesus,
I will tie you to the tailgate if I have to!"
"I'll never forgive you for this," I say.
"Never!"

Buck
From yoke to yoke
the legs give out.
We stop. We kneel.
We bow our heads.

Bright
We feel the heat.
The sun beats down.
Our legs give out.
We kneel and bow.

Virginia Reed: The Princess
I walk. I walk. I walk.
And every few feet I turn to see Billy.
He is on the flat white ground.
His thin legs are folded beneath him.
I see him watch me walk away.
I walk. I walk. I walk.
Now he is a dark shadow magnified by the heat.
The desert is tricking my eyes again.
Three giant shadow ponies rise up on their feet.
Three giant shadow ponies wobble and sway.

Three shadow ponies, on knees as if to pray.
Two shadow ponies crumple to the ground.
One shadow pony falls onto its side.
Billy disappears into the shimmering heat.
I walk. I walk. I walk.

Baptiste Trudeau: The Orphan
Mr. Donner says, "Pull up, boys. We'll leave the wagons here for now."
One more step of hard labor would kill Buck and Bright.
We stop now and release all the oxen from their yokes.
I warn Mr. Donner, Sam Shoemaker, and the others
to secure each ox to a lead.
An ox can smell water a mile away.
Thirsty as they are, they are likely to stampede.
We walk and walk and walk.

Buck	**Bright**
We walk. We walk.	We walk. We walk.
We lay our burdens down.	We must have water now.
We drop yokes. We drop chains.	We leave our wagons on the sand.
We must have water now.	We reach the water and bow down.
One wagon left, two wagons left,	One wagon left, two wagons left,
one and twenty left behind.	one and twenty left behind.
We leave our chains. We walk.	The oxen gather all around.
Drop our yokes. We walk and low.	Reach the water and bow down.

Patty Reed ⟶ *The Angel*
Hastings Cutoff, crossing Great Salt Lake Desert

Dear God,
We waited in the wagons while Pa and the men
took the oxen to the water hole ahead.
Then after one thousand games of pat-a-cake with Tommy,
Pa comes back to say the cattle all ran off!
So we all took off walking. And us with not a drop to drink.
But Pa said, "We either walk or we die."
And Ma said, "James! You'll scare the children."
Pa carried Tommy, but me and Virginia and Jimmy walked.
We walked and walked till it got dark so we could barely see at all.
And I bet we would have froze to death except Ma,
she laid her shawl on the ground, and us children piled on,
and then Ma, she covered us with a blanket, and then Pa,
he started arranging all the dogs on top of us! Every one:
Tyler, Tracker, Trailer, Barney, and even little Cash.
It was a quilt made out of warm, furry dogs!
Then Tommy, he wet his pants and started to cry.
And Virginia, she kept on crying about her pony and saying
how she'll never forgive Ma as long as she lives.
If you meet a pony with cut-up, muddy feet,
that will be our Billy.
I hope you've got a barn in heaven for all them animals.

Amen

James Reed —◆— *The Aristocrat*
Hastings Cutoff, crossing Great Salt Lake Desert

Once the cattle got away from us, we never saw them again.
Eighteen animals gone—all but one ox and one milk cow.
Two wagons abandoned. This is what that means:
I was the richest of our party. And now I am the poorest.
Mr. Graves, Mr. Pike, and Mr. Breen have loaned me four oxen
that I have hitched to the family parlor wagon.
We have saved all the clothing, the food, and the guns.
I've cached whatever I could in the desert.
I've distributed our extra provisions among the others.
From here on out this journey is not about wagons
and calicos and silks and dry goods and good times.
From here on out I will be content
simply to arrive!

TAMZENE DONNER —•— *The Scholar*
Hastings Cutoff, crossing Great Salt Lake Desert

One wagon abandoned.
This is what that means:
We can pick up no more sickly Luke Hallorans.
We can take in no more Jean Baptistes.
It means leaving behind a cookstove never used.
Consolidating foodstuff into fewer bags and barrels.
It means tossing the extra tackle for the animals we don't have.
It means protecting the schoolbooks at all costs.
It means transferring them, all of them,
to the family wagon and walking if we must.
James Fenimore Cooper, Washington Irving, and Charles Dickens.
Keats, Tennyson, Shakespeare, George Sand,
Hawthorne, Emerson, Aristotle, Theodore Weld.
Three copies of Webster's newest dictionary.
Four volumes of McGuffey's Eclectic Readers.
Four volumes of Audubon's *Birds of America*.
I refuse to abandon my Audubon.
I'd just as soon toss out the Bible.

LUDWIG KESEBERG —◆— *The Madman*
Hastings Cutoff, crossing Great Salt Lake Desert

I have abandoned half my wagons.
This is what that means:
It means one half of all we own is lost.
It means more discomfort for Philippine and the children.
I have abandoned half my wagons
and this is what that means:
from now on, Old Hardcoop
must make it on his own.

PATTY REED ⇢◆⇠ *The Angel*
Hastings Cutoff, crossing Great Salt Lake Desert

Dear God,
I have to leave behind every toy I have,
including my dolls. All of them!
Virginia says she don't care because dolls are for babies.
So really what I want to know is, would it be a sin if I was to keep
Grandma Keyes's Angel dolly? It's real small.
And maybe I could keep the little pincushion she gave me?
And maybe a lock of her hair?
But just those three things.
I'll keep them hid in my dress, I promise;
unless you tell me not to.

Shh. This is the part when I silently wait.

Well, since you aren't saying nothing
I guess you must be giving me your blessing.
And a blessing from *you* really means a lot.

Oh. I almost forgot!
Amen

All told, the Donner Party has lost four wagons and thirty-six head of cattle.

When their inventory of food proves too pitiful to sustain them through to California, Charles Stanton and Big Bill McCutchen volunteer to go ahead and bring back supplies. It is heroic but also strategic. The wagonless McCutchen, traveling with only a horse and a mule, is out of food to feed his wife and one-year-old daughter. He agrees to go, so long as the others will take in his family. Leaving his family behind as he does, McCutchen is a good bet to return.

Stanton, on the other hand, is a bachelor with no attachments to any of the others and no incentive, save honor and conscience, to hazard the return. And yet he is trusted by everyone in our party, even suspicious Keseberg.

Unbeknownst to the others, Stanton suffers from a deep sadness that has forced him to flee the city lest he take his own life. Back east he could not live for himself; now he would live for kind-hearted Tamzene Donner, the redheaded Breen boys, strange little Patty Reed, and all the others.

Stanton is scarcely five foot five, and McCutchen is a towering six foot six. Side by side they make a comical sight as they ride off. A big man atop a small horse. A small man atop a big mule. Comical, perhaps, but no one is laughing. You see, last night a storm passed through, blanketing the surrounding mountains with snow. While this bottomland camp is warm enough, the gleaming white peaks are a reminder that our travelers are already more than a week into September. The summer is gone. The clock is ticking.

And so, on the eleventh, they finally break camp. Then they turn their backs to the beautiful spring at the base of Pilot Peak. Every soul among them hungers only for a smooth and easy road.

TAMZENE DONNER —◆— *The Scholar*
Hastings Cutoff, skirting the Humboldt Mountains

Soon after leaving the Pilot Peak spring,
I heard Mrs. Breen and Mrs. Graves speak sharply
against my George and Mr. Reed, accusing them of leading us
on a wild-goose chase—as if George ever twisted anyone's arm.

We went on snapping at one another,
keeping our interactions short, or else not speaking at all.
But in truth we weren't really angry with one *another*.
The truth of it was that we were angry with the men . . . *all* of them.

We have been following Hastings's tracks nearly a week now,
continuing west, from oasis to oasis,
across a monotonous series of short, waterless desert valleys.
Our food, our shoes, our clothes, our very souls are filled with sand.
We breathe it in. We swallow it down. We wipe it from our eyes.
And through it all there are still diapers to change and food to cook.
Today the tracks have led us straight into a range of mountains
stretching north and south as far as the eye can see.
Hastings's tracks turn due south! Where to and how far we don't know.
The only thing us women know is that the men expect us to follow them.
And what choice do we have? We must go where the men go.
In that we are without option.
But that doesn't mean we have to keep silent about it.

JAMES REED —◆— *The Aristocrat*
Hastings Cutoff, skirting the Humboldt Mountains

In my travel journal I have named this place "Mad Woman Camp."
The ladies are not getting along.
They are frightened. They see the snow on the mountaintops.
They feel the chill in the air. And it sharpens their tongues.

After the desert we were supposed to strike the original trail.
But here instead is a chain of mountains Hastings failed to mention.
A chain of mountains *Vasquez and Bridger* failed to mention.

For days we have followed the tracks of a man we had trusted.
Now the tracks suddenly turn south, of all directions!
I suggest perhaps sending two men north in search of a shorter route,
but Keseberg and Snyder laugh, "Another shortcut! No, sir!"

So we press on southward with the mountains on our right.
Snow is clearly visible on the highest peaks.
"Not to worry," Winter says. "I will be there soon."

PATTY REED —◆— *The Angel*
Hastings Cutoff, skirting the Humboldt Mountains

Dear God,
I have never seen full-grown folk so angry and hateful.
So to "sunny things up" I got me a slate from Mrs. Donner.
And Tommy 'n me wrote down an accounting
of our trip's merriest memories so far:

> *The red cliffs by Fort Laramie turned to gold in the sun.*
> *The very large herds of buffalo rumbling the ground.*
> *Tall, skinny Chimney Rock. Duck Duck Goose at Devil's Gate.*
> *Independence Rock with all them names written up there.*
> *Milt Elliott dancing after he drunk too much licker.*
> *Cooking fires made from buffalo poo.* (That one's Tommy's.)

We showed our list to Ma, and she smiled
a big toothy smile like she used to do all the time.
That's why I added *Ma's toothy smile* to my list of merry memories.
'Cause I would trade every last thing on that list,
every single one, for just one toothy smile from my ma.

Amen

PATTY AND TOMMY'S LIST OF FAVORITE MEMOREES

by
Martha Jane Reed,
"Patty" to her friends

and
Tommy

golden red cliffs

bufullow herds

chimnee rock

devils gait

duc duc gooz

independants rock

Milt gets drunk

bufullow poo on fire

ma's toothy smile

BAPTISTE TRUDEAU —◆— *The Orphan*
Hastings Cutoff, skirting the Humboldt Mountains

D-U-S-T spells dust.

For three days I drive Buck and Bright south around the mountains.
At night Mrs. Donner cooks while I play with the little girls.
Later she goes over my letters with me, and I learn to write my name.
I begin to pretend that Mrs. Donner is my mother. The girls my sisters.
Whenever I stand guard duty, I imagine I am protecting my family.

F-A-M-L-E-E spells family.

The mornings come too soon, with more dust, more walking.
John Snyder, teamster for Mr. Graves, runs his mouth—catchin' flies.
Elitha listens to Snyder talk on and on about nothing.
Elitha is the eldest of the five Donner girls.
"Why does Elitha think John Snyder is so clever?" I ask Buck and Bright.
He may be Romeo to the girls, but he is a devil to the oxen.
He curses his animals and hits them with the butt end of his whip.
The whip itself he snaps for no reason but boredom.

In camp the Breen boy, Eddie, who had broke his leg,
takes off the fancy splint Mrs. Breen had made.
We all clap when he stands and walks a few wobbly steps.
I think about all I left behind
and I am glad to be where I am.

These mountains, called the Humboldt Range, are well known to the Shoshone who inhabit them. The Shoshone live like royalty in this kingdom of rock and dust and sage. No one knows the land better; the Shoshone are *part* of it.

The members of the Donner Party are dour-faced and awkward, out of place, overdressed, ill prepared. Just as they are weighed down by their many possessions, they are weighed down by their sense of entitlement. Had the white strangers not looked upon them with such disdain, the Shoshone might have offered directions, six days back, to an easy pass at the northern end of the range that leads straight to Mary's River and the established California Trail.

Instead, like obedient oxen, the members of the Donner Party breathe in alkali dust and follow Hastings's trail as it loops for seven unnecessary days around the Humboldt Mountains, southward through three days of dust. One day west against grit-filled wind. North through three more days of mud.

Finally, on September 26, the wagons of the Donner Party squeeze through the northern end of a perfect snake trail of a canyon that has grown more and more narrow until it now empties them out onto the bank of a river, maybe one rod wide, with water as stagnant and still as a pond. And along the opposite shore, more wagon tracks. But not the ghostly tracks they had been following for weeks. These tracks are well-worn ruts. They have not seen tracks like these since leaving Bridger's Fort, nearly two months earlier.

"From the look of these tracks, I'm guessing we've finally reached Mary's River," announces James Reed. "We have completed the Hastings Cutoff."

"Hastings Cutoff, my ass!" jokes John Snyder. "It's more like Hastings Add-on!"

PART THREE

—◆—

While the Bodies Are Still Warm

September 26–November 8, 1846
Mary's River to Truckee Lake

Hastings Cutoff was meant to save as much as three hundred miles and offer an easy, well-watered road. Instead the party is exhausted from *building* a road over the most inhospitable terrain imaginable. They have actually *added* about one hundred fifty miles. They are more than a month behind schedule. And they are now racing to beat what looks like an early winter.

George and Jacob Donner's wagons have pulled well ahead. John Snyder and the Graves family come next. Keseberg's wagon is just behind. Mrs. Keseberg, slight as she is, helps Old Hardcoop into the wagon when her husband is distracted. In the rear, the Reed family's parlor wagon lurches along with its one large oxen and one small cow.

There is nothing to do but keep moving. And so they do. The sooner they can reach the Sierra Nevada, the sooner they can cross over into California, and the sooner they can all be rid of one another. As long as they keep moving.

And as long as nothing else goes wrong.

Virginia Reed —◆— *The Princess*
On the California Trail, following Mary's River

The Donners, up ahead, are making good time, I guess,
for we haven't seen them now for a couple of days.
But for the rest of us the going is slow on Mary's River.
We have paused today in order to get the wagons over a steep hill.
Milt Elliott and Pa are hitching up extra oxen for better pulling.
John Snyder is talking as loud as usual and giving unwanted advice.
The adults have all been bickering like this for weeks.

I know Ma probably needs me back at our camp,
but I've slipped off to be alone and think about Billy.
I can't get the sight of him out of my mind,
him stuck in the mud and watching me leave him behind.
Just then, I'm startled from my thoughts by the sound
of a horse's hooves . . . and a familiar voice.
"Well, I'll be! If that ain't the biggest sage hen I ever did see!"

"Eddie!" I shout so loud, I even surprise my*self,* grinning ear to ear.
I try to frown and start over. "Hello, Edward. I see you're walking."
But I can't help grinning again, like a fool.

Edward, who is grinning the same as me, says,
"Well, to be specific, the *horse* is walking; *I* am riding!"
Then Edward catches himself, his face becoming serious.
"I'm sorry about Billy," he says. "He was a good pony."

"I'll never forgive Ma and Pa," I say. "We coulda saved him."

"I don't know, Virginia. We lost a lot of animals in that desert."

"Whose side are you on, Eddie Breen?" I practically spit the words.

"I'm on *your* side," Edward says. "That's why you can count on me
to tell you the truth, even though it may not be what you want to hear."

Edward puts out his hand. "Clamber up here, Princess Virginia."

Edward swings me up onto his horse, and I settle in behind him.
And he spurs the horse into a gallop as I hold on for dear life.
We ride off across a flat plain,
empty of anything but sagebrush and a few lone trees.
In the distance I can see antelope leaping, and all of a sudden
I am aware of my arms, holding tight, around Edward's waist.
Aware of his shoulders. The warmth of his back.
My hair flowing. Another bonnet lost somewhere in the sage.

VIRGINIA REED —◆— *The Princess*
On the California Trail, following Mary's River

Not an hour later, we return to our group to see
the long tongue of Keseberg's wagon is set on end.
It looks out of place and ominous against the twilight sky.
I think I hear a crane calling out for its mate,
but it isn't a crane at all. It is Mary Ann Graves kneeling
over a man who is sleeping in the sand next to our parlor wagon.
As we ride up closer, I see that the man is John Snyder,
and he is covered in blood.
A group of men stand conferring around Keseberg's wagon.
Keseberg's voice bites through the murmur, "String him up!"
And I realize he's turned his wagon tongue into a gallows!

I jump down from Edward's horse and run
toward a second group of adults, who have clustered near our wagon.
Mr. Eddy is loading his rifle and handing a pistol to Mr. Breen.
Milt Elliott is cradling a double-barreled shotgun and glaring at Keseberg.
"Milt," I say. "What's happened to Mr. Snyder?"
"I'm afraid he's dead, darlin'," says Milt.
"He's *dead*? What has happened?" I ask.
Then Pa steps out from behind Milt with his hand against his forehead,
and I gasp at the sight of him, his shirt, his face, his eyes—
all covered in fresh blood. I can smell it.
It pours in a river down his cheeks. It drips from his beard.

I begin to speak. "Pa—?"

"I'm sorry, Princess," Pa blurts out. "I am so, so sorry . . ."

JAMES REED —◆— *The Aristocrat*
On the California Trail, following Mary's River

I tell my daughter, "I need you to tend this cut on my head."

"But Pa? What happened? What have you done?" Virginia pleads.

I have no idea what to say. What *had* happened?
Why was I covered in blood? Why was John Snyder lying on the ground?
As Virginia runs back to the wagon for the doctoring supplies,
I try to recall the terrible events of the last half hour:

Milt Elliott is driving a triple team of oxen up the steep hill.
And for some reason John Snyder has pulled alongside.
"For God's sake, Milt, just let me get on by," he says.
"I can do with one team what you can't do with three!"
And he's passing Milt, on his right, and he's spooking the oxen.
You see, there's a certain order to a thing. The wagons go up one at a time.
You unhitch the yokes and send them down for the next wagon.
That's how the thing is done. But Snyder is too impatient.
The oxen balk and collide, and Milt's job isn't an easy one.
It is up to Snyder to avoid the collision,
yet he rails at Milt as if moving eighteen oxen was a lark.
Snyder is being squeezed between the two wagon teams
and raises his whip, beating the animals to left and right.

And that is when I snap.

"John! Stop abusing those animals. This is not your place!"
I dismount from Glaucus and rush over to Snyder.

"I think you should climb back on your fancy nag," says Snyder.
"I'm done answering to you."

"Let us settle this once we reach the top of the hill," I say.

"Why not settle this right now?" he says. He runs at me,
and he strikes me across the forehead with the butt end of his bullwhip.
I can hear the blow from inside my skull like a barn door slamming.
And suddenly I'm on my knees, and I hear a roaring in my ears.
And I'm struck again. More slamming. More roaring. And now blood.
And just as suddenly, my wife, Margret, is there between me and Snyder.
She's screaming and holding up her hands, placing herself between us.
Before I am entirely blinded by the blood pouring from my forehead,
I see Snyder's whip handle come down across Margret's face,
knocking her to the ground with a grunt. Her eyes are wide with surprise.

But Snyder's surprise is greater still.
Surprised that this woman was there.
Surprised that he had struck this woman
who had always showed him kindness.
Surprised, most of all,
by the hunting knife suddenly between his ribs.

We both look at the knife handle protruding from his chest.
We look at my hand around the knife handle—then look at each other.
Snyder considers the knife for an instant and lets out a short laugh.

I remove the knife, hoping to erase the sharp, thin slip of steel.
But then comes the blood.
It pulses from Snyder's chest. A bubbling spring.
Snyder looks down at the spreading blood.
He turns up the steep hill, taking twenty-some careful steps
before his legs shake, then fail, then buckle.
Mr. Graves's son, William, catches John Snyder as he falls.
Mr. Graves himself rushes in to cradle Snyder's head in his lap.
Then Mary Ann is there, screaming. Wailing. "What have you done?

What have you done? What have you done? What have you done?"
The question released, repeatedly, into the air for God, for Snyder, for me.

I had liked John Snyder from the moment we met. We all liked him.
He was a man's man. A straight shooter. A troublemaker to be sure.
But always ready to lend a hand, to tend a child, to put out a fire . . .
to help me find my oxen in the desert—when few others would.
Always making everyone laugh. He was a joker. He was a cad.
And he was an arrogant, belligerent, bullheaded son of a bitch.
He had a big mouth. He was bossy. He was . . .

just like me.

PATTY REED —•— *The Angel*
On the California Trail, following Mary's River

Dear God,
I need you more than ever now. Not for me
but for Pa and for Mr. Snyder, who Pa kilt with a knife
so long it reached into Mr. Snyder and found his soul.
At first some of the men wanted Pa to hang!
I asked Mr. Keseberg if killing my pa would bring back Mr. Snyder.
And he said, "No. Mr. Snyder will be dead forever."
I said, "God says killin' is wrong." (Sometimes folks need reminding.)
So now they figure they won't hang Pa after all.
Instead they've told Pa he must go into the wilderness alone.
Alone with just his horse, Glaucus, and nary a gun nor bullets.
And Ma just cries and cries and cries. She's come undone.
The Breens are praying as I speak, and I hope you hear it.
Mr. Breen prays so much I bet you have an ear set aside just for him.
With all the world's prayers flying up your way, I suppose
you must have more ears than there are stars in the sky.
If you could aim just one little ear this way, I'd be obliged.

Amen

Virginia Reed —◆— *The Princess*
On the California Trail, following Mary's River

How many times have I watched my father's back as he rides away?
Usually I am sad that he is leaving me behind
or mad that he is leaving me to take care of the children.
But now I am frightened that he might never return.
It had all happened so fast. There Pa was, covered in blood.
There I was, tending the deep cuts in his head while Ma stayed in the
    wagon.
The men conferring. Keseberg cursing. Strange little Patty saying her
    piece.
Mr. Snyder, lifeless and limp. The shovels. The shallow grave.
Mr. Breen's solemn words. Pa drooping like a bent willow sapling.
More whispering and talk. I caught scraps of conversation:
. . . look after the kids . . .   . . . they'll be taken care of . . .
. . . it ain't Christian . . .   . . . okay, a horse, then—but no arms . . .
. . . brought this on himself . . .
Next thing I know, Pa is riding away. His back getting smaller and smaller.
I had never seen Pa so quiet. So low. And with no guns,
how could he hope to defend himself—or even hunt?

I find Ma in the parlor wagon curled up in a ball.
Little Jimmy is crying and tugging at her skirt.

"Ma," I say. "What will we do?" But she just cries.

I wipe the tears from my own cheeks.
I take a deep, deep breath. And I straighten myself.
Then I sit on the wagon floor and hold my mother in my arms.
She clutches at me, sobbing. And I run my fingers through her hair.
I have expected Ma and Pa to stop treating me like a child.
But maybe being grown up isn't about how people treat *you*.
Maybe being grown up is about how *you* treat other people.

Ludwig Keseberg —◆— *The Madman*
On the California Trail, following Mary's River

You may think that I am happy to see Reed go.
And certainly I am glad to be rid of his arrogant manner.
I am sorry for his family. But the *Dummkopf* brought it on himself.
He cannot just kill a man and expect us all to turn the other cheek.
Consider if you will how Reed has treated me:
Can I be blamed if I gloat just a bit at his present demise?
And as he ties his bedroll to his horse, preparing to go—
his head hanging low, finally at a loss for words—I cannot resist.
I cannot help myself. I stand on the other side of Glaucus.

"Mr. Reed," I say, "do you even know who Glaucus was?
Have you even read your mythology enough to know?"

"What is your point, Keseberg?" Reed says. He looks tired.

"Glaucus was a breeder of horses, the fastest in the land," I go on.
"They were aggressive, dangerous beasts. Killers. Devils on four feet.
For Glaucus would starve them and then feed them only on human flesh."

"What are you saying, Keseberg?" Reed says quietly.

"I'm saying that Glaucus finally met a well-deserved end
when he fell among his horses—and because he had taught them so well,
he was devoured by the very animals he had created.
They ate him up, Reed. They tore him limb from limb."

"You are a madman," Reed says to me.

"Perhaps I *am* mad, Reed," I say back.
"But at least I am no murderer."

JAMES REED —◆— *The Aristocrat*
Alone on the California Trail, following Mary's River

I feel helpless without my guns. Hopeless without my family.
I walk beside Glaucus, having determined to travel at night.
I encounter dead cattle along the trail, arrows protruding from their ribs.
It occurs to me that my family is better off with me gone.
It was me who had most wanted to leave Illinois to begin with.
It was me who had put so much stock into Lansford Hastings.
It was me who had urged everyone on when the cutoff looked bad.

I am so distracted by the accusing voices in my head,
I don't hear the sound of footsteps coming up behind me.
I don't notice how Glaucus prances nervously, instinctually
sensing the presence of others watching from the darkness.
Too late. They are on me before I can even think to hide or run.
I have dropped my guard, and now I will die because of it.
Then . . .
"Mr. Reed! Are you okay?"
It is the Breen boy, Eddie, his leg as good as new.
And a girl . . .
"Virginia?" I say. "What are you doing here?"

"I couldn't let them turn you out alone without a gun.
So I snuck out, and Edward stole his daddy's horse," Virginia says.

"Borrowed," corrects Eddie.
Then the Breen boy hands over my rifle and my pistols,
a satchel of powder, lead, and biscuits.

"You've saved my life, boy," I say. "I'm thankful.
That took courage, and I am very grateful to you."

"It is Virginia you should be thanking," he says. "She's persuasive."

"You're both in a heap of trouble if the others find out," I say.
I pull Virginia close and she hugs me back.

Virginia pulls away from me, standing straight and confident.
She looks me in the eye, every bit the woman her mother is,
and she says, "I'll tell you just what I told Edward, Pa.
Sometimes doing the wrong thing is the only thing left to do."

LUDWIG KESEBERG —◆— *The Madman*
On the California Trail, following Mary's River

"Old Hardcoop is looking bad, Mr. Keseberg,"
the little Reed girl, Patty, says to me. "Me 'n Tommy saw him,
just sitting by the way. Groaning and talking to himself."
"That's no longer my concern, child," I say. "Now get along."
Following Mary's River is slow due to sand.
And yet, for the first time in weeks, I feel light as a feather.
Reed is not here to "lead" us, nor bore us with his braggadocio.
I feel satisfaction with the simple task of quietly moving ahead.
There are no turns to take, only miles to make.
My new son, Ludwig Jr., is healthy; my daughter, Ada, a shining pearl.
And my Philippine must be the prettiest woman of them all.
She just holds the baby close and stares ahead. Always walking.
We are all walking. Toddlers. Children. Mothers with their babes.
The oxen cannot carry the goods and carry the people, too.
Four times now I've caught that loafer, Old Hardcoop,
stealing a ride on my wagon. Philippine gave him permission.
I think from now on the old Belgian can walk like the rest of us.
From now on Old Hardcoop can either keep up, or he can die.

VIRGINIA REED —◆— *The Princess*
On the California Trail, following Mary's River

Patty spends half the night staring into the dark,
waiting for Old Hardcoop to catch up to the wagons.
What she sees in that odd old man I just can't tell.
I'm trying to have courage, but things are falling apart.
Today, our milk cow finally gave out. The parlor wagon is too heavy.
So we left it behind and put our few remaining things
into a light wagon owned by Mr. Graves, who seemed glad to do it.
Mrs. Graves smoked and grumbled to show what a saint she was.
Mr. Graves and Mr. Breen loaned us one horse each:
Tommy rode one and Jimmy the other with Ma and me
walking alongside holding their hands. Everyone else walks.
We walked and walked and rarely spoke the rest of the day.
And with every step we left the parlor wagon farther and farther behind.
And I suppose it is still standin' there in the dark right now.
When we pulled into camp this evening we found a note left by Pa!
Proof that Pa was still alive!
Finally Old Hardcoop stumbles into camp and Patty starts to clap.
The old man looks half-dead. Patty feeds him a biscuit
and the poor creature rolls onto his side and falls off to sleep.
I finally lay my own body down and think about Pa.
I wonder how far ahead he's got along? I wonder.
I wonder if he's wonderin' what I'm wonderin'.

JAMES REED —◆— *The Aristocrat*
Alone on the California Trail, following Mary's River

The day I was cast out by my own people
I didn't care whether I lived or died.
But when Virginia came to me in the night, I realized
that it wasn't *my* life that mattered anyway.
On a sheet of parchment I've begun creating a map of the land.
A map that will help future travelers yet to come.
My very first entry depicts a long, steep sand hill,
its uppermost reaches covered with rocks.
"Hard pass," I wrote. "You must double up teams."
I could have written, "This is where I killed a man,"
but I did not. I have to keep my mind upon the living.
I have to stay alive.
When possible I leave optimistic notes and fresh-killed meat.
Without the wagons slowing me down I've made very good time.
And it wasn't long before I overtook the Donner wagons,
George and Jacob and the scrappy Murphy family.
I told them I had set out ahead of the others to bring back supplies.
And it was the truth. And my story made sense.
It had been weeks since Stanton and McCutchen had gone on ahead.
For all we knew, they'd been killed or just got lost.
My only lie was by omission. I did not mention the banishment.
I did not mention the blood. Or the knife. Or the body.
I smiled and laughed and talked the way I talk.
I've talked my way through worse troubles than this.

PATTY REED —◆— *The Angel*
On the California Trail, following Mary's River

Dear God,
Tommy is confused. He says, "What we waitin' fer, Patty?
Are we waitin' fer Mr. Old Hardcoop again?"
And I say, "No, Tommy. Tonight we're waiting for something else."
God? As you know by now, Mr. Hardcoop has fallen behind
for the third night in a row, but tonight he hasn't showed up.
Mr. Eddy and Milt Elliott have built a big fire to lead him in.
They tried to incite a rescue, but that didn't amount to much.
If Pa or Mr. Donner was here, *they'd* do something about it.
Mr. Keseberg said, "That old man is not *my* kin to care for."
Mr. Breen said, "I will send a prayer, but I'll not send my horse."
Mr. Graves said, "There's too many dangers to go searchin' after dark."
Ma asked, "Are we just going to leave that man behind like a lame cow?"
The elders in camp just got quiet and started wringin' their hands.
A while back they buried Grandma Keyes with flowers
and a headstone and green sod and a preacher and a picnic.
Now they're all too mad and tired to even dig a hole.
I guess the picnic is up to you, God, though (no offense)
you don't know *nothin'* about puttin' on a fancy fun'ral.
So I'm keeping watch in the dark now, God.
But I'm not watching for Mr. Hardcoop.
'Cause you an' me *both* know he ain't coming. Is he?
But something else is on the way, in Mr. Hardcoop's place.
I know it's coming. I can feel it in my stomach.

Amen

On the morning of October 9, Lansford Hastings and his sixty wagons, now nearly a month ahead of the Donner Party, are descending into Bear Valley on the western slopes of the Sierra Nevada mountains. Their journey is over. The ninety-one members of the Donner Party, staggered out for miles, are now completely and utterly alone on the trail to California.

On the morning of October 9, the banished James Reed and teamster Walter Herron, who has joined him on his crusade, are far ahead of the Donners and making good time across a forty-mile desert stretch. They are both afoot, hoping to keep the tired horse, Glaucus, from giving out altogether. James Reed cannot believe his pampered thoroughbred has lasted this long. By their own calculations, in three days Reed and Herron's rations will be completely gone.

On the morning of October 9, far behind Reed, along the winding Mary's River, the Donner Party has divided into two distinct groups. The forward group is made up of the Donner brothers, George and Jacob, along with their wives and twelve children.

The Donners are accompanied by another family, ruled by widow Levinah Murphy, with her seven children and three grandchildren. Mrs. Murphy's sons-in-law, William Foster and William Pike, drive the two Murphy family wagons. A handful of unmarried teamsters, Sam Shoemaker and young Baptiste Trudeau among them, round out the members of the lead wagon train.

On the morning of October 9, the Breens, the Kesebergs, the Eddys, the Graveses, the Reeds, the Wolfingers, and still more unattached teamsters make up the Donner Party's rear guard. They are a full day's travel behind. The sand continues, deep and troublesome. They rise at daybreak, after a frigid night, to discover that Old Hardcoop never arrived in camp.

William Eddy, Milt Elliott, and Mrs. Reed suggest a rescue. Keseberg, Breen, and Graves are the only ones left with horses, but each refuses to risk the loss. Eddy and Elliott suggest searching on foot, but

Graves, Breen, and Keseberg refuse to wait. So they leave the old man behind.

Farthest down the trail of all, on the morning of October 9, you'll find Old Hardcoop's broken body, propped against the stunted trunk of a large sage bush. His thin, arthritic legs are stretched out in front of him. His unshod feet are swollen. Cracked. Bloody. Raw red pulp.

On the morning of October 9, after one short hour of stillness, a pair of wolves approach, slinking toward the corpse, their limbs like liquid, their empty stomachs clenching.

JAMES REED —◆— *The Aristocrat*
On the California Trail, far ahead of the others, going west

"Please, let's eat the horse," Walter Herron says once again.
Herron is nearly out of his mind with hunger. And I must admit
my mind is going, too. For days now I have seen, off and on,
the ghost of John Snyder standing before me on the trail.

I saw him last night as I fell asleep.
I saw him this morning when I opened my eyes.
And I see him now, standing near Glaucus
and pointing at the ground as if to say,
To hell with you, Reed. You put me in the ground,
and that's where you are headed, too!
Suddenly my mind clears. And I speak to Snyder's ghost.
"You may see me in hell, John Snyder. But not just yet."
Then I grab my rifle, place the stock to my shoulder,
and aim at Glaucus's temple. He lowers his head as if he knows.
Then a flash . . . from the morning sun. A flash of sunlight
reflects off something on the ground. A bean.
A single. Beautiful. Nutritious. Bean. I uncock my rifle.
Glaucus nuzzles my shoulder as I pick up the bean and examine it.
A few feet along the trail I discover another bean. Then another.
One of Hastings's wagons must have a leaking sack or barrel!

"Herron!" I yell. "Beans!" And I hand him two of the three that I've found.
"We shan't be eating Glaucus today!"
And we resume our travel, examining the path before us with heads
    bowed.

I haven't seen John Snyder since.

The Donner Party continues along Mary's River as the nights grow gradually colder. The flowing water grows more rancid and slow. And then, near the middle of October, Mary's River simply comes to an end. It doesn't empty into a lake. It doesn't join a larger river. It just stops like the cast-off water from a washtub.

The land through which the Donner Party now travels is so desolate not even a river can escape it. Not a drop of Mary's River will ever find its way to the ocean. It remains here, trapped in eternal limbo, a shallow, stagnant swamp with beaches of white alkali sludge and sinkholes.

Patrick Breen's last horse, a fine gray healthy mare, sinks up to her knees. Then up to her flanks—devoured by the hungry muck. This is the very horse that Breen would not risk the loss of to rescue Old Hardcoop. Pity. Oh, pity.

The Eddys are left with just one ox. The Eddys, the Reeds, and many of the others are forced to continue on foot.

The Reeds find room for some of their clothing in the Breen wagons, but all their food has disappeared, dispersed among the many. William Eddy pulls two possessions from his abandoned wagon bed: three pounds of loaf sugar and a broken gun. The former he places in a pack on his back. The latter he tosses into the muck of the Mary's River sink. He also keeps a pouch of bullets and a powder horn. With Reed gone, William Eddy is likely the best hunter among them. A hunter without a gun; the very definition of hunger.

Instead of a gun, Eddy will carry his three-year-old, Jimmy, across the desert. Mrs. Eddy will carry the one-year-old, Margaret.

Thanks to the relentless Salt Lake Desert, the adept Shoshone, and the diligent Paiutes, the Donner Party has already lost over one hundred cattle, oxen, and horses. The next twenty miles will likely claim more. But winter will not wait; they have to press on.

TAMZENE DONNER ⟶⬦⟵ *The Scholar*
On the California Trail, following Mary's River

"We can take the time to bury them if you want," says George.
"No, that won't be necessary," I say. "But thank you for the offer."
George says, "We could make a map. Return for them someday."
But we both know that will never happen.

It is the books. The oxen are dying because of the books.
Two wooden crates of books that I painstakingly collected for months.
To survive we must offer them up as a sacrifice to this desolate land.

It is the books.
The history of our times. The geography of our world.
The philosophy of our souls. The meaning of our stars.
The balance of our equations. The truth of our spirits.

It is the books.
Kirkham's *Grammar*. The McGuffey Readers.
The works of Shakespeare and Aristotle.
James Fenimore Cooper, Washington Irving, and Charles Dickens.
John Keats, George Sand, Lord Byron, Blake,
Hawthorne, Emerson, Theodore Weld.
Four volumes of Audubon's *Birds of America*.
Even the Audubon.
But on a whim
I opt to keep one volume of poems by a fellow named Tennyson.
"Out with the old. In with the new," my husband says, trying to help.
We stack our civilization neatly in the desert. We turn away and walk.
I do not have to look back to see what's been left behind.
The sun beats down. On the books. On our backs.
We are becoming the beasts. Equal to the oxen.
We are yoked to one another with one simple purpose.
Walk. Move on. Stay alive. Walk. Move on. Stay alive.

BUCK AND BRIGHT
THE DONNER PARTY
On the California Trail, following Mary's River

Buck and Bright
We shoulder the yoke. We bow our heads.
Plod our hooves into the road.
Chains pull taut from yoke to yoke,
from pair to pair. We'll take your wagons there.

    The Donner Party
    We shoulder our packs. We bow our heads.
    Plod sore toes into the road.
    Our skin pulled taut
    from bone to bone.
    Our stomachs turn.
    We take our hunger there.

Buck and Bright
One wagon goes, two wagons go,
ten wagons left abandoned on the road.
We drop and die. We rise and go.
Bow and bellow. Slowly go.
We pull the wagons down the road.
From yoke to yoke. From pair to pair.
We take your wagons there.

    The Donner Party
    One wagon, two, three wagons left behind.
    Abandon what's left of what we were.
    There is no was; there's only what's ahead.
    We drop and die. We bow our heads.
    We slowly go. We step. And step. And step.

No time to rest our tired feet.
The sun beats down; it burns our souls.
With little sleep. And little left to eat.
And hunger walks among us as we go.

Buck and Bright

Hunger walks among us as we go.

The Donner Party

Hunger walks among us as we go.

After passing through the fog, in the third week of October, the Donner Party finally comes to the Truckee River. They know this winding river will lead them to the Sierra Nevada mountains. They know from now on, water and grass will be plentiful. But they also know their dwindling food stores will not be enough to sustain them.

They have lost faith that Charles Stanton and William McCutchen, sent ahead so long ago, will ever return. Most of them figure James Reed to be dead. Why else would his happy notes and gifts of food have stopped so abruptly? So Mrs. Murphy's two sons-in-law, William Pike and William Foster, volunteer to forge ahead and try their luck. The Donner Party members trust that Pike and Foster will return, since the two men would be leaving behind wives, children, and a mother-in-law.

I am hunger. And I have no voice. So I have no say. But if I *could* talk, I might remind William Foster that the pistol he now tends has one loaded chamber and a persnickety trigger. Could I speak, I would advise *all* of them that the cattails growing in abundance at the Truckee River's edge (a ready food source) have been providing nourishment to hungry Paiutes for many generations. I would tell them they have been walking over edible soaproot buried just inches beneath their feet. And I would inform them that, only two days earlier, the diminutive Charles Stanton and the massive Bill McCutchen had *indeed* reached the large wooden gates of Sutter's Fort.

Charles Stanton and Bill McCutchen arrived at Sutter's Fort even before Lansford Hastings's lagging wagons. But Big Bill, all two hundred and fifty pounds of him, was overcome with his exertions, became deathly ill, and was forced to put his bulk to bed. It was up to the scrappy Stanton to take charge. The honorable Captain John Sutter, for whom Sutter's Fort was named, is widely known to early emigrants as a philanthropist and a saint—though the local Maidu and Miwok people don't much agree. Upon Stanton's arrival, Sutter readily offered seven fine mules, each laden with dry blankets, dried beef, cornmeal, and roughly ground flour.

It is worthy of note that the honorable Captain John Sutter made it very clear to Charles Stanton that the honorable Captain John Sutter expects to be honorably paid in full for every last hastily ground grain of wheat. And if his seven mules are not returned in good order, then the honorable Captain John Sutter expects to be honorably compensated for his loss.

The same is true of Luis and Salvador, two Indian vaqueros whom Sutter has offered to send along. They are reliable workers. One eighteen years old, the other twenty-three. Both of them Christianized members of the Miwok tribe. They speak Spanish, mostly. Some English. And of course their native language, although Sutter usually frowns upon it.

Salvador and Luis —◆— *The Savior and the Slave*
At Sutter's Fort, Alta California

Salvador
Ah, there you are, Luis—and just in time. I
am nearly done packing the mules, which
we were supposed to be packing *together*.
Where have you been hiding?

> **Luis**
> I would like you to address me as Eema.
> My Miwok name. I have told you this
> before. And I was not *hiding*; I was detained
> by a horse who refused to be broken.

Salvador
Ah, Luis. I fear that *you* are the horse who
refuses to be broken. If I call you by your
Miwok name within earshot of Captain
Sutter, we will both be forced to hide from
the hiding we would receive. Your name is
Luis Antonio, nothing more.

> **Luis**
> Luis Antonio is a name forced upon me as a
> child by a priest who baptized me when I
> was too young to refuse. Just like you,
> Salvador. I have told you my Miwok name;
> now you tell me yours.

Salvador
I am *not* the same as you, Luis. I was
baptized, willingly, when I was eighteen.
I am a true believer.

Luis

Ha! And I truly believe the church would
have killed you if you had not converted.
Tell me your Miwok name, Salvador. Say it
just once. No one is listening. I promise not
to tell.

Salvador

I am Salvador. And nothing else. You are
Luis, and nothing else. Captain Sutter has
chosen us to guide the little man, Stanton,
over the mountains to relieve a group of
women and children. I am going, gladly, to
help save these people from their suffering.

Luis

And I go, gladly. I go in order to get away
from the stink of Sutter's Fort. And
maybe after I've crossed the mountains,
I won't come back.
I know enough about horses
to run a ranchero of my own.

Salvador

Your ranchero would have to be very far
away. Captain Sutter will hunt you down
and castrate you like any other unruly
stallion. I am not so young and strong as
you, Luis, but I have more brains. Captain
Sutter trusts you. Don't ruin it. Or it is back
to the wheat fields and the feeding trough
for both of us.

Ludwig Keseberg ⇥✦⇤ *The Madman*
On the California Trail, following the Truckee River west

Do you believe that certain things are predestined?
Well, I tell you that they are.
For how else do bad things happen to good people?
And how else do good things happen to bad people?
Today we have reached a beautiful place they call Truckee Meadows.
There are wild geese everywhere, and I'm determined to bag one.
My shotgun is loaded and I am excited with the sport.
"Philippine," I call as I set out, "I dare say I am . . . happy!"
But we who are born under evil stars do not stay happy for long.
I am so distracted by the hunt, and eagerly watching the game,
that I do not notice how the willows along the steep bank
have been burned off into short, sharp stubs sticking up like knives.
I feel sudden pain, and just like that, my happiness turns to horror.
I look down, and I see the tip of a sharpened willow
protruding through the top of my buckskin moccasin.
The willow has pierced me, like a tiny spear,
into the ball of my foot, up between the bones of my toes.
I lift my impaled foot off the willow pike, and I scream in pain
as the inside of my moccasin fills up with warm blood.

JAMES REED —◆— *The Aristocrat*
In the Sierra Nevada mountains, west of the pass

"It's the right thing to do, Reed," says Herron. "You won't regret this."
We have long since eaten every bean we found along the trail.
So as night begins to fall, Walter Herron and I descend
into the valley to slaughter poor Glaucus.
Glaucus, who has survived for so long against the odds.
I had been warned all along not to bring a thoroughbred on the journey.
And he has proved every naysayer wrong.
We have come so far. We are so near our destination.
"I'm sorry, old friend," I say to Glaucus as I lead him down the hill.
"I'm afraid there is no other—"
"Hey, look!" Walter Herron interrupts me. "Ain't those wagons?"
There, in the valley clearing—white canvas, glistening through the gloam.
Wagons! Wagons full of people. Wagons full of food!
Glaucus gives a whinny as if aware of another narrow escape.
Walt Herron starts to laugh, then he faints with a thud.

After Herron is revived with a bit of bread and bacon,
I am surprised and happy to discover Charles Stanton among this group.
Stanton, who had set out so long ago with Big Bill McCutchen.
"Captain Sutter graciously loaned these mules to my care," says Stanton.
"We have packed them with as much food as we could."
"And what about Big Bill?" I ask.
"McCutchen took ill," says Stanton. "He had to stay behind."
"And you returned," I say, "to give relief to the families of other men?
You have come all this dangerous way alone?"
"Not alone," says Stanton. "I have Luis and Salvador!"

SALVADOR AND LUIS —◆— *The Savior and the Slave*
In the Sierra Nevada mountains, west of the pass

Salvador
Little Man Stanton says the one with the fine
horse is Reed, their leader.

> **Luis**
> He does not *look* like a leader. He seems
> half-dead.

Salvador
Stanton says they have traveled many days.
He says they are nearly starved.

> **Luis**
> Why did they not just eat the horse?

Salvador
Perhaps the *horse* is the leader, Luis.

> **Luis**
> I've told you, call me Eema, my Miwok
> name. Little Man Stanton does not know
> that Sutter forbids it. There is no harm.

Salvador
Sutter will find out once we return.

> **Luis**
> You mean *if* we return? In these mountains
> we are free men.

Salvador

Free or not, soon we will be *cold* men. See
how that ring of light encircles the moon?

> **Luis**
>
> I can see it, my friend. I know what it means.

Salvador

The sky cannot hold back much longer.

> **Luis**
>
> Snow is on the way.

JAMES REED —◆— *The Aristocrat*
On the road to Sutter's Fort, west of the pass

I left Walter Herron behind to recover in Bear Valley
while I continued my journey west on a fresh horse,
nursing poor loyal Glaucus on a lead along the way.
I began to pass fields of newly planted winter wheat.
And today, nearly three weeks after my unfortunate
dustup with poor John Snyder, I cross
one final river and follow the trail up a hill
to the massive white walls of Sutter's Fort.
And standing in my path, as if on cue, is a man in his forties,
in a finely woven hunting frock, with a well-groomed mustache,
long, full sideburns, and a large-brimmed white straw hat.
"Hello, Mr. Reed," says the stranger. "I understand you are in trouble."
"How is it that you know my name?" I ask.
"My name is Captain John Sutter, sir. At your service.
And nothing happens within a hundred miles of New Helvetia
that I do not know about. I, Sutter, am the law."

He shakes my hand and graciously escorts me across a small bridge
and past several small adobe corrals teeming with horses.
He gestures to the animals with kingly confidence.
"You can see, Mr. Reed, that in this land there is no need
to hang on to any beast beyond its usefulness."
He pats poor wheezing Glaucus on the rump and says,
"Be it a plow horse, a pack mule, or a field hand.
Replacements grow here as abundantly as wheat!"

VIRGINIA REED —◆— *The Princess*
At Truckee Meadows, east side of the Sierra Nevada mountains

We arrive at a beautiful camp that the men call Truckee Meadows.
And I'm told that from here we will finally ascend into the mountains.
Eleanor and Lovina Graves, both about my age, have joined us.
The beautiful Mary Ann Graves is with her little sisters.
Mary Ann lost a lot of her spark once John Snyder died.
But even *she* seems to sense that our nightmare is coming to an end.

"What will you girls do once you reach California?" asks Mary Ann.

> *I will heat water in a hundred kettles*
> *and have a long soak in a washtub!*
> says Mary Murphy.

> *I will be a schoolteacher like my mother!*
> says Elitha Donner.

> *I will dance!*
> says Eleanor Graves.

> *I will get me a husband and a dozen babies!*
> says Lovina Graves.

> *I will get a dozen husbands and NO babies!*
> says Mary Ann Graves.

> *I will eat a dozen fresh eggs!*
> says Leanna Donner.

I will race horses by the ocean!
I add to the chorus.

Then—*BANG!*

Our game is cut short by a loud report.
Followed by the sounds of a man in anguish.
Frantic shouts come from the Murphy campfire.

"Something's happened," says Mary Murphy.
And she runs to where her brother-in-law, William Pike,
lies writhing on the ground. Her other brother-in-law, William Foster,
stands above him with a gun in his hand.

"It just discharged as if on its own," says William Foster.

Pike's wife, Harriet, kneels over her husband, removing his jacket.
"I cain't see where the bullet's got to. We gotta get this off!" she screams.
Mary Ann Graves, standing at a distance, looks on blankly.
Half a dozen helping hands succeed in exposing the wound.
Mr. Pike's back shows little blood, but a neat round hole tells the tale.

"It hasn't come out anywhere I kin tell," says Mrs. Murphy.
But by now blood is coming from William Pike's mouth.
He chokes. And he sputters. And he squirms in pain and panic.

"What happened?" says Eddie Breen, suddenly standing beside me.
But I don't have to answer. Edward sees the blood and gasps.

"Come on, Pike!" says William Foster. "Come on, Pike, get up!"

By the time the sun begins to go down on this beautiful day,
in this beautiful meadow, we have buried the body of William Pike.

A bright white halo rings a near-full moon.
And as if the winter sky is weeping at the scene,
soft snow flutters down to cover up the fresh-dug grave.

◆ SNOW ◆

snow

snow

snow

mous

snow

snow

snow

william
pike

snow

mous

john
snyder

luke
halloran

old
hardcoop

sarah
keyes

snow

LUDWIG KESEBERG —◆— *The Madman*
At Truckee Meadows, east side of the Sierra Nevada mountains

Hear me out. I feel badly for Mrs. Murphy and her family.
Her son-in-law was a good man as far as I could tell.
But to delay one instant more might spell our doom.
The snow has many of us spooked and rightly so.
Other families share my sense of urgency.
And so Philippine, Ada, Ludwig Jr., and myself have set out, finally,
with the Breens and their redheaded boys in the lead.
With us also is Mr. Denton, the stonecutter from England.
Also Reed's old friend, William Eddy, plus Eddy's wife and children.
Augustus Spitzer drives my wagon since I am injured.
My foot is swollen, red, and painful to the touch,
and walking is not possible. But I can ride a horse
with my foot bound up against the saddle.

We leave the Murphys and Pikes behind to grieve—
the Graveses, the Reeds, the Donners, and the others.
They will have to catch up as they can. We are racing the snow.
But before we go ahead even half a day's march
we run up on two Indians coming toward us with a half dozen mules.
William Eddy starts to panic.

Then, out from behind the mules, comes the familiar voice
of Charles Stanton, who had left us so long ago to get help.
Stanton says, "Stay calm, Mr. Eddy. Say hello to Luis and Salvador.
They're here to save your life."

SALVADOR AND LUIS ━◆━ *The Savior and the Slave*
At Truckee Meadows, east side of the Sierra Nevada mountains

Salvador
Let go of your anger, Luis. The child who
shares your saddle is as blameless as the
mule you ride.

> **Luis**
> That man Eddy would have killed us back
> there had Stanton not stopped him. We are
> risking our lives to save them, and that is
> how they repay us?

Salvador
Fear causes the bonds of their tribe to
weaken. They are leaderless. They no
longer travel together as they should.

> **Luis**
> The children were grateful for the food. And
> grateful for the news that their leader, Reed,
> is still alive. The faces of the young ones lit
> up like the sun when they heard.

Salvador
White children love their parents as deeply
as do Miwok children. The love between
parent and child exists in every nation.
Even the white man can feel love.

> **Luis**
> You sound more like a padre than a
> vaquero, Salvador.

Salvador

I am no padre, Luis. But I do believe in what
the padres' Bible has to teach.

> **Luis**
>
> Bahh! The padres teach us the ways of the
> Bible so that we Miwoks will love the white
> men even in the face of their cruelty. The
> padres tell us to turn the other cheek when
> the white men whip us. The padres tell us
> we must turn our eyes toward heaven as the
> white men take our land.

Salvador

The young children who now cling to us,
they are innocent children. They have no
blind hatred. Their eyes are open. Their
hearts are pure. And the little girl
with her arms around your waist—
she is smiling at *you*. I think she likes you.

> **Luis**
>
> I think she likes the lump of sugar I gave
> her. Loving children become hateful adults.
> This rain that is falling down on us is
> harmless in this meadow. But rain in the
> meadow becomes snow on the mountain.

Salvador

Children are not water nor rain nor snow.
They are like seeds of the wheat we
grow at Sutter's Fort. Nurture them now,
and later you will have bread in return.

Luis

Do you mean the padres' Bible teaches us to nurture our children now so that we can eat them later?

Salvador

Ha! Something like that.

Luis

All I know, Salvador, is that we could leave these people. Ride away as free men, and seven mules richer.

Salvador

And all *I* know is what is in my heart. And my heart tells me if you abandon innocence, you abandon all hope. And without hope, whatever path you take, you will never be free. Your spirit will be hungry forever.

Luis

All your white god's hope may be worthless as long as this rain continues. Rain in the meadow means snow in the mountains. And snow in the mountains means there will be no path left at all.

Patty Reed ⟶◆⟵ *The Angel*
At Truckee Meadows, east side of the Sierra Nevada mountains

Dear God,

Thank you for returning Mr. Stanton with food and mules.

The food disappeared as fast as it was put out! It did!

Thank you, also, for sending Mr. Salvador and Mr. Luis.

There was mules enough for me to hitch a ride with Mr. Luis.

(Mr. Luis is a grumpy goose, but I think he's just pretending.)

And Jimmy doubled up behind Mr. Salvador, who was very friendly.

(Did you know *Salvador* is the Mexican word for Savior!)

Tonight I took hot coals around to Mr. Luis and Mr. Salvador,

who laughed and called me Too-Lee-Loo, which Mr. Stanton

says is an Indian name of a white-footed mouse who stole fire

from the valley and carried it in a little flute to the mountains.

I danced and made like playing a flute and even Mr. Luis smiled.

It was the perfect ending to the best day in a while.

But better than food, mules, or white-footed fire mice

was the news, from Mr. Stanton, that Pa and Glaucus are both alive!

So wherever Pa is tonight, God, look in on him and keep him well.

Amen

JAMES REED —◆— *The Aristocrat*
At Sutter's Fort, Alta California

From a distance Fort Sutter had been a warm, welcoming sight.
Now up close the fortress had a cold, inhospitable look.
The massive walls were eighteen feet high and three feet thick.
A severed head, its eyes removed long ago,
stood blind watch, a frightful silent sentry—a doorman to hell.
Two large cannon stood ominously on either side of the entrance.
As we passed through the gate, we were met by more large guns,
mounted on wheels, with muzzles that seemed to follow us as we walked.
A group of Indians of every age (laborers in from the field)
crowded around a wooden feed trough carved out of a log.
Later, in a two-story adobe building from which Captain Sutter
oversaw the running of his own private kingdom,
two young servant girls entered the room and poured us whiskey.
(They weren't any older than my own Princess Virginia.)
And without ever looking away from the girls, Sutter said,
"Whatever you want, Mr. Reed. I'm happy to provide it."
The whiskey was as smooth as the finest back home.
But I was drinking with the devil.

Virginia Reed —◆— *The Princess*
Sierra Nevada mountains, Truckee Lake, east of the pass

Milt Elliott rode up with word that the Donners
had fallen even farther behind, delayed by a broken axle.
Our group now included the Graves and Murphy families,
Eliza and Baylis Williams, Luis and Salvador, and a few other single men.
After two days' travel we finally caught up
to the Breens, the Eddys, and the Kesebergs.
All of them gathered at the shore of a beautiful little lake.

I found Edward helping his ma with the cookin'.
"We tried to make it over the mountain," he said,
"but the snow was too deep and we lost our way.
I have never been so cold in all my life!"

Luis and Salvador warned that more snow was coming.
And Mr. Stanton was anxious to try it again.
So after lunch we set out once more but didn't get even two miles
before the snow got too deep for the wagons.
Mr. Keseberg said we should pack our possessions on the oxen
and try to make it out on foot rather than perish in the snow.
Stanton, Luis, and Salvador rode ahead.
Those of us who remained argued over what to bring and what to leave.
This woman wanted to bring calico. This man wanted tobacco.
This one wanted a feather bed. That one wanted a set of tools.

Ma said, "Oh, for heaven's sake. The children are turning blue."
And she spread out a buffalo robe upon the ground.
She commanded us to lie down, and we did as we were told.
Then Ma spread a second robe over the first with all of us in between.
"There," she said. "All of my worldly possessions—two robes, four
    children."

"And five dogs!" said Patty.

"Come on, dogs," said Ma. "Do your duty."

Obediently, all five dogs did as they were told.
Tyler, Tracker, Trailer, Barney, and even little Cash.
They all circled and shifted and jostled for position in the pile.
And despite our miserable situation, we all giggled.
And we lay there warm as corn kernels in a roasted husk.
And we watched the newly loaded oxen bellow and buck
and rub their massive backs against the trees
and kick and fling the packs in every direction!
For warmth, Mrs. Breen set fire to a half-dead pitch pine
and Edward and his brothers all gathered round it, laughing.
Mr. Keseberg, who has a hurt foot, fell off his horse into the snow,
yelling something in German that needed no translation.
Mr. Stanton, Luis, and Salvador returned to find half the camp in chaos,
the other half in bed.

SALVADOR AND LUIS —◆— *The Savior and the Slave*
Sierra Nevada mountains, approaching the pass from the east

Salvador
Only white men would risk the lives of their
children to carry with them so many useless
things. Boxes of nothing. Bags full of rocks.

        Luis
        The Miwok work for a month in order to
        buy a shirt or a pair of pants from Captain
        Sutter's store. The white man hardly works
        at all and lives like a king. Perhaps if we had
        such wealth we would understand.

Salvador
If they were not burdened by so many
possessions, they would have crossed the
mountain weeks ago.

        Luis
        Do you never wish for possessions,
        Salvador?

Salvador
I have two possessions. And that is all I
need.

        Luis
        What do you possess?

Salvador
I possess my own soul. And I possess this
fine wool blanket.

Luis

And what will you do with your
possessions?

Salvador

I shall wrap my
soul in this blanket and rest against this tree.
Wait for the snow . . . and die.

Luis

Why don't you give me the burden of that
fine warm wool blanket and you will die
much more quickly?

Salvador

Because I want to be as warm as possible as
I freeze to death.

Luis

Since you are about to freeze to death, will
you tell me your Miwok name?

Salvador

No.

Luis

After you are dead, and I have stolen the
blanket from your frozen corpse, and you
have risen to haunt me, will you tell me your
Miwok name?

Salvador

No. Now stop talking and let me freeze to
death in peace.

◆ SNOW ◆

snow

snow

snow

snow

snow

snow

snow

MOUS

MOUS

snow

snow

MOUS

snow

MOUS

snow

You haven't heard from me in quite a while. Trust me, I've been right here all this time. Nor have I forgotten the Donner brothers, now tending their broken wagon.

George and Jacob Donner are no strangers to wood. They have built everything from rocking chairs to coffins. They know their way around a wagon's complex undercarriage, but a broken axle is no lark. Even though Jacob has one spare axle left, the ends will need tapering to fit into the smaller wheel hubs of his big brother's wagon.

And, for an instant, George hungers to be holding his wife instead of this damned axle, which causes his concentration to waver. And in that same instant, Jacob, hungering only for the tedious job to be done, lets slip the sharp tip of the chisel as he swings his hammer.

Neither brother knows, at first, why Tamzene Donner is screaming and rushing toward her husband. Or why she is grabbing George's hand that way. Or where all the blood is coming from—fresh and warm and steaming in the chilly air.

In fact, if not for an expertly wrapped bandage (applied by Tamzene herself), George can "hardly believe the wound is there a'tall." The brothers finish their axle, and the two Donner families move on a full sixteen miles before finding a suitable camping spot. Nearby is a creek and a thick stand of alders.

Young Baptiste ties up his beloved Buck and Bright and the other oxen to make it easier to collect them in the morning. He notices the telltale ring around the moon. He notes, with annoyance, the soft rain beginning to fall. Then the orphan turns in, laying his tired body down among the other single men. And the whole camp sleeps. And the wound on the back of George's hand is all but forgotten by everyone . . . except me.

Specifically, the cut is four inches long. A jagged quarter-inch wide. A full half-inch deep in places. Jacob's chisel was sharp (thanks to Old Hardcoop), but it was dirty. And that dirt was alive with thousands of thriving invisible creatures whose hunger is as insatiable as it is silent.

Only eight miles away to the west, around Truckee Lake, two feet of snow has fallen in two hours. Six miles farther still, four-foot drifts have begun to obscure the trail that ascends to the pass.

Here we find the remainder of the Donner Party. The ones who refused to follow Charles Stanton and Luis and Salvador over the pass. The ones who wanted just one night's rest, an escape from the cold, before proceeding on. And of course, unlike me, these weary souls are only human after all. We can hardly blame them for wanting to sleep or wanting to be warm.

Neither can we blame the snow for wanting to fall. And fall. And fall. All through the night the snow comes down. Silent. And soft. And slow.

Salvador leans against his tree, shrugging tiny white peaks from his shoulders. Luis sits beside Salvador, slumped forward onto his knees, the brim of his hat pulled back to keep the snow from falling down his shirt. The hat itself resembles a perfectly round, white-frosted cake. Margret Reed rises throughout the night to brush the accumulation from the children and the dogs. As does every other mother in camp. But eventually even the mothers give in.

And in the morning the travelers awake to a weight pressing down on their chests. Wake up to find themselves buried alive. From their vantage point against the tree, Salvador and Luis look over the empty campsite as men, women, and children pop up through the smooth white surface, one by one, like bewildered dead men rising from their graves.

Whatever slim chance of passage they may have had the day before is certainly gone now. After morning reconnaissance, Salvador and Luis report that the pass ahead is now buried under snow. Some *fourteen feet* of snow. There is nothing to do but gather whatever possessions and cattle they can find. Then they will walk back down the mountain and regroup at the lake, where the snow is less deep.

The women sense it first. The women always do. Being surrounded by children makes it worse. All those innocent faces with wide yearning eyes and empty mouths. The women know for certain now hunger is walking among them.

TAMZENE DONNER —◆— *The Scholar*
At Alder Creek camp

"Wake up, Momma! Momma, wake up!"
Frances, Georgia, and little Eliza push, pull, shove, and shake me awake.
"Look at all the snow, Momma! Look it. Look it. Look it!"

We had passed the night tolerably in makeshift tents.
But the snow had fallen a good twelve inches or so,
which makes breakfast preparations challenging to say the least.
We are surprised after breakfast by Milt Elliott, the Reeds' man,
who brings us news that frightens the very breath from my lungs.
"The pass over the mountain is closed off by snow," Milt says.
"And if the soupy sky west of the ridge is any indication,
we're about to get a second storm—and soon.
The rest of us are building shelters around Truckee Lake."

"We'll gather up our things and head out early," says Jacob.
"No, Mr. Donner," says Milt. "You don't understand.
I ran all this way to tell you that the pass is gone!
There's no hope of moving your wagons even one more mile!
Your time is better spent building cabins right here."
"This is impossible," says George. "Hastings's book said
the snows *never* come until the end of November."
"I guess maybe the snows can't read," answers Milt.
"'Cause the snow is here. And it's got here a whole month early.
And there's more of it on the way."

VIRGINIA REED —◆— *The Princess*
At Truckee Lake camp

Ma told me not to wander off but I did anyway.
This time it's not my own fault, because
Number One: That old curmudgeon Mr. Graves is building us a cabin
near half a mile from the cabins at the lake
and he can't expect me to live like a hermit.
Number Two: Patty and Tommy ran off first,
so I figure I'm just helping out by running off in pursuit.
I find Tommy and Patty down by the shore of the lake.
Tommy is jumping up and down, saying, "Them's fish!"
And he is pointing to a school of skittish trout just below the surface.
But Patty is lost in thought again, staring out across the lake.
"He's out there, Virginia," Patty says without looking away.
"Pa is on the other side of those mountains. I can feel him."
As I've always said, Patty Reed is a strange child.
But looking up at the mountain
I almost think I can feel Pa out there, too.

JAMES REED —◆— *The Aristocrat*
In the Sierra Nevada mountains, west of the pass

Big Bill McCutchen, whom Stanton left behind at Sutter's Fort,
was now fully recovered and determined to rescue his family.
On the third day of November, we left Sutter's Fort together,
with nine horses, clothing, and as much food as we could carry.
On the fifth day of November, we reached Bear Valley
and found it blanketed in eighteen inches of snow.
A pioneer couple was waiting out the weather in a makeshift cabin.
They offered McCutchen and me bowls of delicious soup.

"What is it?" asked Big Bill McCutchen as he served himself seconds.
"That's what's left of Old Rambler," the woman said.
Her husband added with great solemnity, "He was loyal as they come."
McCutchen kept a serious face and said, "Yes ma'am, loyal *and delicious*.
I know Old Rambler would have wanted it this way."
"He *was* a good dog." The woman spoke with a faraway look.
"Of course the flavor is mostly in the sauce."

I had a full stomach and no complaints,
for I had vowed never again to complain about food,
no matter what it was. We thanked the couple for the sustenance
and we continued on our way east toward the pass.

Patty Reed ‑‑✦‑ *The Angel*
At Truckee Lake camp

James Reed ‑‑✦‑ *The Aristocrat*
Just west of the pass

Patty Reed
I know Pa is out there, Tommy.
I can feel him. I know he isn't alone.

> **James Reed**
> On the fifth day of November the snow is
> three feet deep.

Patty Reed
I know Pa is out there, God. He has food
and horses and he's looking for us.

> **James Reed**
> On the sixth day of November, more deep snow.
> We leave our horses tied to trees.
> We put whatever we can on our
> backs and we set out on foot.

Patty Reed
I can feel Pa out there
on the other side of the mountain.
Tommy and me make snow angels
to show Pa where we are.

> **James Reed**
> On the seventh day of November
> the snow is up to our shoulders.
> Even Big Bill can't muscle through this.

Patty Reed

More snow angels, Tommy.
We need more snow angels.
He will see them. I know it.

        James Reed

        On the eighth day of November.
        We are hopelessly stuck.
        The snow over our heads.
        To go on would be suicide.
        McCutchen and I stand helpless.

Patty Reed

I know he can see us.
I know he can see the angels.

        James Reed

        We can see perfectly well
        the notch in the mountain
        through which we need to cross.
        I can see it plain as day.

Patty Reed

He sees the angels.
But he can't reach them.

        James Reed

        But there's no way to reach it.

Patty Reed

Lets go back to the cabin
for now, Tommy.

James Reed
We are forced to retreat
back to Sutter's Fort for now.
We are finished for now.

Patty Reed
We are finished for now.

Patty Reed   **James Reed**
But we'll be back.   But we'll be back.

PART FOUR

—◆—

Hunger Walks Among Us

November 8, 1846–January 17, 1847
Truckee Lake, Alder Creek, and the Snowshoe Party

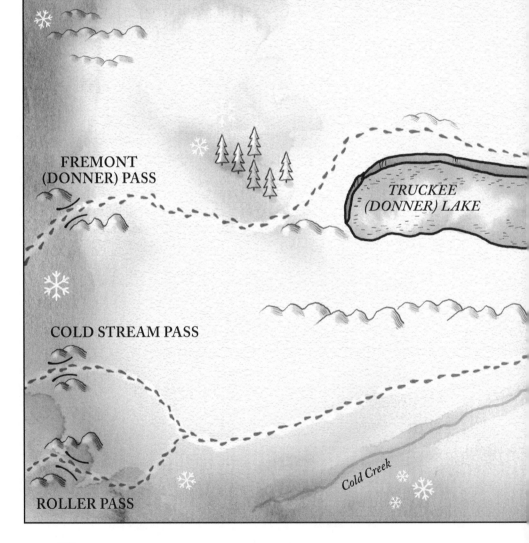

DONNER PARTY CAMPS AT TRUCKEE LAKE AND ALDER CREEK, WINTER 1846-1847

We may never be 100 percent certain of the actual trail taken by the members of the Donner Party in the winter of 1846–1847. The same is true of the actual locations of the cabins and tents, especially those occupied by the Donner family near Alder Creek. There is also some debate as to how many tents the Donners occupied.

▬▬▬▬ Probable trails taken by Donner Party members and rescuers

FREMONT (DONNER) PASS

TRUCKEE (DONNER) LAKE

COLD STREAM PASS

ROLLER PASS

Cold Creek

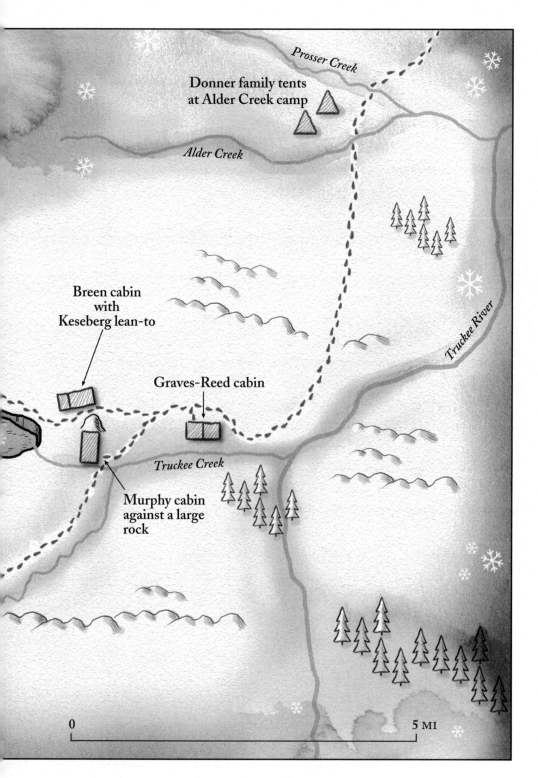

Prosser Creek

Donner family tents
at Alder Creek camp

Alder Creek

Breen cabin
with
Keseberg lean-to

Graves-Reed cabin

Truckee River

Murphy cabin
against a large
rock

Truckee Creek

0   5 MI

Virginia Reed ⟶ *The Princess*
At Truckee Lake camp

The whole camp is hammers, axes, and saws.
Dragging trees and notching logs.
Our lakeside camp is really three camps in one.
First off, there's the Breens. They were luckiest of all
because they got to the lake before anyone else
and moved into a small cabin already waiting like a little gift.
And Mr. Breen commenced to slaughter his beeves
to put up the meat and to use the skins as a cabin roof.
In fact every cabin constructed among us was covered
with pine boughs, canvas, and cowhides.
Mr. Breen begrudgingly allowed some of the Germans to build
an elaborate lean-to against the Breens' ready-made cabin.
Closer to the lake, maybe two hundred yards from the Breen cabin,
Mrs. Murphy's son-in-law, William Foster, helped Mr. Eddy
to build a three-walled cabin against the flat side of a boulder.
The third cabin, the one that I'm living in now,
is nearly half a mile away, out of sight of the others.
Mr. Graves says he chose the site
because it was near wood and a handy little creek.
Mr. Graves's son, Billy, and son-in-law, Jay Fosdick, helped out.
Mr. Stanton, Luis, and Salvador all lent a hand.
The finished dwelling is a double cabin that shares a center wall.
We can hear Mrs. Graves complaining through the logs.
But at least we don't have to look at her pinched-up face.
Mr. Stanton, Luis, and Salvador are bunking on our side of the cabin,
as is Milt Elliott, Eliza Williams, and her brother, Baylis.
Mrs. Graves has four other young'uns. Ma's got her three.
Add to that Mrs. McCutchen's little baby and you've got
eight children under the age of eight, plus nine boys and men,
plus nine girls and women, making for about twenty-six souls
all under one leaking roof—and don't *even* get me started on the dogs!

Baptiste Trudeau —◆— *The Orphan*
At Alder Creek camp

P-O-N-E-E spells pony.

The snow came on so sudden that we had to abandon cabin-making.

There it sits, the walls just four logs high, and there it shall remain.

At least until we chop it up for firewood.

R-I-F-U-L spells rifle.

I am trying to write a note to send along with Milt Elliott.

Milt and some of the others will try their luck over the mountain.

Uncle George and Uncle Jake are making out a wish list, too.

Promissory notes for oxen, mules, flour, beans, and sugar.

N-U-T-H-I-N spells nothin'.

I've got nothing to offer but my rifle.

I'd cross the mountain myself except for Buck and Bright.

O-R-F-I-N spells orphan.

I'd cross the mountain myself except for the girls.

Well, I guess they're like sisters to Buck and Bright.

And Uncle George and Mrs. Donner has been just like a ma and pa.

But mainly I'm concerned about Buck and Bright.

There's too much talk of slaughtering the cattle for the winter.

No way I'm leaving Buck and Bright behind for dinner.

The Orphan's Note

I am but a poor orfin with nuthin
I will giv my riful
for a ponee or a mule to rid

Jean Baptiste Trudeau

George Donner's Note

I, George Donner, hereby authorize
Millford "Milt" Elliott to purchase for me
six yoke of work cattle and three beeves,
for which I will pay cash or goods
on arrival in California.

George Donner

Jacob Donner's Note

Milt,
Please bring me five mules to pack
also four low priced active ponies
suitable for women & children to ride,
200 weight flour, 2 bushels beans,
2 gallons salt, 3 dollars worth sugar
if it can be had on reasonable terms,
and a cheese.

Jacob Donner

Virginia Reed — *The Princess*
At Truckee Lake camp

We've been snowed in at the lake now for nearly two weeks.
Milt has come in from the Donner camp at Alder Creek,
saying they weren't able to build proper shelter before the snow hit.
Here at Truckee Lake my family has shelter but little else.
Our cabin is cramped. Mrs. Graves is a grump.
Today Ma lets me escape toward the lake, snow or no snow.
I meet Edward outside chopping firewood with his brothers.
The two of us walk down to the lake with a willowy fishing pole.

"Me and my brothers have been trying to snag us a fish for days,"
Edward says. "But they shy away from every type of bait.
They've put on their winter appetites, I'd guess.
Lake's starting to freeze over anyway, so I guess it won't matter."

"At least your folks got plenty of food," I say.
Edward laughs, "Have you seen how much me and m'bruthers eat?"
"At least your cabin ain't packed tight as a woodpile," I try again.
"Ha!" says Edward. "We're cozy enough with Muther 'n Da, us six lads,
my baby sister, *plus* Mr. Spitzer and Dutch Charley! It's cozy."
Edward tosses his fishhook in the water as he talks.
"*And* Mr. Keseberg built a lean-to up against one end of our shanty.
He bangs on the walls if we even yawn, and he says, 'You woke the baby!'"

"My ma has sick headaches," I say, trying to keep the conversation going.
"My da has the gravel," Edward counters. "It hurts like the devil.
But he says all his prayers; he pees out a stone and then he's right as rain."

Patrick Breen's Diary
At Truckee Lake camp

Friday, November 20, 1846

Came to this place on the 31st of last month. Snow so deep we were unable to find the road when within 3 miles of the summit. Then turned back. Returned to shanty it continuing to snow all the time. We now have killed most part of our cattle having to stay here until next Spring.

LUDWIG KESEBERG —◆— *The Madman*
At Truckee Lake camp

So cold. Yet so hot. I am ice on fire.

Shhh–shhh–shhh.
Through the wall I can hear it, the nib of Mr. Breen's pen
scratching across the paper as he writes.
That's how quiet it is right now.
Silence, utter and complete; silent camp, silent cabin,
but that *shhh–shhh–shhh* in my feverish skull.
Philippine is sleeping. Ada is sleeping.
Little Ludwig Jr. is sleeping.
The boisterous Breen boys have gone to get wood.
Mrs. Breen has stopped weeping. Mr. Breen has stopped praying.
And the snow (the cursed snow) absorbs every sound.
My injured foot throbs. Just as Hardcoop's feet must have throbbed.
It is easy to hide one's fear amid the noisy bustle of survival.
The wagon wheels, the chains, the animals, the children wailing,
the chaos of construction, brutal bargaining, slaughter, chopping wood.
Every sound, for now, is swallowed by the snow.
Every sound save the sound I've been trying not to hear.
Mr. Breen's pen across the paper? No. Something else.
Old Hardcoop . . . scraping his knives to a keen sharp edge.
I close my eyes and see the old man. Miles away. Slowly approaching.
Bloody footprints. Bloody streaks across the snow.

Shhh–shhh–shhh. Shhh–shhh–shhh.

Patrick Breen's Diary
At Truckee Lake camp

Saturday, November 21, 1846

Fine morning. 22 of our company are starting across the mountain.

Another cold attempt to cross the mountain.

With William Eddy and the fearless Charles Stanton as coleaders, they set out with an ambitious crew of nearly two dozen. Salvador and Luis drive Captain Sutter's borrowed mules ahead. Around the perimeter of the lake, the beasts break a path for the humans to follow.

Back home in Chicago, about a year ago, Charles Stanton had his first thought of suicide. His melancholia, a constant companion, had been attractive in his youth. He was fiercely loyal. He was empathetic. The truest of friends. And he inclined toward poetry. But the mundane and demanding responsibilities of manhood had created in him a deep, unshakable feeling that something was missing. Ah, dear reader. Dare I say Mr. Stanton hungered for something? Something more? Perhaps he didn't even know what it was. But he knew it was not in Chicago.

In this snowy world Mr. Stanton is transformed. He is a man of purpose. Leading a group of fellows-in-need. A hero to the rescue. He has no blood relative among these companions. But he feels as though he matters. Thoughts of suicide no longer enter his mind.

William Eddy reconnoiters ahead and returns with good news: although the snow at the pass is too deep for the mules, at this moment it is frozen over just enough to support the weight of human feet. Not only that, the snow has ceased, at least for now.

"Let's leave behind the mules and carry what we can," says Eddy. "If we make haste, we'll get across before the surface ice melts."

But Stanton hesitates. "Leave the mules?" he says. "But I promised Mr. Sutter I would return these mules in good order."

"Look at them clouds, Stanton," Mr. Eddy says, pointing. "This ain't about wagons and mules anymore! This may be our last good chance to make it through before that snow pins us down for the winter."

The first rule of hunger: you cannot have your cake and eat it, too. Or to be more prosaic: you cannot satisfy hunger without devouring something first.

PATRICK BREEN'S DIARY
At Truckee Lake camp

Monday, November 23, 1846

The expedition across the mountains returned after an unsuccessful attempt.

JAMES REED ━◆━ *The Aristocrat*
Return to Sutter's Fort

With a heavy heart McCutchen and I arrived back at Sutter's Fort.
We reported at once to Captain Sutter.
"You've done all you can for now," he said.
"Rain in the valley means snow in the mountains—
and the locals say winter has never come on so early.
You'll have to wait it out."
"But if we had more men," urged McCutchen,
"we could make a go of it."
"Men?" said Sutter. "Look around you, Mr. McCutchen.
There *are* no men. They've gone off to fight.
The United States has declared all-out war with Mexico."
"With whom will you side, Captain Sutter?" I asked.
"Whichever side wins, of course," he replied.

So the weather had won, at least for the moment.
McCutchen and I will spend the next few weeks waiting for the thaw
and scouting the area for the best land,
a place to build a home to come home to.
I calculate the Donner Party should have plenty to eat
as long as they ration it properly, as long as they share it kindly,
and as long as they've lost no more oxen along the way.

Patrick Breen's Diary
At Truckee Lake camp

Sunday, November 29, 1846

Killed my last oxen today. Will skin them tomorrow. Hard to get wood. Still snowing. Now about 3 feet deep.

VIRGINIA REED —◆— *The Princess*
At Truckee Lake camp

Ma is turning red-faced as she bargains with Mrs. Graves.

"I can't believe my ears, Mrs. Graves.
You say you will sell me this near-dead skin-and-bones steer
in exchange for two *healthy* ones once we get to California?"

"Them's the terms, Margret. Under the circumstances,
they's fair."

"Fair? You told my husband you'd look after us, Mrs. Graves."

"I have to look after *my* family first, Mrs. Reed."

"Mr. Eddy says you charged him twenty-five dollars for a dead
ox carcass.
When you know good and well you can buy two, alive, for half
that amount!
I can't *believe* you're taking advantage at a time like this."

"And I cain't believe you're passing judgments at a time
like this.
You don't know me, Margret. You don't know nothin'
about me.
If you want to eat, you know the cost."

Patrick Breen's Diary
At Truckee Lake camp

Monday, November 30, 1846

Snowing fast. About 4 or 5 feet deep. Looks as likely to continue as when it commenced. No living thing without wings can get about.

JAMES REED —◆— *The Aristocrat*
At Sutter's Fort, Alta California

Captain Sutter has introduced me to what little "society" exists at the fort.
He has helped me acquire some fine land in Napa Valley.
He invites me to dinner on a regular schedule and shares
his fine wine, his good whiskey, fat beef and succulent lamb.

With Captain Sutter's help I have been assigned a position in the army.
My job will be to travel along the valleys gathering up recruits.
And as I travel I'll make arrangements for a rescue in the spring.
On the last evening before taking up my post, we dine one final time.
"I must be honest with you, Sutter," I say. "I should be the first to tell it.
I did not leave the Donner train solely to ride ahead for provisions."
I confess my story—the business with Snyder, the banishment, all of it.
"I wanted you to know the truth," I say. "You have befriended a killer."

To my surprise, Sutter bursts out laughing. Then he draws in smoke
from a huge cigar. He exhales pensively and looks me in the eye.
"Reed, you have often complained that Hastings did not tell you the
    truth.
You have often complained that Bridger and Vasquez did not tell the
    truth."

I say, "Bridger, Vasquez, and Hastings all knew the cutoff was untested,
and yet they urged me to take it anyway. And that's as good as lying!"

Captain Sutter laughs again.
"Let me tell you what I know about The Truth, Reed.
The Truth . . . is entirely in the telling."

Patrick Breen's Diary
At Truckee Lake camp

Tuesday, December 1, 1846

Snow lies about 5½ or 6 feet deep. No going from the house. Our cattle all gone but three or four of them. The horses & Stanton's mules gone. Lost in snow. No hopes of finding them alive.

BAPTISTE TRUDEAU —✦— *The Orphan*
At Alder Creek camp

S-N-O spells snow.
Long days of cold and firewood, smoke and snow.
Mrs. Donner says, "I can't work on your reading tonight.
Uncle George's hand isn't healing as it should."
Her worried face tells me it's bad.
None of the girls never smile no more.
Jake Donner's tent is no better off, and maybe worse.
Sol and Will Hook, Jake's stepsons, say he has stopped being a father,
or being anything. He just sits all day and night, his head in his hands.
I go back to my spot in the bachelors' hut only to find the fire's gone out!
Every pathetic occupant has just downright given up!
I dig three times a day to keep the tents from being buried.
In the morning I cut stair steps into the snow to rise up from the pits.
Three more feet fell last night. Three more stairs this morning.
The morning fine and clear and—Buck and Bright . . .

They're gone. They're gone. My whole life, gone.
My whole life swallowed up by the snow.

Patrick Breen's Diary
At Truckee Lake camp

Sunday, December 6, 1846

The morning fine & clear. Stanton & Graves manufacturing snow shoes for another mountain scrabble. No account of the mules.

Salvador and Luis ⬩ *The Savior and the Slave*
At Truckee Lake camp

Salvador
The mules are gone, Eema. Little Man Stanton
would rather perish in the snow than go back on
his word to Captain Sutter. And now the mules
are gone anyway.

> **Luis**
> You called me Eema. Aren't you afraid?

Salvador
If you run away to start your own ranchero,
Captain Sutter will hunt you down. So I have
decided to call you whatever you wish.

> **Luis**
> I have decided not to run away. The mule
> that I had hoped to borrow has been eaten by
> the snow. And if you return without me,
> Sutter may kill you for not stopping me.

Salvador
You have saved my life
then, Eema. Thank you.

> **Luis**
> Since I have saved your life, and
> since you are calling me Eema, will you
> now tell me your Miwok name?

Salvador
No.

Patrick Breen's Diary
At Truckee Lake camp

Wednesday, December 9, 1846

Snows fast. Scant supply of beef. Stanton trying to beg beef for his Indians & Self. Not likely to get much.

Scant. A little word that means . . . little.

The stores of food are scant. And yes, our pioneers are hungry.

Physical hunger now dwells in every cabin along the shores of Truckee Lake and in every tent under the boughs of Alder Creek.

At the Alder Creek camp, Jacob Donner is first to cross over, though his body writhes and sighs and tries for days to stay alive. He takes his last breath sitting up, head in hands, as if trying to think of a reason not to die. His soul empties out. And death moves in to fill the void.

James Smith, a young unmarried teamster for the Reeds, has been giving up since the very first snow. Although he is physically healthy and just twenty-five, his commitment to quitting is absolute and unshakable. Had he placed even a tenth of the effort he took to die into staying alive, he might have lived another hundred years.

Sam Shoemaker, another young bachelor who has been driving for the Donners, dies soon after Smith. Or maybe just before. It is somewhat difficult to tell. And barely a day later the bachelor Joe Reinhardt, in the throes of death, says in German, "*Es tut mir leid.* I am sorry. I am sorry. I am sorry."

And then, with eyes wide open, Reinhardt dies.

Just in time to witness these four men die in such quick succession, Milt Elliott, the Reed family's loyal wagon master, has arrived from the lake in the company of a boy who hired on with the Donners back in Illinois, Noah James. Noah is sixteen, the same as Baptiste, although Noah has not been hardened into an early manhood by circumstance as Baptiste has been. To watch these older men pine and fade away only strengthens Noah's resolve to keep breathing. Likewise, Baptiste himself has no intention of giving in so easily, even as he grieves the loss of his beloved Buck and Bright.

What separates the survivors from the quitters? What gives some souls the will to stick it out to the end? Strange little Patty Reed might say angels. Baptiste Trudeau might say family. Devout Patrick Breen might say God the Almighty. Tamzene Donner might say intellect. Ludwig Keseberg might say luck. James Reed might say power and prestige.

Jake Donner. James Smith. Joseph Reinhardt. Sam Shoemaker. Whatever these four men lack, I am certain they do not die from starvation alone. The cold weather, yes, is an accomplice in their death. The fatigue of the previous months of travel, too. But none of the four should be gone so soon.

In the end it is likely hopelessness that dealt the final death blow. For even with a stomach empty of food, a person might stay alive many weeks. But a person whose soul is empty of hope . . . is already dead.

◆ SNOW ◆

snow

snow

james
smith

joseph
reinhardt

snow

sam
shoemaker

jacob
donner

snow

snow

snow

snow

snow

snow

snow

william
pike

snow

john
snyder

luke
halloran

old
hardcoop

sarah
keyes

Baptiste Trudeau —◆— *The Orphan*
At Alder Creek camp

B-I-Z-E-E spells busy.
Mrs. Donner keeps saying we got to keep busy.
"People who stay busy don't have time to die," she says.
So I learn my letters by pinecone candlelight.
And at the first crack of day I wake up Noah James.
And we cut whatever new snow steps need cuttin'.
Then we wade, waist deep, through more snow to the woods.
We are eye level to limbs probably fifteen feet from the ground.
(I know Buck and Bright are somewhere below my feet.)
We hack off the easiest branches with an ax.

Then Noah goes to the family tents to feed the fires
as I go about my work with a fishhooked nail
fastened to the tapered end of a twelve-foot pole.
I stab the snow here. I stab the snow there.
Then lift the hook looking for blood or hide or hair.
Stab here. Stab there. Stab and pull and check. Repeat.

> *I stab the snow here.*
> *I stab the snow there.*
> *Then lift the hook looking*
> *for blood, hide, or hair.*

This is my purpose from noon to night.
Searching for some trace of Buck or Bright.

Patrick Breen's Diary
At Truckee Lake camp

Sunday, December 13, 1846

Snows faster than any previous day. Wind NW. Stanton & Graves with Several others making preparations to cross the Mountains on Snow shoes. Snow 8 feet deep on the level.

Wednesday, December 16, 1846

Fair & pleasant. Froze hard last night & the company started on snow shoes to cross the mountains.

SALVADOR AND LUIS ⸺◆⸺ *The Savior and the Slave*
On the snowshoe expedition

Salvador
You walk very funny in those snowshoes,
my friend.

> **Luis**
> But I could not look half as funny as you.

Salvador
It is a small price to pay so that I may walk
on water. I walk on water like a savior.

> **Luis**
> But it is no miracle. Just wooden frames
> and rawhide strips fastened to your feet.
> Better than any miracle. With these I could
> run away many miles. Only the birds could
> travel farther.

Salvador
I fear Little Man Stanton's travels may
soon be over. He falls behind. He is not
well. A body cannot walk so much as he
has while eating so little.

> **Luis**
> I see he has dropped behind yet again.

Salvador
Once we make camp we will build up the
fire. We will build up the campfire to show
him the way.

VIRGINIA REED —◆— *The Princess*
At Truckee Lake camp

I had watched Mr. Graves for days as he fashioned snowshoes
by carefully cutting the U-shaped oxbows in two
and weaving the halves together like a split-bottom chair
with endless rawhide string. And all the while he would sing
or tell lively stories about his days as a boy
back in the snowy Green Mountains of Vermont.
I guess he was happy to dwell on happier times.
For now our food was *mostly gone.* Cheekbones jutted *out.*
Eyes were *red and sunken* in. Once-rosy faces had turned *ashen gray.*
Sleep was near impossible, yet we were *forever sleepy.*
We had to *do something* or die. And we figured if eighteen of us left,
that meant eighteen *less mouths to feed* in camp.
Stanton, Luis, and *Salvador* went, of course, as the guides.
They set out two whole *days ago,* yet here I'm in bed *with a fever.*
And *I feel like a ghost* in this sad little cabin.
The same double flannel bloomers that I put on for *the journey.*
But on the *morning of our departure* I couldn't *rise* from my bed!
And here I stay. *I seem* to weigh three hundred pounds.
What's wrong with me, Ma? I say. *I'm panicky as a cat.*
My legs won't hardly move. Can't catch a breath. Or lift my head.

"Princess," says Ma, "I'm afraid you are starving."
Ma starts to cry when she hears herself say it.
And Eliza Williams calls out from the corner pallet.
"Baylis! Can you hear me?" she screams. *Baylis is mysterious.*
Nocturnal and quiet and pale. Like a ghost. "Baylis!"
"He's dead, Mrs. Reed!" Eliza says. "My Baylis is dead!"
Quiet. "My Baylis is dead." *Like a ghost.*

Patty Reed —•— *The Angel*

At Truckee Lake camp

Dear God,
If you notice a new soul up there with you,
and he looks like he's made out of ivory and gold,
that's probably our man Baylis Williams.
His hair is yellow corn silk and his eyes are the palest blue.
Baylis don't like the light at all. It hurts his eyes.
And we all know how bright it is up your way,
so could you maybe arrange a special shady spot for this one?

Ma thinks Virginia is dying, too, but I know otherwise.
Because Eddie Breen paid her a visit, and she's very much revived.
A little from the food he brung, but mostly just from Eddie.
And thank you for bringing Willy Murphy back safe.
And thank you for bringing Dutch Charley, too.
No snowshoes to help them keep up with the others.
Dutch Charley says the snow measured eighteen feet.
That means the snow is three graves deep!

Amen

◆ SNOW ◆

snow

snow

snow

baylis
williams

snow

james
smith

snow

joseph
reinhardt

sam
shoemaker

snow

jacob
donner

snow

snow

snow

william
pike

snow

snow

john
snyder

luke
halloran

old
hardcoop

sarah
keyes

JAMES REED —•— *The Aristocrat*
At Sutter's Fort, Alta California

I can see the snow accumulating on the mountains
as it rains on us here in the valleys.
I think of my family daily, and I'll go to them in time.
But I must wait till the spring for the snow to subside.
Meanwhile I play soldier and recruit men to fight the Mexicans.
Captain Sutter surrendered his fort to the United States
as soon as he realized that the Americans outnumbered him.
Thus Sutter was never unseated from the throne of his empire.
But Sutter's lordly mien masks a darker savagery.
Though he is jubilant and cordial as he offers you a drink,
it is best to take your leave before he drinks too much.
A few of his vaqueros and managers are treated well.
But at the height of the wheat harvest, Sutter "employs"
over five hundred local men, women, and children—
at best, in a state of indentured servitude;
at worst, in a state of de facto slavery.
"I am civilizing the wilderness," Sutter says.
"Can you name one civilization that wasn't born of savagery?"

BAPTISTE TRUDEAU —◆— *The Orphan*
At Alder Creek camp

I stab the snow here. I stab the snow there.
I lift the hook looking for blood, hide, or hair.
> I have wrapped up the three Littles in my blanket,
> same way my pa would wrap *me* up—safe.

Stab the snow here. Stab the snow there.
Lift the hook looking for blood, hide, or hair.
> I sit them on a log to wait and watch and giggle.
> And I remember my father—

Lift the hook looking for blood on the snow.
> I remember my father wrapping me tight.
> That night, long ago, when some bad men came.

Stab the snow here.
> Do not make a sound, boy. Whatever you hear.
> Stay rolled in Pa's blanket. Stay hidden right here.

Blood on the snow.
> Could be that they're friendly.
> I'll see what they want.
> Don't make a sound, boy. Whatever you hear.

I stab. I stab. I stab. I stab.

> Looking for Buck and Bright.

Forced to abandon their families for now, James Reed and Big Bill McCutchen settle into a twilight life at Sutter's Fort.

In the snow-cloaked Sierras, our imprisoned pilgrims have begun to die. Near the shore of Truckee Lake and under the trees of Alder Creek, they pray. They gather. They hide, hoard, and ration. Sometimes they hunt, but what little is caught is never enough for so many stomachs.

The seventeen members of the snowshoe expedition had set out on December 16 with eight pounds of poor beef each. On the first day, they made it to the far end of the lake. On the second day, Dutch Charley and little Willy Murphy, unable to keep up, fell back to the cabins exhausted and defeated. On the third day, the remaining fifteen snowshoed across the high granite spine of the Sierra Nevada. On the fourth day, Charles Stanton, snow-blind and depleted, fell behind himself. But he stumbled into camp after dark, guided by Luis and Salvador's signal fire. On the fifth day, the food was gone. All of it.

On this, the sixth day, Charles Stanton falls behind for good. He sits up against the rough bark of a tree, a cloth tied tight about his head to soothe his swelling eyes. He smokes his pipe and listens to the others walk away. The snowshoers' final view of Little Man Stanton is his bushy beard, the pipe, and the placid smile. There is a pile of wood beside him that Luis and William Eddy gathered. But Little Man Stanton hasn't the strength to lift the tiniest twig. And he dies happy and content.

He dies mostly of the cold. And extreme fatigue. Oh, he *had* begun to starve; I assure you of that. But his soul was perfectly bursting with hope.

Finally in death, Charles Stanton has found something to live for.

Salvador and Luis —✦— *The Savior and the Slave*
On the snowshoe expedition

> **Luis**
> Little Man Stanton did not arrive in camp
> last night.

Salvador
I fear we will never see him again, Eema.
Look down the mountain that we just
ascended. See the lake below?

> **Luis**
> I can see the smoke from the lake cabins.
> Little Man Stanton should be *there* now
> instead of sitting frozen against a tree. We
> should not have let him come.

Salvador
See how the lake looks like the eye of God
staring up at us? God is watching over
Little Man Stanton.

> **Luis**
> It *does* look like an eye. But I prefer my
> god to watch me from above. That way he
> can tell me which way to turn. For I am
> now completely lost.

Salvador
I am afraid we may need more than faith to
find our way through so much snow.

Luis
Whatever you do, Salvador, do NOT tell
these people we are lost. For if they know
we are lost, we are no longer guides—we
are rations on the hoof!

Salvador
These people are good at heart. They will
not harm us.

Luis
I hope you are correct, my friend. For all of
the food is gone. This is the time for dying.
Only when their stomachs are empty
will we see what's in their hearts.

Patrick Breen's Diary
At Truckee Lake camp

Monday, December 21, 1846

Milt Elliot got back last night from Donners camp. Sad news. Jake Donner, Sam Shoemaker, Joseph Rinehart & James Smith are dead. The rest of them in a low situation. Snowed all night with a strong SW wind. Continued to snow all day with some few intermissions. Had a severe fit of the gravel yesterday. I am well today. Praise be to the God of Heaven. Snow shoe expedition gone now near a week.

On the seventh day of the snowshoe expedition, Luis and Salvador mistakenly turn south to follow the North Fork of the American River. Had they only pressed due west up the ridge before them to the slight gap above. Had they only then followed the gentle descent, dropping seven hundred feet into Bear Valley. They could have then followed the Bear River all the way to Johnson's Ranch.

Instead they follow the wrong river in the wrong direction. The mistake will add seven days to their nightmare. A week of unspeakable miseries.

But on this their third day without food, their situation is already grim enough. And someone (was it William Foster?) speaks of "a final contingency"—to assure the group's survival through a voluntary sacrifice, some individual (chosen by lottery) whose body might deliver the rest from death.

Hmmm. Let us pause and ponder the thought.

As Luis and Salvador stand off a good distance, the rest of the men even go so far as to draw paper lots. Patrick Dolan, the cheerful bachelor from Dublin, picks the slip of paper with the sole black X. But no one has the heart to end his life.

"Why sacrifice one of our own," whispers the half-crazed William Foster, "when we could sacrifice one o' *them* two?" He gestures to Luis and Salvador.

"Because it's murder," says William Eddy.

"It wouldn't be murder," says Foster. "It would be survival. Think of your kin, Eddy, back at camp. You got a wife and children. Do you want to ever see them again?"

And so they walk on, leaving the problem unresolved but planting a tiny seed in each traveler's mind. A seed that will grow, and grow, and grow—with every hungry step.

SALVADOR AND LUIS —◆— *The Savior and the Slave*
On the snowshoe expedition

Salvador
I can no longer find my way through this
snow, Eema. We should have seen the pass
two days ago.

> **Luis**
> This is not good, Salvador. The white men
> play a game of chance to choose a sacrifice.

Salvador
That does not concern us, Eema. They will
not let us participate, even if we would
agree to it—which I will not. Besides,
they did not follow through with it. There
is hope for them yet.

> **Luis**
> They are cowards for gambling. A man
> should volunteer himself willingly.

Salvador
No man *wants* to die.

> **Luis**
> Especially if there are two skinny Miwoks to
> be had. And Little Man Stanton is not here
> to stop them.

Salvador
My faith tells me these men are good and
they will not harm us.

Luis
My *faith* tells me that these men
are hungry and they will not harm us—*until*
they discover that their guides have no idea
where they are going.

On the ninth day, as the fourteen remaining showshoers crest another rise, a storm comes on suddenly and violently. Luis and Salvador quickly gather and arrange green branches atop the snow to form a dry base upon which to start a fire. But the wind will not allow it. William Eddy even attempts to ignite some black powder. The wind will not have it.

Without immediate shelter they will all perish within the hour.

Salvador and Luis, using what little English they have, instruct the others to form a circle upon the platform of branches. They shepherd the whites to sit with feet facing inward as closely as possible. Then with Eddy's help, the Indians cover the shivering group with whatever blankets are to be had. They lay branches on top of the blankets, thus adding a roof to this makeshift cave with human walls. Then Eddy, Luis, and Salvador finally take their places inside the circle.

Patrick Dolan, the once-cheerful bachelor from Dublin, falls deep asleep and dreams that he is choosing lots, the only living person in a circle of dead men. Then he wakes with a gasp. He is suddenly very hot. While he fumbles for the buttons of his waistcoat, he stumbles upon (what is this?) the X-mark he won earlier while choosing lots. It strikes Patrick Dolan, all at once, that this may be the first time he has won anything in his life. He begins to laugh.

It is Christmas Eve.

BAPTISTE TRUDEAU —◆— *The Orphan*
At Alder Creek camp

No one mentions Santa Claus.

Mrs. Donner has forbidden any talk of Christmas Eve.
Visiting her hut, I write the date on my slate.
"Ha! *Date* and *slate* are spelled the same!" I realize aloud.
Mrs. D smiles at me. Warm smile. Sad eyes.
And all the while Uncle George snores.
A sweet, putrid smell comes from his bandaged hand.
Mrs. D is lost in thought. Her mind is far away.
She does not teach tonight.
I roll the three Littles up tight in Pa's blanket.
They fall asleep, and I think of my father.
Tomorrow at daybreak, Christmas or not,
I will look for Buck and Bright.

> *Lift the hook looking*
> *for blood, hide, or hair.*

Near sundown of December 24, Christmas Eve, the fourteen remaining members of the snowshoe party are now huddled in a ring under blankets and branches. No fire to warm them. Only the heat of their own bodies. Their food supply long since gone. The relentless whiteness has nearly hidden them altogether from God's view.

The mad wind howls. The snow comes down, whipping in every direction. The sun is blown out of the sky. Night falls. Inside the darkness of this living wigwam, a teamster, hired on at Fort Laramie, begins to murmur a prayer in Spanish. His name is Antonio. Thirteen-year-old Lemuel Murphy begins to sob. Patrick Dolan, the cheerful bachelor from Dublin, has become more and more deranged, complaining of the intense heat. He escapes the shelter into the howling storm, removing his clothes as he goes, laughing.

Dolan shouts into the wind, "I won! I won! I won!"

Mr. Eddy, with help from Luis and Salvador, manages to wrestle the half-naked man back to the warmth of the tenuous shelter. Patrick Dolan finally calms down, yet still jabbers to himself. He mistakes Sarah Fosdick for a girl he had once loved in Dublin. Sarah Fosdick does not answer.

Sarah Fosdick and her young husband, Jay, hold hands. Sarah is the Graves family's eldest daughter. She married Jay Fosdick just a week before her family set out west. It was meant to be the honeymoon of a lifetime. Sarah's father, Mr. Franklin Graves, now slumps. His head falls onto the lap of his other daughter, the beautiful Mary Ann.

"I am not long for this life, Mary Ann," he says. "Be strong. You must do whatever you have to in order to survive. Use my body that you may live."

"No," says Mary Ann. She soothes her father's forehead. "You must stop that sort of talk, Papa. Tomorrow will be Christmas."

Patrick Breen's Diary
At Truckee Lake camp

Friday, December 25, 1846
Christmas Day

Snowed all night & snows yet rapidly. Great difficulty in getting wood. John and Edward has to get it. I am not able. Poor prospect for any kind of comfort spiritual or temporal. Offered our prayers to God this Christmas morning. The prospect is appalling, but hope in god. AMEN.

VIRGINIA REED —◆— *The Princess*
At Truckee Lake camp

Just knowing it is Christmas Day creates the tiniest
breath of excitement, like a bell chime in the air.
Aside from me, Ma, Patty, and the two little boys,
we still have Eliza, the cook, of course. And Milt Elliott.
Mr. Denton, the Englishman, is a constant resident as well.
So Christmas morning is something of a family affair.

The weather has made it nearly impossible to move about.
But that didn't stop Edward Breen from bringing me a morsel of beef
as "an early Christmas gift" when I was sick in bed.
Edward's visit pepped me up as much as the food.

All the cattle in camp have been eaten.
We have broken every bone to extract the marrow.
Then we have boiled and boiled every broken bone.
Then we have burned the bones black and boiled them again.
Christmas breakfast is strips of ox hide boiled into a glue.
It is the awfulest-tasting stuff you ever did eat,
but we are all of us too hungry to care.

Tamzene Donner —◆— *The Scholar*
At Alder Creek camp

George has somehow found the strength to rise and dress.
He begins a slow climb toward the light above. I call after him,
"Remember, George Donner. You are sworn to silence."
"Yes, ma'am," George answers in his easy North Carolina drawl.
"I'll not breathe a word . . . about Christmas."
He whispers the word "Christmas" loud enough to annoy me
but soft enough that the others don't hear.
George speaks with a Southern twang reminiscent of Tully,
and perhaps I was drawn to that. Drawn to the drawl. Ha.
George smiles my way, but decides not to push his luck.
My husband knows to leave me alone when I get the Christmas blues.
December 24, you see, was the day God took my Tully from me.

The older girls, Elitha and Leanna, whisper and climb up the stairs next.
Frances and Georgia, giggling, follow close on their half sisters' heels.
Then Baptiste says, "I'll see if Uncle George needs a hand."
I watch sixteen-year-old Baptiste ascend the stairs and imagine him to be
my own son, dead these sixteen years, ascending the stairs.

Suddenly I am alone with Eliza, the sleeping toddler.
It dawns on me that my family must be up to something.
Then I hear the cries from above.
I gather up Eliza and hurry outside—
to scold George for not tending the children.
But, to my surprise . . .
they are all laughing!

"Merry Christmas, Momma! Surprise!" says everyone at once.
"See here, Momma," says Elitha. "We've made ourselves a Christmas
    banquet."

Look, Momma. Snow apples!
         See, Momma? Snow corn!
Snow stew. Snow steak.
                  Snow watermelon!
Snow sweet potato pie!

The girls have made themselves a feast of fallen snow.
George is grinning. A light flickers in his sunken, red-rimmed eyes.
All five of my girls are now gathering to conspire;
now they're rushing upon George and Baptiste, a snow potato in each
      hand.
Well targeted, George and Baptiste are pummeled into snowmen.
Now a snowball battle erupts as the men retaliate.

And somehow, Christmas has found its way into hell.
Snow apples. Stew. And sweet potato pie.
Somehow Christmas has found its way.

On Christmas Day, somewhere west of the pass, far away from the merriment, the fourteen remaining members of the snowshoe expedition begin to die.

In truth, Mr. Franklin Graves is dead before daybreak—what little daybreak there is. The storm goes on unabated, blotting out the sun. Fifty-seven-year-old Mr. Graves had never been sick a day in his life. And all the while living in Vermont, he would venture out, no matter what the weather, to tend to business or help a neighbor.

Patrick Dolan complains of the heat. He removes his heavy coat and shirt straight down to his bare-skinned chest. Then he dies calling out the name of the girl he had loved in Dublin.

Antonio, the teamster, simply closes his eyes. Mutters a final Spanish prayer. Then slumps forward, dead.

Thirteen-year-old Lemuel Murphy removes his coat and makes as if to leave. He says to his sister, Sarah Foster, "I smell fresh biscuits. I'll go get us one. An' we'll share it." He bolts out into the storm.

By the time Salvador drags him back inside, young Lemuel Murphy is shirtless like Patrick Dolan. The boy rests his head in Sarah Foster's lap. She sings to him. Before the second verse, the boy dies without closing his eyes. She stops singing to listen for his breath.

The ten remaining members of the snowshoe expedition spend the remainder of the day in silence waiting out the storm, the living and the dead passing the time together, as they listen to their own bodies breathing.

Or not breathing.

VIRGINIA REED —◆— *The Princess*
At Truckee Lake camp

By the time the sun began to set
we had long since eaten our nasty Christmas glue.
Then Ma starts to smile a big toothy smile and says,
"Now, children. You close your eyes and don't peek till I say so."
And we all close our eyes and start to giggle
because Ma is grinning and we know it is still Christmas.
Jimmy and Tommy and Patty and me are all squeezing hands.

"Okay," says Ma. "Now open your peepers. Merry Christmas!"

And there, laid out before us on a white linen cloth . . .

FOOD!

A tin cup full of dried beans,
11 slices of dried apple (we counted),
a bit of tripe (the size of Patty's fist),
and a small piece of bacon!

Tommy and Jimmy and Patty begin to dance!
"Ma," I say, "where did you—?"

She says, "No children of mine shall go
without a proper fancy Christmas dinner!
I've been hiding it. I saved it bit by bit."

So all that evening we watch the magical ingredients cooking in the
    kettle.
The little boys squeal whenever a chunk of tripe or a bean breaks the
    surface.

It is great sport, and the cabin fills with the most wonderful aromas.
Darkness comes on outside, and our Christmas feast is nearly ready.

Ma and I hug each other tight, which makes the tears flow.
"It's a proper royal banquet for my princess, eh?" Ma says.
She doesn't call me Princess as much as Papa does.
I think she is worried that I will get spoiled and bratty.
But to hear her call me Princess now—*her* princess—
well, I have never felt so close to my mother
as at this moment. And I would not be surprised at all
if the Graves family next door can see sun rays shining through
the gaps in the log wall that separates our families.
And outside,
into the darkness,
rays of sunlight bursting forth across the snow.

On the eleventh day, the ten remaining members of the snowshoe expedition wait for more to die, but none do. Those men who are left alive take turns going out into the cold to shake the accumulating snow from the blankets.

On the twelfth day, the storm finally breaks. The snow ceases. The winds go away. The sun comes out. Mr. Eddy, Luis, and Salvador stumble out onto the snow, approach a dry brown pine, and set fire to it with powder, flint, and steel. The dead resinous timber goes up quickly. The heat is like a siren's song. It draws the remaining snowshoers out from the horrific hollow where they have been huddling. Now they gather round the conflagration as near as the searing heat will allow.

They turn their backsides to the blaze and look back on the site where they had just spent three hellish days and nights. A shallow pit has formed, now strewn with blankets and four dead bodies. Bodies that used to be people, but now are not.

The milky-white skin of Patrick Dolan's exposed chest and arms fairly gleams in the sun. As does the naked back of young Lemuel Murphy.

The heat from the burning tree warms our sufferers' stomachs. They begin to realize they are alive. Then they realize they are hungry. For to be alive is to be hungry.

The massive crackling tree begins to shed its branches like flaming fallen angel wings. The burning limbs drop all around, hissing against the snow, but our travelers do not flinch or even notice.

Their eyes are transfixed on the bodies of the dead.

PATTY REED —◆— *The Angel*
At Truckee Lake camp

Dear God,
I have begun to cook little pieces of the rug by the fireplace.
Just the tiniest bits around the edges so as not to be missed.
While pulling out a bit for Tommy and Jimmy I discovered gold!
It wasn't much. Just a flake or two beneath the "dinner rug."
Mr. Denton says to Ma, "Why, Mrs. Reed, I am certain this is gold!"
Mr. Denton carved Grandma Keyes's headstone, you might recall.
And he is a gunsmith and metalworker by trade.
So he must know his business, and he scooped up
about a thimbleful of gold dust and flakes and wrapped it up in a cloth.
Mr. Denton says it must have come from the river
where the hearth rocks done come from.
He said, "I'll find more later. Ha, ha. If I ain't dead."
Ma said, "What good is gold? I wish you'd found some bread."

Amen to that, God.

Amen

Patrick Breen's Diary
At Truckee Lake camp

Wednesday, December 30, 1846

Fine clear morning. Froze hard last night. Charley died last night about 10 O'clock. Had with him in money $1.50, two good looking silver watches, one razor, 3 boxes percussion caps. Keseberg took them into his possession. Spitzer took his coat & waistcoat. Keseberg all his other little effects. Gold pin, one shirt, and tools for shaving.

Ludwig Keseberg —◆— *The Madman*
At Truckee Lake camp

Shhh–shhh–shhh.
I dream Old Hardcoop is making his way
across the frozen lake while he sharpens his blades.
Then I wake, once again, to the sound
of Breen scratching words into his book.
Shhh–shhh–shhh (sharpening the knife edge).
Writing about *me* no doubt, the busybody.
Breen sits on his hoard of food and says his prayers
as all the rest of us starve. *Shhhh–shhhhh–shhhhh.*
I try to stay awake. But sleep takes me. And Hardcoop is there,
limping toward me like a devil. And he's holding a knife—
James Reed's big skinning knife, the one he stuck in John Snyder's heart.
And Hardcoop is sharpening the knife blade—
shhhhh–shhhhh–shhhhhh—over and over against a whetstone,
and his bloody feet leave a trail of red along the snow.

On the thirteenth day, after the Christmas blizzard lifts, the snowshoe party goes about the grisly task of harvesting the flesh and organs of their dead. I will not dwell upon it, at least not now. For now you need only know that they linger in camp two whole days, weeping and butchering and eating and drying whatever meat is left for the next determined march.

The desire to stay alive can drive a person to untold extremes. And that's how our hopeful snowshoers overcome their revulsion. Don't think their disturbing repast tastes good. It does not.

On the fourteenth day out, with parcels of flesh prepared for travel, they finally resume their journey. They descend into the American River canyon. Their wool and cotton clothing remains constantly wet from rain, from snow, and from their own sweat. Their garments freeze and thaw with the whims of the weather. They have not been warm, nor comfortable, nor unafraid for weeks.

On the fifteenth day, out of desperation they leave the American River and head directly up the canyon's steep western wall. They pull themselves up by grasping shrubs and rocks. The climb is nearly perpendicular. They spend the entire day at it. Finally at the top they construct the usual platform of green logs so their fire will not sink into the melting snow.

On the sixteenth day, the sun reveals a perfect view of the Sacramento Valley. Still far away, but finally within sight! So they walk. Mary Ann Graves takes from her pack the last rations of flesh from their earlier grim harvest. She takes comfort that it hadn't come from her father's bones. For the group had taken care, as much as possible, to avoid ingesting the clay of their own relations.

They descend into a valley and follow along its western side, letting a pleasant river lead them on. The deep snow gives way to shallow snow with intermittent patches of grass. The first hint of earth they have seen in weeks. One after the other, Mary Ann Graves, Luis, Salvador, Mr. Eddy, Mr. Foster, and the rest remove their awkward snowshoes.

Still, their feet are frozen. Swollen. Bleeding. Cracked. By now many have no shoes at all. They wrap their feet in torn strips of blanket to protect themselves from the rocks that now protrude from the drifts. The crust of ice atop the snow cuts their ankles and shins with the efficiency of a knife. Salvador's moccasins are the bloodiest of all.

On the seventeenth day, it dawns on our travelers that they are following, finally, the much anticipated Bear River. This river, they know, will lead them to Johnson's Ranch, and salvation. But once again, every scrap of food has been consumed. They travel on, making seven miles before they camp.

Jay Fosdick has fallen behind. His newlywed bride, Sarah, walks back to find him. Around the campfire this night, Salvador unwraps a black and frostbitten foot. The man winces as the last knuckle of his pinky toe falls to the ground. He picks it up. Examines it. Shows it to Luis, then tosses it into the fire.

On the eighteenth day, they cook and eat the rawhide strings from their useless snowshoes. William Foster is becoming increasingly irrational. Hunger has replaced his humanity. Half joking, William Foster suggests to Mr. Eddy that they make a meal of Mary Ann Graves.

Also on the night of the eighteenth day, Jay Fosdick does not return to camp. His wife, Sarah, is missing as well.

William Eddy will not go look for them. He assumes they are dead. Finally before lying down, William Eddy (holding the group's only gun) pulls Luis aside.

Salvador and Luis —◆— *The Savior and the Slave*
On the snowshoe expedition

> **Luis**
> Salvador. Wake up.

Salvador
Eema, for the last time, I am *not* going to tell
you my Miwok name. Now go to sleep.

> **Luis**
> It is not that, Salvador. You must wake up.
> Now! We have to run. They mean to kill
> us!

Salvador
You must be having a nightmare, Eema.
These people are our friends. We risked our
own lives to *save* them.

> **Luis**
> Friends or not, they mean to make a stew of
> us. Four of them were gracious enough to
> die all on their own. But the meat is now
> gone. And William Foster plans to kill us
> both!

Salvador
Mr. Eddy will not allow it. The others will
not allow it. The others will stop William
Foster. We are their friends.

Luis

Salvador. Your eyes are open, and yet you still sleep. Wake up! Mr. Eddy has given me a warning. I know you want to help these people. But they will repay you with your own blood. We must go, Salvador. We must go. NOW.

On the nineteenth day of the snowshoe expedition, our hungry travelers wake to find Luis and Salvador gone. Mr. Eddy, an expert tracker, might easily discover where they'd gone. But William Eddy is not William Foster.

Instead Mr. Eddy discovers and shoots a deer, a large near-dead buck that he kills with a lucky shot. Also on this nineteenth day, Jay Fosdick lies dead in the morning sun, having died in the night listening to his wife's voice. His bride, Sarah, had wrapped his lifeless body in their only blanket and waited all night to die as well. But she rose in the morning to find herself still alive.

And on the night of the nineteenth day, the seven remaining snow-shoers eat poor venison from Mr. Eddy's unlucky buck. And they dry the rest of the meat in the cooking fire's smoke. And into the venison they mix a sweeter meat, though still somewhat gamey to the finer palate. For Jay Fosdick's body has been butchered as well. The arms, the legs, the spongy lungs, the soft, gelatinous brain.

Sarah Fosdick sits, as if in limelight, contemplating the fire and wondering, *Where did it all go?* She had just gotten married, just before leaving Illinois. She and her new husband had made love under the stars with the blessing of God. Now she sat on a log a thousand miles away, a widow and a cannibal, watching her husband's heart. Removed from its precious nest. As it roasted on a stick.

Or maybe it is the heart of the buck. Sarah Fosdick suddenly grasps the absurdity of her situation. And on the night of the nineteenth day, Sarah Fosdick begins to laugh. Uncontrollably. At first the other four women look on with concern. Then they notice the roasting heart. And oddly enough, they all begin to laugh. With frowning, confused faces, William Foster and William Eddy look at each other for clues.

About one day's hike away, having escaped with his life, Luis is digging for acorns. In luck, he finds a few. Salvador is sitting against a tree, completely snow-blind. But he can feel that he has lost a second toe to the frost.

SALVADOR AND LUIS —◆— *The Savior and the Slave*
On the snowshoe expedition

Salvador
You should leave me here, Eema.

        Luis
        I will not.

Salvador
Leave me. Run to the mountains and find a
good wife. Start your own ranch. Raise
your own horses. Be your own man. Own
yourself. Leave me here.

        Luis
        I cannot leave you here, old man. Not until
        you have revealed your Miwok name.

Salvador
If I tell you my name, do you promise to
save yourself and leave me here to die?

        Luis
        Yes, of course.

Salvador
You are lying.

        Luis
        Yes, I am. I will not leave you here to die.

Salvador
You are beginning to sound like a Christian.

Luis
I should kill you myself for saying so.
It has begun to snow again.

Salvador
I can feel it on my face. Like angel kisses.

Luis
Perhaps your angel kisses will cover our
bloody tracks in the snow.

◆ SNOW ◆

snow

jay
fosdick

snow

lemuel
murphy

patrick
dolan

dutch
charley
burger

antonio

franklin
graves

snow

snow

charles
stanton

baylis
williams

snow

snow

sam
shoemaker

joseph
reinhardt

snow

james
smith

snow

jacob
donner

william
pike

snow

john
snyder

old
hardcoop

luke
halloran

sarah
keyes

Patrick Breen's Diary

At Truckee Lake camp

Monday, January 4, 1847

Fine morning. Mrs. Reed, Milt, Virginia, and Eliza started out about ½ hour ago with prospect of crossing the Mountain. May God of Mercy help them. Left the children here. Tommy with us. Patty with Kesebergs family. And Jimmy with Graves folks. It was difficult for Mrs. Reed to get away from the Children.

Virginia Reed —◆— *The Princess*
Preparing to leave Truckee Lake camp

Ma makes her mind up not to watch her children starve.
Figures to go on foot but leave the three little ones behind.
Neither Tommy nor Jimmy will let Ma go.
They cling to her skirt and cry and have a fit.
But in the end we promise them if they let us go now,
we will bring them back a loaf of bread each.
Jimmy is to stay with the Graveses. Tommy with the Breens.
Patty right next door with Mr. and Mrs. Keseberg.
It is good to see Edward at the Breen cabin.
I know my face is red as a beet when we hug each other goodbye, and
    Edward's brothers laugh.
But that don't matter. None of that matters no more.
Only thing that matters is I'm dressed in my walking bloomers
and I've set my cap for stayin' alive.

PATTY REED —◆— *The Angel*
At Truckee Lake camp

Dear God,
I love to help Mrs. Keseberg tend to her babies,
and Tommy and I can touch fingers through cracks between our cabins!
Mr. Keseberg is sad on account of him hurting his foot by
stepping on "a gall-danged som'bitch spiky willow stub."
He tries to not like me, but he likes me anyway.

Today, Mr. Keseberg, in the bed, turned his face to the wall.
"Wanna see what I got from Grandma Keyes?" I said to his back.
"This here dolly is named Angel. An' here's a little pincushion
that Angel uses for her pillow. An' this here's a lock of Grandma's hair."
Mr. Keseberg don't turn around but he starts to shake and cry, quiet-like.
Then I put Angel on the bed next to him. Propped up against his back.
"This is me," I said. "I know it's just a wooden doll. But it's me, too."
Then Mr. Keseberg turned his face around and handed Angel back to me.
He said, "You keep your doll. No angels for me. I am cursed."
I said, "I can make you your very own angel in the snow.
Snow angels, when made with care, can counter *any* curse."
Mr. Keseberg looked at me like I had three heads. Ha!
But I know what I know so you know what I did?
I made them all snow angels of their own.
Ma, Virginia, Eliza, and Milt. That should keep them safe.
Oh, and of course I made one for Mr. Keseberg, too.
But I s'pose you saw.

Amen

Patrick Breen's Diary
At Truckee Lake camp

Friday, January 8, 1847

Very cold this morning. Mrs. Reed & company came back. Could not find their way on the other side of the Mountain. They have nothing but hides to live on. Patty is to stay here with us. Milt & Eliza going to Donners'. Mrs. Reed & the 2 boys going to their own shanty & Virginia. Prospects dull. May God relieve us all from this difficulty if it is his Holy will. Amen.

Virginia Reed —◆— *The Princess*
Back at Truckee Lake camp

Climbing the mountain had been difficult.
There were many granite ledges to clear.
But I felt hopeful to be doing something, *anything*.
Anything but sitting still waiting to be rescued . . . or to die.
I was colder on that mountain than I had ever been.
We stopped nearly a whole day to make snowshoes
from materials we had brought along for that purpose.
Eliza complained loudly the whole way, finally turning back.
The rest of us kept on, but the path was erased by the snow.
Ma dropped to her knees and cried. Milt was speechless.
With heavy hearts we made a retreat back to the cabins.

Now a storm has come on with hurricane winds
and, of course, more snow. More snow. And more snow.
And we realize that by returning we have likely saved our lives.
And we realize that those in the snowshoe party,
who crossed the mountain before us, are probably all dead.

On the twenty-fourth day, the seven remaining members of the snow-shoe party are out of food again. It took just two days to devour the meat they had taken from William Eddy's buck and from the corpse of Sarah Fosdick's husband. For the next three days they had walked without eating, the intense hunger made worse by their recent feasting. For nothing disheartens a prisoner more than a brief taste of freedom.

On the afternoon of the twenty-fourth day, William Foster sees the obvious tracks of blood in the snow. Two sets of bloody tracks now. Two humans moving slow, from the looks of it. Foster comes to a tree set back in the woods where the snow has melted away to bare ground. He notes the telltale signs of acorn excavations. And a bed of leaves, still holding the shape of the two bodies that had occupied it the night before.

The trail of blood disappears around a bend up ahead. Foster feels lucky for the first time in weeks.

The ten-pound rifle grows lighter in William Foster's hands. He is done asking opinions. He has the gun. He cocks the hammer. And he moves forward.

Though his companions are far behind, they all know where William Foster is going. They all know what he intends. But this time no one raises an objection. This time no one talks about humanity. Or honor. On the twenty-fourth day, they sheepishly shuffle their own bloody feet. This time nobody, not even Mr. Eddy, lifts a finger to stop what happens next.

SALVADOR AND LUIS —◆— *The Savior and the Slave*
The snowshoe expedition

> **Luis**
> Here, Salvador, I have warmed a
> blindfold over the fire. The heat will help
> revive your eyes.

Salvador
QuéYuen.

> **Luis**
> What did you say?

Salvador
QuéYuen.

> **Luis**
> What do you mean?

Salvador
That is my name, QuéYuen. You asked me
my Miwok name, and now you know it.

> **Luis**
> QuéYuen. I am happy to know it. A
> wonderful name!

Salvador
So what does that change? Am I a different
man than I was before? Are QuéYuen and
Salvador not the same dying man? They are
both very cold, that is the truth. They are
both tired and hungry and blind.

Luis

It is nice to meet you, QuéYuen.

Salvador

And you too, Eema.

Luis

And now my friend, QuéYuen. You have
been asleep for some time. And luckily we
are sitting against a very generous oak tree
who has left us three acorns. I ate one while
you slept. You may have this second one
all to yourself. The third acorn we will
split.

Salvador

I cannot see, Eema. How can I be sure
you haven't found *ten* acorns? How do I
know you aren't keeping the rest for
yourself?

Luis

Faith, QuéYuen. Ha, ha.
You must have faith in me.

Salvador

What is that? I hear footsteps. I hear a
man breathing. And the cocking of . . . a
rifle.

Luis

Do not worry, QuéYuen. It is only William
Foster. He has . . . brought us . . . something
to eat.

Salvador
You do not have to protect me from the truth of this, Eema. Remember, I am blindfolded . . . but I am not blind. Thank you for the acorn.

> **Luis**
> I am sorry I could not make it into bread, QuéYuen.

Salvador
The acorn is perfect just as it is, Eema. It is everything I need.

⇀ Hunger ⇀

On the twenty-fourth day, William Foster succumbs to the hunger of his soul.

CRACK! Surrender is a musket blast, sounding over the snowbound slopes. Violent and loud. An explosive report, then a ghostly echo, ebbing to a whisper.

CRACK! Surrender is a second musket blast. As violent, as loud, and as true as the first. Rebounding from the opposite mountain.

Luis's unfolding fist.

A single acorn upon Salvador's open hand.

◆ SNOW ◆

salvador

luis

snow

snow

jay
fosdick

dutch
charley
burger

snow

snow

lemuel
murphy

patrick
dolan

franklin
graves

antonio

baylis
williams

snow

sam
shoemaker

snow

charles
stanton

snow

joseph
reinhardt

james
smith

snow

jacob
donner

william
pike

snow

snow

luke
halloran

john
snyder

old
hardcoop

sarah
keyes

On the twenty-fifth day, the seven remaining members of the snowshoe expedition strip Luis's and Salvador's flesh, then dry it over the fire. Thus stocked, they resume their journey. The fearfully deep snows give way to lesser drifts. On the twenty-sixth and twenty-seventh days, they see more earth than snow. They travel an amazing seventeen miles. And just as they eat the last of Luis's and Salvador's flesh, they leave the snow behind for good.

On the twenty-eighth day, they come across a path and follow it. On the twenty-ninth day, they stumble into a village of mountain Miwoks who treat them kindly and feed them acorns. I cannot tell you if William Foster, or *any* of our grateful travelers, feels the slightest pang of guilt or irony. This Miwok village, called a *ranchería* in Mexican parlance, is one of many, housing the Miwok workers tied to nearby ranches as seasonal labor. *Rancherías* also provide relatively safe havens for Miwoks who are escaping the hospitality of Sutter's Fort. Just the sort of oasis Luis had been hoping for.

On the thirtieth day, the kindly Miwoks lead them to another trail and another *ranchería*. Through sign language, an elder of this village tells the whites that Johnson's Ranch is about fifteen miles away, an easy walk for a healthy body. But on the thirty-first day, they begin to give out. None can rise to resume the journey. None except William Eddy. He leaves his companions behind. And he presses on with a single Miwok escort.

Finally, on the thirty-third day, Mr. Eddy nearly gives out himself. But rather than falling down, he stays upright. And he walks. He can scarcely lift his feet past a shuffle. He stumbles. He stops frequently, leaning against trees to rest. He does not sit, lest he not be able to get back up. But he keeps moving forward. His feet begin to bleed, as Salvador's had bled. He wraps them in rags, but still they bleed. They both burst open. Still he will not stop.

He does not stop until reaching the first cabin on the outskirts of Johnson's Ranch. His escort calls to the cabin from the yard. The young woman who comes to the door is Harriet, the teenage daughter of Colonel Matthew "Dill" Ritchie. This is his place.

The sight of Mr. Eddy—the sunken eyes, the wasted frame, the skeletal face and hands—takes Harriet Ritchie's breath away. She manages only to gasp.

"Please," whispers William Eddy. "May I have bread?"

To hear the horrific thing before her speak in such a spectral voice makes Harriet Ritchie's fear complete.

She screams.

This article will appear later in one of the only two newspapers in Alta California.

Distressing News

A messenger was sent down from Johnson's Ranch, with the astounding information that five women and two men had arrived entirely naked, their feet frost bitten. Their main company, The Donner Party, became snowbound near Trucky's Lake on the east side of the mountains, and fearing starvation, sixteen of the strongest, (11 males and 5 females) agreed to start for the settlement on foot. Scantily clothed and provided with provisions they commenced that horrid journey over the mountains that Napoleon's feat on the Alps was child's play compared with.

After wandering about a number of days bewildered in the snow, their provisions gave out. And as they died the company went into camp and made meat of the dead bodies of their companions. After travelling thirty days, 7 out of the 16 arrived. Nine men died and seven of them were eaten.

The company left behind, stranded in the mountains, sixty odd souls; ten men, the balance women and children. They are in camp about 100 miles from Johnson's Ranch, the first house after leaving the mountains, or 150 from Sutter's Fort.

PART FIVE

—◆—

CLOSER TO HEAVEN

January 17–February 28, 1847
Truckee Lake and Alder Creek

Patrick Breen's Diary
At Truckee Lake camp

Sunday, January 24, 1847

Ceased snowing yesterday about 2 o'clock. All in good health thanks be to God for his Mercies endurath forever. Heard nothing from Murphys camp since the storm. Expect to hear they suffered some. Mrs. Keseberg here this morning. Lewis, Junior died today. Mr. Keseberg sick, will not get out of bed.

LUDWIG KESEBERG —◆— *The Madman*
At Truckee Lake camp

Shhh-shhh-shhh, my little one.
My little Ludwig. My little me.
Your mother wails inconsolably.
Your sister, Ada, cries out from hunger.
And yet you sleep. You sleep and sleep.
And from this day on you will never wake.
You have arrived at one final horizon
that will not fade. You are in a place
where you will be warm and well-fed forever.
With a father who can care for you and protect you.
A father who will succeed where I have failed.
Your mother wails. Her baby will not wake.
Shhh-shhh-shhh. Old Hardcoop had a hand in this.
Somehow. While I slept.
This is his doing. He wants me to know
how it feels to be left behind.
He has taken my son. He has taken my baby.
Will he destroy everything and anyone that I love?
Shhhhh-shhhh-shhhh.

PATTY REED —◆— *The Angel*
At Truckee Lake camp

Dear God,
Please welcome little baby Lewis
and be sure to keep him warm
and be sure to let him know
that I will be here to take care of his father.
I heard Mr. Keseberg crying through cracks in the wall.
I passed my doll, Angel, through to him.
He pushed it back and said, "No! No angels for me."

So I went out and made a snow angel
'specially for Mr. and Mrs. Keseberg.
Can you see it?
Can you see it from where you are?
It is a right handsome angel. The snow was fine as flour.
It looks so real gleaming in the sun.
I think I can hear it sing.

Amen

◆ SNOW ◆

ludwig
keseberg
jr.

BAPTISTE TRUDEAU —◆— *The Orphan*
At Alder Creek camp

A sunny day. Icicles gleam in the lookout tree.
From high in the branches I can see the smoke from the lake cabins.
As usual I see no sign of mules, or men, or rescue.
Below I see Solomon Hook, Betsy Donner's boy, wandering alone.
So I climb down the branches. I gather him up,
and I return him, blind and babbling, to Aunt Betsy's hut.
The stench in that terrible hole is unbelievable.
It now falls on Noah James and myself to do much of the work,
though Milt helps out, too, during his visits from the lake.
After each big snow, we dig back out.
At night more reading and letters by pinecone light.
Mrs. Donner carries on with her teacups and smiles
as if we was all just on a family picnic in the spring,
as if we all wasn't wasting away to nothing,
as if Mr. Donner isn't going to die.

Noah James says he's leaving first chance.
But I can't leave Buck and Bright lost in the snow.
I know they ain't alive, but I just want to know.
I just need to see it to believe it.

TAMZENE DONNER —◆— *The Scholar*
At Alder Creek camp

As if it never existed, one of Elitha's shoes disappears.
Just one. It is a beautiful sunny day, finally.
Finally it *could* have been a normal and pleasant afternoon.
And yet, a shoe is missing. But it is a beautiful day.

And I have brought out the good china for a tea party!
It is a beautiful, sunny day. But a shoe is missing.
Baptiste probes the snow looking for the carcasses of buried cattle.
And a shoe is missing.
All the girls are out in the common between the huts.
They are throwing a stick to our little dog, Uno.
I have dubbed this little common area "Harvard Square."
Anything to make the girls forget the horror of our situation.

Then Uno begins to cough and gag. Then he vomits a shoelace.
And a shoe is missing. And a shoe is miss—

—that's when it strikes me as funny that this little dog
is somehow still walking the earth with meat on its bones
while human folk are starving to death all around us.
I have made a meal of my botanical specimens:
the lupine, the larkspur, the primrose, the eardrop—
each dried bloom had been a record of a better place and time.

My daughters are the only *specimens* George and I have left!
Eliza, three, and Georgia, four, have dark-brown eyes and hair like their
    father.
Frances, six, has my own blue eyes and fair skin.
Leanna is now eleven and makes an attentive nurse to her father.
I have raised Leanna and Elitha as if they were my own.
But Elitha has never let go of her real mother.

Elitha has never truly let me in.
And a shoe is missing. And a shoe is miss—

That's when it strikes me: I've never truly let George in.
I know George has sensed it, how I have struggled to live in the present,
how I have kept Tully's memory pressed and dried,
like a specimen to illustrate the perfect man, the perfect love.
Perhaps Elitha, being the oldest, has sensed it, too, all along.

Ha. More than just Elitha's shoe has disappeared.
The little girl who Elitha used to be is gone as well.
Now thirteen years old, she is taller than me by half a foot,
and her menses had begun even before we set out from Illinois.
But of course there are no menses *here* among the starving.
Here in this hell of missing shoes and shoelace-vomiting dogs.

I go to Elitha and I hug her and I say, "I see you, Elitha."
She looks at me (and rightly so) as though I have lost my mind.
I am angry that I have lost so much time.
I am angry that I have made my family share me with a dead man.
I am angry that Uno ate my stepdaughter's shoe.
I am angry because we could have eaten the shoe ourselves.
I am angry that we have been reduced to eating shoes.
I am angry that my teacups and china and books
cannot keep us from becoming animals.
I am angry at Jacob Donner for cutting George's hand,
only to give up and die. And I am angry
with George for getting hurt and angry
with the wound for failing to heal. Angry with myself
for being unable to make my husband better.
Angry that I did not love him fully while he was alive!
"Mother, what is it?" asks Elitha. "Are you ill?"
I want to scream vulgarities. I want to break every last teacup.
A shoe is missing.

"No, dear," I say instead. "I'm just . . . *A shoe is missing.*"
"Mother, you don't seem yourself," says Elitha.
I begin to shake. Anger is welling up inside me.
"POETRY!" I shout as I rush into the hut, possessed.
"Poetry is what we all need. To remain calm!"

"We *are* calm, Mother," says Elitha. "But you're scaring the Littles."
In reply I open my book of Tennyson,
still marked on the page I once shared with Mr. Keseberg.
I read aloud. I spit the words like venom . . .

> *I am a part of all that I have met;*
> *Yet all experience is an arch wherethro'*
> *Gleams that untravell'd world whose margin fades*
> *Forever and forever when I move.*

Something inside of me breaks.
And a shoe is missing.
Something like the cracking of a wagon axle in my chest.
And a shoe is missing. A shoe. A shoe. A shoe.
"Where is Uno?" I scream. My voice echoes through the woods.
"Where is the special little dog who eats my daughter's shoes
while my daughter has nothing and starves?"

Baptiste quickly brings forth Uno.
The special little dog wags his tail at all the attention.
I throw the book of Tennyson's poems onto the fire.
Flames devour the poetry as I bring the kettle to a boil.

Patrick Breen's Diary
At Truckee Lake camp

Sunday, January 31, 1847
Landrum Murphy died last night about 1 O'clock.

Friday, February 5, 1847
Eddy's child, Margaret, died last night.

Sunday, February 7, 1847
William McCutchen's child, Harriet, died 2nd of this month. One of the most severe storms we experienced this winter. The snow fell about 4 feet deep.

Monday, February 8, 1847
Augustus Spitzer died last night. We will bury him in the snow. Mrs. Eddy died on the night of the 7th.

Tuesday, February 9, 1847
William Pike's child, Catherine, all but dead. Keseberg never gets up, says he is not able. My son, John, went down today to bury Mrs. Eddy & child.

Wednesday, February 10, 1847
Milt Elliott died last night at Murphys shanty about 9 O'clock. All entirely out of meat but little we have. Our hides are nearly all eat up.

catherine
pike

milt
elliott

margaret
eddy

augustus
spitzer

eleanor
eddy

snow

harriet
mccutchen

snow

salvador

snow

landrum
murphy

snow

ludwig
keseberg
jr.

luis

dutch
charley
burger

lemuel
murphy

jay
fosdick

franklin
graves

patrick
dolan

snow

baylis
williams

snow

sam
shoemaker

antonio

charles
stanton

snow

joseph
reinhardt

james
smith

jacob
donner

william
pike

snow

luke
halloran

old
hardcoop

snow

john
snyder

sarah
keyes

JAMES REED —✦— *The Aristocrat*
At Sutter's Fort, back from the war

With the war now mostly over,
Big Bill McCutchen and I are free to attempt another rescue.
These past weeks, while recruiting soldiers for the US Army,
I've also been gathering comrades for my own relief effort.
In Sonoma I recruited five men and ten good government horses,
saddles, bridles, tents, and other supplies. At Napa, two more horses
and three more men, including none other than Caleb Greenwood,
the legendary mountain man familiar with the country.
In Yerba Buena, a group of citizens raised money and supplies.
Midshipman Woodworth of the US Navy will sail these supplies upriver
and set up a field station near Johnson's Ranch.
McCutchen and I will travel overland with the horses and men.
And we'll gather more along the way as we can.

Our mission is now more urgent than ever,
for until Mr. Eddy escaped the mountains to tell his tale,
we had been under the impression that the Donner Party
was well supplied with meat for the winter.
But now the truth is clear: our families . . . are starving.

VIRGINIA REED —◆— *The Princess*
At Truckee Lake camp

I have shared living quarters, off and on, with the Breens
since returning from our failed attempt across the mountain.
"With God's help, spring will smile upon us," says Mr. Breen.
For all his horsing around, I know Edward is a good Catholic.
And I don't intend any ill will toward Edward nor his kin,
but when Milt Elliott died, I did not pray for spring.
When Ma and I dragged Milt's body up from the cabin,
Ma pulling on his shoulders, me pushing at his feet,
I did not pray for spring. When I buried him in the snow,
commencing at his toes, patting the cold powder down
until I reached his eyes, I did not pray for spring.
Milt was a big brother to me. It broke my heart to cover his face.
What sort of a Father would allow such a thing?
You know what *I* think? I think spring will come
whether God wills it or not. That's what *I* think.
Shall I pray to God for the sun to rise,
then shout hallelujah when it does?

~ Hunger ~

By now, even the most patient of our snowbound sufferers is losing patience. Even the most faithful, losing faith. The most hopeful, losing hope. Even the most well-sewn seam will fail eventually if stretched too far.

But take heart, dear reader. At this very moment, a relief party of courageous men is trundling eastward toward the pass. Led by a Mr. Reason Tucker, this rescue party is now reduced to just seven. Each rescuer is equipped with a single blanket, a tin cup, a hatchet, and sixty pounds of dried meat. They wade through snow up to their waists. They walk atop the deepest patches using snowshoes of pine boughs and rawhide.

The route is anything but straight, skirting the denser stretches of forest and winding around the steeper mountains and hills. Reason Tucker pushes a fifteen-foot pole down into the snow. It does not reach bottom. They travel single file, the leader breaking through the soft snow to ease the way for the others. Even with snowshoes the frontrunner's feet sink into the powder to his knees, making every step tedious. Once exhausted, the leading hiker drops to the back, replaced by the second in line.

They set fire to several dead pine trees along the way to mark their path for the return journey and to direct future relief parties. They progress only four to six miles each day. Every third day, they stop to hang small bundles of dried meat from a high branch. They do so in anticipation of their hunger on the way back as much as to lighten their heavy packs.

They struggle on this way until sunset of the sixteenth day, when they find themselves walking across the frozen surface of Truckee Lake. They approach the easternmost shore, where William Eddy had told them they would find the surviving pioneers.

But there is no one there. Not a soul. Not even a single cabin.

"Halloooooo!" Reason Tucker calls out. No response. Barely even an echo. Tucker's shouts are absorbed, devoured if you will, by the ubiquitous white drifts.

"Halloooooo!" Mr. Tucker repeats. He scans the whiteness for signs of life.

"What's that?" asks one of Tucker's companions. The man raises his gun instinctually, for game has been scarce.

"Put down the rifle, Glover," says Tucker. "That's a woman."

The cabins at Truckee Lake are now hidden beneath eighteen feet of snow. The lone woman attempts to walk, but the snow makes it impossible to progress. So she stands and waits for Reason Tucker and his six men to approach. Behind her, several others begin to emerge, blinking. They are women and children, mostly. Maybe one grown man among them.

Tucker and his men, though a hardscrabble lot, are not prepared for the ghastly spectacle presented by these ashen-faced, famished creatures. They have no words.

Finally, Mrs. Breen speaks. "Are you men from California? Or do you come from heaven?"

Patrick Breen's Diary
At Truckee Lake camp

Friday, February 19, 1847
7 men arrived from California yesterday evening with some provi-
sions but left the greatest part on the way. Some of the men are gone
today to Donner's Camp. Start back on Monday.

TAMZENE DONNER —•— *The Scholar*
At Alder Creek camp

They say I have to choose.
I try to hold my tongue. I try to be gracious.
"There are seven of you?" I ask. "And no mules or horses?
How can seven men rescue so many sufferers,
many of them children who cannot walk on their own?"

In the end I decide to send away the oldest of the children.
My precious stepdaughters, Elitha and Leanna. Eleven and thirteen.
The three Littles—Frances, Georgia, and Eliza—will stay with me.
They are too small. They would have to be carried much of the way.
If George was fit, we could manage I guess. But George . . .
the infection in his hand has spread past his elbow.
The fever and pain have left him bedridden,
and no, I will not leave him (no matter how he tries to persuade me to).

My sister-in-law, Betsy, must make the same choice.
Her oldest, Solomon Hook, is still recovering from snow-blindness.
She sends away William Hook, who is twelve, and George Jr., just nine.
She keeps Mary, Isaac, Samuel, and Lewis, all under seven years old.
Young Noah James will be leaving us,
but thankfully Baptiste is going to stay.
I don't know how we would get along in camp without him.
He is bent on finding his buried oxen.
He says they are the only family he's got.
But I think he has grown attached to the girls.
And certainly *they* have grown attached to *him*.
And, yes, I have my own attachment, too.
Perhaps it is selfish to ask a sixteen-year-old boy to stay behind.
But I don't care.

Virginia Reed —◆— *The Princess*
Walking west toward the pass

The seven men who have come to our relief
seem nearly as starved and exhausted as us who are being saved.
We will be leaving very little meat behind for the others.
And many are so weak in camp they cannot hope to make the walk.
In the end we set out with twenty-three of us,
six adults and seventeen children.
Edward is joining us with his little brother, Simon,
but every other Breen will stay behind.
"Da has the gravel again," says Edward. "And Ma won't leave 'im."

Our rescuers have snowshoes and walk in the lead.
We follow behind along the packed snow trail.
We are all wore out from lack of food. Tommy cries.
Ma and I take turns holding little Tommy, but Jimmy is too big.
Patty, also, is too heavy to carry and she starts to fall behind.
Until finally Mr. Tucker says we have to send them back.
One of the rescuers volunteers to walk them safely to the lake.
But my mother's heart is breaking and mine is breaking, too.
Patty says, "Don't worry none, Ma. You do the best you can.
And if me and Tommy die, we'll see you soon in heaven."
Tommy says, "I don't wanna go to heaven!" And he starts in crying.
How can Patty think that God will give her heaven after she's dead
if God offers nothing but hell while she's alive?

PATTY REED ⟶◆⟵ *The Angel*
Back at Truckee Lake camp

Dear God,
When the man brung us back to the cabin I was glad.
I was glad to be there for Tommy while he cried.
I told him all about the in-the-middle growing time:
when you're too big to get toted and too little to walk.
Mrs. Breen pitched a fit when the man brung us back,
but she finally relented and let us come in.
And now here we are eating Towser stew.
I said, "Don't be sad, Mrs. Breen. We ate up our own little Cash
a couple weeks back. We ate up every *bit* o' that little dog.
I'm sure Towser's happy to help. Now he's in heaven with God."
Mrs. Breen scolded me for saying that dogs go to heaven,
but I bet heaven is swimmin' with four-legged angels.
Between all them Breen boys, there wasn't much of Towser to go round.
Tommy and I appreciated little Towser's sacrifice, all the same,
for he tasted much better than bits of roasted rug.
Please pass on our respects. And our grateful thanks.

Amen

Patrick Breen's Diary
At Truckee Lake camp

Tuesday, February 23, 1847
Shot Towser today & dressed his flesh. I had to shovel the snow off our
shanty this morning. We hope with the assistance of Almighty God to
be able to live to see the bare surface of the earth once more. O God of
Mercy, grant it if it be thy holy will. Amen.

VIRGINIA REED —◆— *The Princess*
Crossing the pass, walking west

Mr. Breen says our suffering is all God's will.
But what of the McCutchen babe? The Eddy babe? The Keseberg babe?
All innocent creatures pure as snow themselves? God's will?
I can no longer feel my toes. My heart feels frozen, too.
Ma can barely stand from the grief of leaving Patty and Tommy behind.
God might as well have asked her to tear off her own arm.
Oh, I promise right here and now in the eyes of heaven
that I'll become a Catholic *myself* if my family survives this hell.
But for now I'll place my faith in my earthbound pa rather than God.
What use is a Father in heaven when all of us are here on earth?
I try to hold my tongue. I try to be gracious.
But all I can say is "Where is my father?"

JAMES REED —◆— *The Aristocrat*
At Johnson's Ranch, heading east

After we set out from Napa Valley, the road conspired against us.
Dirt turned to mud. Mud to molasses. Molasses to swamp water.
My caravan of men and horses followed the swollen Cache Creek
until we finally forded the torrent, the water up to our horses' backs.
We sloshed on across flat bottomland that had become a perfect swamp
until we reached the shore of the mighty Sacramento River—
the very spot where we were to meet the supply ship from Yerba Buena.
We camped and we waited. And we waited. And we waited.
We waited for a ship that never came.
Luckily we were able to cross with the aid of a passing barge.
One more day's ride and we reached Johnson's Ranch.
We dried more meat. We rested the horses.
With hand-cranked coffee grinders, we turned wheat into flour.
Finally today, the twenty-first of February, we will resume the rescue.
It is a Sunday, but I refuse to wait one more second—not even for God.
"Come on, men," I bark. "You can pray while you walk."

Patty Reed —◆— *The Angel*
At Truckee Lake camp

Dear God,

Tonight Tommy was hungry and cried himself to sleep.

Then I heard more crying through the cracks in the wall.

I whispered, "Mr. Keseberg? You want my doll now?"

The crying stopped, but Mr. Keseberg didn't say nothin'.

I said, "I'm sorry you feel sad."

He didn't say nothin'.

Then he says, "I am alone. My son is dead.

Mrs. Keseberg and Ada are gone to safety.

I know it is selfish to want them back. But I do."

I told him, "Come daylight, we'll make snow angels.

One for Mrs. Keseberg. One for Ada. One for baby Lewis.

A snow angel each, to keep them safe.

I'll make an angel for you, too!"

"No angels for me," he says through the wall.

"Old Hardcoop is coming for me. I left him behind.

I can hear him outside every night, sharpening his knife."

"That's just the wolves," I said. "Digging at the snow."

Mr. Keseberg says, "You are a good and kind person."

Then through the wall comes a serving of flour on a silver spoon.

"Take it," he said.

And, God, it was the best thing I ever did taste!

"Good night, Mr. Keseberg," I said.

"Gute Nacht, mein Engel," Mr. Keseberg said.

That's how you say "Good night, my angel" in German.

But you probably already know that, too.

Amen

Patrick Breen's Diary
At Truckee Lake camp

Thursday, February 25, 1847
Froze hard last night. Fine and sunshiny today. Wind W. Mrs.
Murphy says the wolves are about to dig up the dead bodies at her
shanty. The nights are too cold to watch them. We hear them howling.

BAPTISTE TRUDEAU —◆— *The Orphan*
At Alder Creek camp

Last night I heard the wolves howling by the lake.
    Stab the snow here.
If only I had a wolf's nose.
    Stab the snow there.
The snow has melted some.
    Stab the snow here.
But still there is nothing on the end of my hook.
    Stab the snow there.
Until—
    Stab the—

I gasp. My hook has found something! Buried in the snow.
Hair! Dark hair. At the end of my hook.
I shout, "Buck and Bright!" I've found them. At last.
And I dig. With my hands at first. Then a shovel from the firepit.
I dig. And dig. And dig. Until finally—
a face. A human face. The fleshy face of a man.
I see the face of my father. I had forgotten what he looked like.

"That'd be Sam Shoemaker," says a voice behind me.
It's Mrs. Donner with her arms crossed.
How long she'd been there watching I do not know.
I want to tell Mrs. Donner how I saw my father's face.
I want to tell Mrs. Donner how much I want him back.
Instead I say, "I'll never see Buck or Bright again, will I?"

"No, my sweet boy," says Mrs. Donner. "And I'm sorry."

"So I guess I ought to stop looking," I say.

"No," says Mrs. Donner. "I want you to keep looking,
but not for Buck and Bright." She hands me a red cloth.
"Joe Reinhardt and Jim Smith should be laid out pretty near Sam.
Once you've found their bodies, mark the location
with a long stick and a red flag. That way we'll know
where they are but still keep them away from the wolves."

"What about Sam?" I ask Mrs. Donner. "Shall I rebury him?"

"No," she says. "I want you to finish digging him up.
I'll go get Aunt Betsy and we'll help you.
This location will do fine. Away from the eyes of the children."

"What do you mean?" I ask. "This location is fine for what?"
But I know the answer before the question leaves my lips.

By now the hunger is deeper than the snow.

The first relief, led by Reason Tucker, tramps away from the lake. The second relief, led by James Reed, heads *toward* the lake. The Donner family at the Alder Creek camp prepares to butcher Sam Shoemaker's corpse. At the Truckee Lake camp, the Murphys, the Graveses, Keseberg, and the Breens squabble over the dwindling scraps of hide. And the children. The children cannot fathom why the adults cannot feed them. The adults cannot fathom how they came to be so helpless.

Reason Tucker now leads the first relief out of the mountains, reversing his hellish trip of the week before. The snows have diminished somewhat and the surface is frozen, which makes for easier travel. The large burned pines help the travelers keep their bearings. Oh, how they anticipate the caches of food they had so carefully secured on the journey in. And, oh, the bitter disappointment to find the first cache mostly devoured by animals.

The day after escaping over the pass, John Denton, the good-natured Brit, gives out and cannot rise from his resting place of the night before. His companions sit him up near a fire on a platform of green saplings. They give him pen, paper, and pipe. They murmur all around how another rescue will surely be by soon. And they move on, knowing full well that John Denton is as good as dead. He scratches out a poem, from memory, with his numb fingers. A verse that had always taken him home. Finally his body falls onto its side, spilling from his breast pocket the gold dust he had discovered in the rocks of Mrs. Reed's hearth.

Meanwhile, a few miles ahead, rescuer John Rhoads carries the two-year-old Pike baby strapped to his back. Ada Keseberg is passed from rescuer to rescuer until the whining child goes limp. Philippine Keseberg is called for. And for the next mile, the grief-stricken mother refuses to let go of her daughter's lifeless body. Finally, their muscles burning with exhaustion, Reason Tucker and his men bury the child in the snow, wrapped in a remnant of calico.

Six-year-old Jimmy Reed, too heavy to tote, is forced to walk behind as the grown-ups break the path ahead. With every laborious step, he thinks how he is closer to seeing his father again. His stepsister, Virginia, cheers him on.

After three days of tramping west they come to a second cache of food. This one has been devoured like the first. Ah, hunger.

Meanwhile, tramping east, James Reed and his men are better fed, but just as cold.

As the gold spills from John Denton's pocket, Reed and his men have entered the snow. As the body of little Ada Keseberg is buried in calico, Reed and his men are forced by the deep drifts to abandon the horses and put what provisions they can on their backs. Big Bill McCutchen, all two hundred and fifty pounds of him, falls backward into the snow and flails his limbs frantically like a toppled turtle. "A horse! A horse!" he bellows. "My kingdom for a horse."

Despite themselves, the men laugh until the tears come.

Meanwhile, at the Alder Creek camp, young Baptiste Trudeau continues to search for the bodies of the dead. He marks the location of each new discovery with a sturdy staff topped by a length of red cloth that snaps in the chilly breeze. As best he can, he does not watch as the two Donner women go about the grisly task of butchering Sam Shoemaker's corpse. The three Littles are not allowed in this part of the campsite, the land of the red snapping flags.

And meanwhile, eight miles away at Truckee Lake, the hungry wolves lurk in growing numbers. Here the emigrants began to die only after the first terrible snows, so the corpses are not buried so deep as at Alder Creek. The smell of them is all the more strong. All the more intoxicating. At night the wolves paw at the snow. As if to show the stupid, helpless humans how to survive.

They howl all night in disbelief.

"Smell the abundance," the wolves seem to sing. "The wealth of easy sustenance. Here, let us point you the way. Why would you allow hunger to win? With such a banquet as this right beneath your feet?"

◆ SNOW ◆

ada
keseberg

john
denton

eleanor
eddy

margaret
eddy

augustus
spitzer

catherine
pike

snow

snow

salvador

snow

milt
elliott

snow

luis

harriet
mccutchen

ludwig
keseberg
jr.

dutch
charley
burger

landrum
murphy

lemuel
murphy

jay
fosdick

patrick
dolan

franklin
graves

snow

snow

baylis
williams

sam
shoemaker

antonio

charles
stanton

snow

joseph
reinhardt

jacob
donner

snow

james
smith

snow

william
pike

john
snyder

luke
halloran

old
hardcoop

sarah
keyes

PATRICK BREEN'S DIARY
At Truckee Lake camp

Friday, February 26, 1847
Hungry times in camp—Mrs. Murphy said here yesterday that she
thought she would commence on Milt & eat him. I don't think that she
has done so yet. It is distressing. The Donners told the California folks
that they would commence to eat the dead people if they did not succeed
in finding their cattle then under ten or twelve feet of snow & did not
know the spot or near it. I suppose they have done so ere this time.

TAMZENE DONNER —◆— *The Scholar*
At Alder Creek camp

When I moved to the wilds of North Carolina,
I first witnessed the slaughter of a large sow.
The unceremonious bullet to the head.
The undignified upside-down suspension from a chain.
The blood drained from the neck into a bucket.
The underside slit from breastbone to crotch.
The contents of the gut spilling onto a tarp.
The poor beast sacrificed for my own wedding feast.
How Tully laughed when I refused to eat the pork.
Years later, by the time I married George Donner,
I could dismember almost any creature in kitchen or classroom.
To my own children, I would point out the mysteries
of the Christmas goose's internal anatomical structures.
But here now in front of me was this man. Our friend. Sam.
My sister-in-law, Aunt Betsy, had long gone mad with grief.
"Seems funny—to eat the flesh of a man who starved?" she says.
We look down and consider the lifeless body at our feet.
"It's the face that makes it Sam," I say.
We consider removing the head first—to make the task less personal.
"Too much work," says Aunt Betsy.
She sets down the cleaver. She sets down the saw.
Then she covers Sam's face—with her white lace apron.
And we begin.

At first they had the meat of the oxen to eat. They had eaten an emaciated bear, a lame coyote, a deer, three ducks. Even an owl. But before long the ox meat was consumed. The wild game gone. Small meals were made of a dozen famished mice that happened into cabin or tent in search of food themselves. One by one the faithful dogs were killed and dressed. First the work dogs and then the precious pets. The feet. The haunches. The tails. The heads. Parts that would be tossed away back home were treated as rare delicacies here—priceless and precious.

When the meat was gone, they turned to the bones. Broke them open for the nutritious inner marrow. Boiled them into soup. Burned them black. Pulverized them into powder. Boiled them again into jelly.

In the beginning the ox hides had been stretched over cabins as a roof. But even the hides themselves were taken down for food. Cut into strips and turned into a barely palatable glue. The hungry occupants were literally eating themselves out of house and home.

They drank large amounts of water in an attempt to fool their stomachs. They chewed on twigs. They smoked tobacco. Roasted bootlaces over coals. Toasted bits of a rancid buffalo robe.

During the snowshoe expedition weeks before, the decision to eat the dead had been urged on by the severe cold and the immediate need to keep walking, no matter what. But at the sedentary camps, the travelers, trapped in their prison of snow, have had weeks to contemplate their slow, lingering descent into the full bloom of starvation. And so they have had weeks to consider the horror of what they are about to do.

The ideals of humanity and community are now spread as thin as the hides that used to cover the cabins. Social order has broken down. A transformation has taken effect. Those who lacked the drive to survive are already dead. Those who are left will stop at nothing.

JAMES REED ━◆━ *The Aristocrat*
Walking east toward his daughter

VIRGINIA REED ━◆━ *The Princess*
Walking west toward her father

Father
I will not stop. I will stop at nothing.
The rising sun shines in our eyes.

> **Daughter**
> I will not stop. I will stop at nothing.
> The setting sun lies just ahead.

Father
Walking east, we finally leave the grass
behind and reach the snow. Not long to go.

> **Daughter**
> Walking west, we tramp over slopes as steep
> as stair steps. Snow up to our knees.

Father
Eleven horses and mules lightly packed.
Leave the rest to set up a way station.
Make fifteen miles. Deep snows. Hard
labor for the horses.

> **Daughter**
> We leave John Denton writing poems
> beneath a tree. He barely sees. I fear the
> bright snow may blind us all. Abandon the
> poet beneath the tree.

Father

We abandon the animals. Packs on our
backs. Man becomes the mule. Ten more
miles hard labor for the men.

> **Daughter**
>
> The men stumble, children clinging to their
> backs. The children beg for bread.

Father

We stop to eat and rest our weary feet. Big
Bill entertains us by quoting Shakespeare
as he's wont to do. "In winter with warm
tears I'll melt the snow. And keep eternal
springtime on thy face!" And then he farts.
And we laugh. We laugh until Big Bill
begins to weep.

> **Daughter**
>
> We rest our feet. The Keseberg girl is laid to sleep
> in the snow. Mrs. Keseberg wails and weeps.
> "Jimmy, catch up! One step closer to Pa!"

Father

Every step takes me closer to my family. Arrive
at the head of Bear Valley. Ten miles today.

> **Daughter**
>
> The bears have eaten half the food. I lag behind
> and Edward holds my hand.

Father

Halfway up Bear Valley now. I see
travelers approaching up ahead.

Daughter

Halfway down the valley now. I see travelers
approaching down below.

Father

We go. We double march. I scan the
approaching figures for clues. My wife's
steady, measured gait? My daughter's lilt?
The sway of her hips? Watch for little
Patty, holding little Tommy's hand.
Tommy's other hand in Jimmy's.

Daughter

I watch the men approaching ahead. I search
the silhouettes for Pa. His old flop hat? His
shoulders back? Lanky? Tall? And lean?

Father

Closer . . .

Daughter

Closer . . .

Father

Jimmy! . . . and my wife! . . .

Daughter

Mr. McCutchen! . . . and my pa!

Father

. . . and Virginia, my princess!
"Oh, my family. Dear God, here you are!"

Daughter
"Pa! You're here! It's really you!"

Father and Daughter
We embrace.
A family, minus two.

Father
There is no choice.
There's nothing left to do
but keep moving onward to the lake.

Daughter
There is no choice.
There's nothing left to do
but stay and watch my father go.

Father
For Patty's and for Tommy's sake.

Daughter
I watch my father disappear across the snow.

Father
Farther and farther apart . . .

Daughter
Farther and farther away . . .

Father and Daughter
I give one final wave,
then I turn and look away.

PART SIX

— ◆ —

ANGELS IN THE SNOW

February 28–May 16, 1847
Truckee Lake and Alder Creek

We might do well to pause a moment to contemplate the usual stages of starvation.

The first two days are likely the worst. The body is strong and vigorous, so the cravings of the stomach are commensurately brutal. On the third and fourth days, the stomach's incessant craving gives way to weakness and nausea. If even the smallest morsel is swallowed, it feels like a living lobster inside the gut.

On the fifth day, the eyes become wild and glassy. The skin is pale and ashen. The stomach commands that the legs find food. The legs are too weak to obey the command. The different parts of the body are at war. Food occupies every waking thought and every sleeping dream.

On the sixth day, fantastical imaginings of food possess the sufferer like a host of demons. Dizziness overtakes the head. The limbs are like lead. To rise from bed is a Herculean deed.

By the seventh day, the body has begun to devour itself. The vital organs are shutting down. The fat stores are mostly gone. The muscle shrunken and shriveled. By now a listlessness has transported the mind to a state of near euphoria. The needs of the body have fallen away. The spirit almost shimmers through the gray gossamer skin.

And this, dear reader, is how otherwise civilized people are driven to consume the flesh of their dead. In fact it is easy. The very cells of the starving body will dictate what parts of the corpse to harvest. The sugars in the brain. The proteins in the muscle. The life-giving iron in the liver and the heart.

So do not judge them, lest you suffer a similar fate. Instead, let us celebrate that small, yet mighty spark of life. That half-full bucket waiting in the depths of the well. That last bean lingering at the bottom of the empty barrel. Do not judge them.

Let them eat.

LUDWIG KESEBERG ⟶ *The Madman*
At Truckee Lake camp, now at the Murphy cabin

After the first relief party took away Ada and Philippine,
my welcome with the Breens wore thin.
And anyway, they nearly drove me mad
with their incessant, vociferous prayers
and *praise-be-all-merciful-God!-Amen-Amen-Amen!*

So I've arranged to stay in the Murphy shack.
Poor Mrs. Murphy is sickly and sullen.
And, God, how the babies wail. It seems every babe in camp is here.
I hold them in my lap when I can
and rest beside them on their filthy pallets.
My only solace is when they sleep.
I watch them breathe, chests rising and falling.

Though my foot is still very painful and swollen,
today I go out to gather wood. I limp, hatchet in hand,
to the low-lying limbs like a frostbitten Quasimodo.
And I happen on the Reed girl, *mein Engel.*
She is with her little brother making angels in the snow.

I scold them loudly, half in jest, half in earnest.
"You children and your silly angels! You will freeze.
Do you know there is fifteen feet of snow on the ground?"

"And what do we say to *that*, Tommy?" Patty says.
Thus prompted, the boy says,
"Fifteen feet of snow on the ground;
fifteen feet closer to heaven."

"You can join us, Mr. Keseberg," the little girl says.
"Me 'n Tommy will teach you how."

"No, thank you," I say. "I've no time for angels.
Unless your angels are made of firewood.
Can you not see, I am busy—trying to stay alive?"

"I will write the instructions down, for later, if you like," she says.
"I will write them neatly on a little slip of paper," she says.
"I'll draw a little picture of your family, too, to make it specialer.
You can make your angel later, when you finish your chores."

Nineteen out of twenty-one rescued emigrants have made it out of the mountains alive. But they have a few days' travel yet to go, and food is still scarce. The rescuers now have an added task of keeping the starved wretches from eating too fast and eating too much. This is hunger's greatest irony. Those whose stomachs have been so empty for so long can literally eat themselves to death if they do not proceed with caution.

Aquilla Glover stands watch over the delicious bundles of food. But Aquilla Glover hungers for sleep, and so he feasts on slumber. He slumps into a heap and softly snores. And young William Hook, now very wide awake, hungers for something more. *Everyone is asleep,* William thinks. *Just a finger or two of beef. No more, I swear.*

The boy is barely twelve years old. He creeps, so cautiously. Opens the bag. One sliver of dried meat. Oh. Oh. Oh.

And another one just to tide him over till dawn. And oh. Oh. Oh. How can anything taste so exquisite? A thousand glands within his mouth begin to burn awake with salt and fat and sustenance. His throat is in immaculate pain. His stomach churns. Within his gut the lobster comes to life.

Elitha Donner, William Hook's cousin, finds the boy at daybreak on his knees by his bedroll. His head is bowed as if he will puke, so she places a comforting hand on his back. But William Hook is dead. She discovers his pockets stuffed with biscuits and dried meat.

◆ SNOW ◆

*william
hook*

That same day, back at Alder Creek, William Hook's mother, Betsy, and his aunt Tamzene are busy drying the thin strips of muscle they have managed to remove from Sam Shoemaker's lifeless legs. Betsy laughs despite herself. Tamzene envies her sister-in-law's waning sanity. But Tamzene is determined to keep her wits. She must keep her children alive.

That same day, at Truckee Lake, a Washoe scout comes within twenty feet of Mr. Breen, who has emerged from his buried shanty to take in the air. The man smiles and says something that Mr. Breen cannot understand, before placing three large tubers of soaproot in the snow. Then the visitor turns and disappears across the drifts on small bark snowshoes, expertly crafted.

Truckee Lake is well known to the Washoe, for this is where they gather to hunt and fish. They call the lake *awegia behzing*, the small watchful eye. The Washoe near the lake that day have all heard stories of how these white men shoot at anyone who dares approach to offer help. And there are rumors of cannibalism. The Washoe call the whites *mushago*, people to be feared.

That same day, Patty Reed sits on the roof of the Breen shanty that has begun to emerge from the melting show. She can dangle her feet and easily touch the white surface. She stares at the mountain gap through which, her faith tells her, her father will come.

That same day, her father, James Reed, breaks camp on the other side of that very gap. Reed, leading the second relief party, observes half a dozen Washoe men leaving the lake area.

"No time to lose, gentlemen," says Reed. "We're nearly there."

That same day, after a short descent, James Reed and the second relief are already crossing the frozen lake.

JAMES REED —•— *The Aristocrat*
The second rescue party, arriving from the west

Soft, powdery snow had slowed us considerably.
Had our loved ones already starved to death?
Had I brought this on myself when I raised my hand to Snyder?
Was this Keseberg's fault for speaking against me?
I am certain I could have guided the whole Donner Party
safely to California had I just been allowed to stay and lead.

And finally I've reached the camp, and I see
my little Patty, sitting easy as you please
atop the cornice of the Breens' snowbound house.
And something breaks inside of me.
Relief is cracking open like a clay water jug.
I can feel its contents spilling out, filling my chest.
Patty is alive. Smiling. And wide-eyed when she sees me.
We run to each other and embrace, and it's hard to let her go.
"I knew you were coming," she says
as we descend into the buried Breen cabin.
I send three men—Cady, Clark, and Stone—ahead to the Donner camp.
Mr. Breen tells me that Keseberg has moved to the Murphy cabin;
he says the crotchety German has a nasty abscess on his foot.
So I sling a pack of supplies on my back and set out.

Patrick Breen's Diary
At Truckee Lake camp

Monday, March 1, 1847

Today fine & pleasant. Froze hard last night. There has 10 men arrived this morning from Bear Valley with provisions. We are to start in two or three days & cache our goods here. There is amongst them James Reed, Bill McCutchen, and some old mountaineers. They say the snow will be here until June.

Thus Patrick Breen's diary abruptly stops. Its author is too busy preparing. Patrick Breen believes in the power of prayer, but he also believes in preparedness. His latest bout of kidney stones is over, and he feels strong. He and his wife and their five remaining children will risk the trip.

Patty and Tommy Reed remain with the Breens while James Reed helps Big Bill McCutchen rebury his infant daughter, Harriet. She had been laid to rest near the Graves cabin, but the body had been disinterred by wolves.

The Graves family, like the Breens, has kept mostly to itself. Mrs. Graves had once been known to travel many miles in any weather to help a sick neighbor. But her present desperate situation has transformed her into a closefisted hermit. James Reed, like Reason Tucker before him, tells Mrs. Graves that her husband is alive. But she knows in her heart it isn't true. Mrs. Graves and her four remaining children will all return with Reed across the mountain.

A few yards away, the situation in the Murphy cabin leaves Reed speechless. Outside the entrance, the corpse of one-year-old Catherine Pike lies partly exposed by the receding snows. Descending into the tiny room, Reed is overcome by the stench. Mrs. Murphy has risen to greet him only to fall backward, feebly, onto her cot. Her grandson, Georgie Foster, and William Eddy's son, Jimmy, sit together wailing in their soiled crib. Both toddlers are crawling with lice. Mrs. Murphy's eight-year-old son, Simon, sits on his haunches like a living gargoyle in the corner, rocking methodically. And Ludwig Keseberg is laid out by the hearth on a pallet of his own, reading a book, his throbbing foot propped up above his head.

Keseberg and Reed lock eyes. For half a minute neither looks away.

Then Reed sets to work making soup in the pot. Portioning it out by the spoonful like an elixir. He assigns a man to guard against overeating. One by one he washes each child with water warmed on the fire. One by one he dresses them in fresh, clean clothes. He shaves their lice-infested heads. He burns their filthy clothes in a firepit on the surface. He offers Mrs. Murphy fresh clothing, too. She declines with a hoarse laugh, saying, "That's not a good color on me, Mr. Reed."

Finally, James Reed turns his attention to Ludwig Keseberg. He pulls a thick rawhide strap from his bag of supplies. He looks at Keseberg's foot for a moment, then faces the ornery German who had once called for Reed to be hanged.

"I need you to come on up outside, Keseberg," Reed says, the corners of his mouth turned down. "I don't want the children to see."

"Very well," Keseberg sighs, and he rises to his feet, wincing.

Once at the surface, Keseberg sits on a campstool by the firepit where the infested clothing and bedding still smolder. Reed stands above Keseberg and, without speaking, pulls the large knife from his belt. Keseberg takes in the sight of it and gasps. The polished blade comes to life with a flash of sunlight.

"Stretch out your leg," Reed finally says. And Keseberg does as he is told. Reed produces a flask from his bag and holds it out.

"Nein," says Keseberg. "I don't need it."

"Suit yourself," says Reed. He sets the flask down within Keseberg's reach, then plunges the knife's blade into the fire's glowing coals. Then Reed unwraps the bandages, exposing Keseberg's swollen foot. He hands Keseberg the rawhide strap. "You'll want to bite down on that," Reed says.

Keseberg does as he is told.

With a practiced hand, Reed picks up the knife and quickly jabs it into the top of the big German's swollen foot. Keseberg screams at the back of his throat. Bloody pus gushes from the wound and sizzles against the hot rocks that circle the firepit.

"God almighty, Keseberg!" says Reed as he picks at the rancid flesh, cutting away dead skin. And after a time, he lifts out a bloody shard of willow sapling, a full two inches long, that had been tormenting Keseberg for so many weeks.

"It festered its way from bottom to top, all the way through your foot," Reed says in disbelief. "That's really something."

Then, with a clean cloth, warm water, and soap, Reed begins to wash

Keseberg's foot. He packs the wound with lint to help it drain. He bandages it slowly at first, picking up speed as the layers grow thicker.

Then Reed reaches into his bag and pulls out a comb. And he begins to run its teeth, gently, through Keseberg's matted hair. Reed had learned from Keseberg's wife that their daughter, Ada, lies buried in a drift just west of the pass. But Reed says nothing.

My daughters are still alive and well, Reed thinks. *What would be gained by telling him the truth? He'll find out soon enough.* Instead Reed says, "With rest, and luck, that wound may heal quickly. We can only leave behind provision enough to last four days, if you ration it. Another relief will be along soon."

Keseberg reaches for the flask and takes a long pull. He winces as the liquor burns its way down. Then he clears his throat and says, "Tastes like horse piss." And he smiles.

"Mmm-hmmm," says Reed. And the corners of his mouth turn up. Just barely. But they do.

JAMES REED —◆— *The Aristocrat*
The second rescue party, at Alder Creek and Truckee Lake camps

After leaving Keseberg, I hike eight miles to the camp at Alder Creek.
Bill McCutchen, Charles Cady, and Nicholas Clark travel with me.
The sight that greets us takes our breath away.
The bodies of Jacob Donner and Sam Shoemaker (perhaps one other)
lay upon the snow in various stages of dismemberment.
The flesh is stripped to the bone in places.
The torsos have been cut open and robbed of their organs.
The by-products of the butchery are cast about pell-mell;
thus arranged by human or animal we cannot tell.
We set to work passing out flour and soup and clean blankets.
We remove each tent to higher ground to mitigate the damp.
I tell them what I hope is true: that more relief is on the way.
The food I have to offer will last, maybe, four or five days.
Betsy Donner is much too weak to travel.
But she agrees to send with us her oldest three children.
George Donner, I'm afraid, is practically an invalid.
He cannot rise from bed, let alone walk through snow.
He urges his wife, Tamzene, to escape and take their daughters,
but she insists she must stay with her husband.
And her three girls will not leave without their mother.
And the young man, Baptiste, will not leave without the three girls.
Cady and Clark agree to stay to help Baptiste attend to each tent,
cutting wood, cooking, and rationing food.

By day's end I return to the lake to make final arrangements.
Mrs. Graves and her remaining four children prepare for departure.
She smokes her pipe as she instructs my men to dismantle her wagon,
revealing eight hundred dollars in gold and silver coin hidden in the
    floorboards.
Mr. and Mrs. Breen, in relative good health, are bustling as well.
Though Mrs. Breen is loath to leave the safety of her cabin,

her boys have eaten the final tiny morsels of hoarded food.
So she knows the only food left would be the bodies outside in the snow.
Mr. Breen has cast off a sack that was once filled with meat.
I thaw its frozen fibers over the fire and scrape the traces from the seams.
In all I recover a full teaspoon of nourishment,
and I tuck it into the very tip of my mitten's thumb.
A final contingency, I think.

And so the next day, we go.
We leave behind Charlie Stone, one of the relief party,
to tend to all those still laid up in the Murphy cabin,
including Keseberg, still sleeping off the fever of his healing foot.

LUDWIG KESEBERG —✦— *The Madman*
At Truckee Lake camp, the Murphy cabin

After Reed removed the splinter from my foot,
I slept for what seemed like days.

> *I dreamt I was home back in Berleburg.*
> *In my father's house, seated at a sumptuous banquet.*
> *Philippine was there, singing to baby Ludwig.*
> *Ada and Mathilde, one girl for each knee. The twins giggling.*
> *And there was music and light and warmth.*
> *And then the girls began to cry. Their faces melt away—*

Jimmy Eddy and Georgie Foster are crying in their tiny crib.
Mrs. Murphy is still in bed, her face to the wall.
Her son, Simon, stands up, staring at nothing,
rocking from foot to foot with a monotonous hum.
"How long have I been asleep?" I ask. No answer.
The fire, though just coals, shows signs of tending.
As I rise to go up and gather wood, Simon speaks.
"She's gone," he says. "That little girl left with her daddy."
I climb to the surface and stand in the sun.
My foot is healing. A little tender, but the painful infection is gone!
As I set out to find firewood, for just a moment I feel happy.
But then, just as suddenly, I am stopped in my tracks:
There, near the entrance to the cabin, I see the faint outline of a dozen
weather-blown snow angels. And at the very center of this host,
the snow is churned up, the angels erased by erratic wolf tracks,
a single human arm, from elbow to hand, emerging from the snow.

Tamzene Donner —◆— *The Scholar*
At Alder Creek camp

Mr. Reed and his men have taken three of Betsy's children.
That has left just twelve of us at the Alder Creek camp.
Betsy shares her tent with her little boy, Lewis,
along with Baptiste and two men Reed left behind to help.
My own tent is still crowded with George and me,
our three girls, and Betsy's other boy, Sammie, just four years old.
Aunt Betsy is coming unraveled in the mind,
so we've taken Sammie in to ease the strain.
George is now fevered all over, his arm green to the shoulder.
I'm going to die, Tamzene, he whispers. *My blood is poisoned.*
I say, "You could still get better."
He says, *You cannot correct this like a misspelled word.*
I say, "Mr. Reed assures me help is on the way."
George says, *I love you, Tamzene.*
But if our children don't reach California with their momma . . .
then what will I have died for?
It has taken this nightmare to make me realize
how lucky I am to be loved and cherished
by this living, breathing, wonderful man named George Donner.
I had wanted to come west as much as he did. Maybe more.
How can I leave him behind to die alone?

JAMES REED —◆— *The Aristocrat*
The second rescue party, east of the pass going west

I left Truckee Lake with a motley crew
of nine rescuers and fifteen grateful survivors.
After a day's slow march we camped at the lake's north end.
There Mrs. Graves slipped away, alone, to bury her coins.
I distributed the day's rations: one and a half pints of tasteless gruel.
Mrs. Breen complained. The Breen boys cried.
Mrs. Graves returned, quietly, without the burden of her heavy coins.
Now, this morning we are busy preparing to cross the pass.
But the sky is dark with snow clouds. The air is heavy and damp.
Patty and Tommy giggle, catching something on their tongues.

Snow?

We are suddenly silent, listening to the terrible sizzle
of fat snowflakes falling into the flames of our small morning fire.

More snow is on the way.

More snow.

More snow.

More snow is on the way.

"We've no time to lose," Reed tells his party of two dozen. "We have to get well over the mountain in case more snow sets in."

But it takes nearly all of that day for our pioneers to make the arduous climb over the pass. Here they enter the small prairie at the head of the Yuba River, where they find a collection of thick green branches set tightly, side by side, atop a level patch of snow. It is a fire platform left behind, no doubt, by Reason Tucker and the first relief. It is constructed so that a fire might be made on top of the deep snow without it melting through.

"We will stop here to build a fire," says Reed. "The temperature is dropping. And I don't like the looks of those clouds."

Patrick Breen thanks God for the ready-made platform, for it saves the men much labor and allows them to start a blaze quickly. The snow, which had begun the day before on the eastern side, begins now to fall, tenfold, on the western side. The ominous clouds blot out the sun. And without warning, the wind becomes a perfect blizzard. Reed, Big Bill McCutchen, and Hiram Miller build up a bulwark of snow around the group of people huddling with their feet to the fire.

They are now caught out in the open without shelter, and they are situated at the narrow end of a small, funnel-shaped prairie, a contour that intensifies the already explosive bursts of wind. The snow fills the air utterly and absolutely, the gale blasting small, sharp ice crystals in every possible direction all at once.

James Reed discovers himself suddenly snow-blind and unable to see the flames that dance not five feet in front of him. At some point in the night, he gives out altogether and nearly falls into the fire. Bill McCutchen and Hiram Miller shake him awake and place a bit of loaf sugar on his tongue. Reed revives but is useless for the duration of the storm. Patrick Breen and many of the others pray.

"Perhaps God could lend us a hand with the damned fire," McCutchen spits.

In order to survive, our stranded pioneers must continually tend not just the fire but also the platform that holds it up. The whole apparatus sinks a few inches every hour as it melts the snow beneath. Care has to be taken to keep the base branches level so the entire conflagration will not topple into the snow or onto the cowering refugees.

The storm will rage this way for more than two days. And when a break finally comes, five-year-old Isaac Donner will be dead. He will remain propped up for hours between his sister, Mary, and little Patty Reed.

PATTY REED —◆— *The Angel*
With the second rescue party, stranded west of the pass

Dear God,
Can you see us? Can you tell that we're here?
You've sent along a powerful fierce wind.
I know you watched us go over the pass.
And I thank you for leaving behind
a ready-made platform for our fire.
But why this wind and terrible snow?
Maybe you forgot we was still here.
I know you have a whole world to look after,
but it's been blowing now for a day and a night.
The wind is so loud you might not hear Mr. Breen's prayers.
And I'm scared. You see, Isaac Donner is sittin' to my right.
And Tommy's sittin' to my left. And they're about the same age.
Only Isaac, as you probably know, died a little while ago.
Please make a solid shield of me, God,
so death will not leak through.
I hope that you are satisfied
and don't take Tommy, too.

Amen

◆ SNOW ◆

isaac donner

TAMZENE DONNER ⟶◆⟵ *The Scholar*
At Alder Creek camp

It was the worst snow of the winter so far.
Not long after Mr. Reed's relief party had gone,
the dark clouds swept in low. And then came the snow.
Some three feet or more. Covering the corpses. Covering the tents.
The snow literally buried us. It was impossible to gather wood.
For three days and two nights we went without fire.
The wind blew like a hurricane. We'd never seen the likes.
The huge pine trees all around us thrashed as wild as prairie grass.
In the darkness we could hear uprooted trees crashing to the ground.

When the storm finally broke, Aunt Betsy came to our tent,
and she laid the lifeless body of little Lewis in my lap.
"Fix him up, Tamzene," she said. "Make my boy better.
I cain't lose another one. I just cain't lose one more!"
With the help of Baptiste and Mr. Clark, we cut a grave
in the fresh fallen snow and laid little Lewis to rest.
Aunt Betsy then put herself to bed and would not rise.

We've come too far to give up now, George finally whispered.

"I'm *not* giving up," I snapped. "And I'm *not* leaving you alone!"

I won't be alone. I'll have Baptiste and Mr. Clark, said George.

"But Mr. Clark won't stay," I replied. "I've heard him talking.
And Baptiste doesn't say it, but I know he wants to go, too."

George said, *If you won't leave for yourself, then leave for the girls.*
I hate to even say it, Tamzene, I really do—
but we could all be dead before the next rescue.
Don't risk our daughters' lives to hold a dying man's hand.

So today, when Mr. Stone and Mr. Cady come to my tent
and declare their intention to make their way back
before the next big storm hits, I come up with a plan.
Perhaps God has decreed that George *is* to die.
And perhaps it *is* wrong to choose a dying man over my living children.
But sometimes doing the wrong thing
is the only thing left to do.
And perhaps, just perhaps, there is a way to do both.
George is right. We *have* come too far to give up now.
And as God is my witness, I will *not* be cheated of a single second
of whatever time George and I have left together.

◆ SNOW ◆

lewis
donner

Do you see how Tamzene Donner's hunger for more time keeps her alive? Just one more day. One more hour. One more second of life. For *that* she will do anything.

The very same storm that now pins down James Reed and the second relief has given Tamzene Donner time to think. And the more her husband pleads with her to leave him behind, the more she knows she will stay with him to the end.

So when Mr. Cady and Mr. Stone declare their intention to escape before the next big storm, Tamzene Donner offers them the princely sum of five hundred dollars to escort her girls safely over the mountains.

Charles Cady, Charlie Stone, and their friend Nicholas Clark had all proven their courage when they crossed the mountains to bring relief to the suffering emigrants. They further proved their courage by staying behind to look after those left in both camps. Before the storm Nicholas Clark had shot a young bear, a week of flesh and fat. But Nicholas Clark was gone for now, away with Baptiste on the hunt for more meat.

Surely Cady and Stone have proven themselves worthy of the task at hand. They readily agree to Mrs. Donner's terms. She clothes her three daughters in fresh dresses, woolen stockings, and warm quilted petticoats. Next come the cloaks, three-year-old Eliza and four-year-old Georgia in garnet-red twill with white thread. Six-year-old Frances in a thick blue shawl. Then Tamzene covers their small heads with matching knit wool hoods.

She shepherds her Littles up the snowy steps. And once out in the open air, she lines them up and kisses them one by one. She has been talking all this time, to no one in particular. For all of the proceedings are quite lost on the children.

Finally she speaks to the air. "I may never see you again, but God will take care of you."

This last statement settles into the six-year-old mind of Frances Donner, who will replay the phrase again and again, chewing on it. *God will take care of you.* For she had been waiting for this God person to appear and give her something to eat.

Tamzene has packed a bundle containing silks and silver spoons. Three glorious fancy skirts. A number of pretty white-lace day caps trimmed with dainty ribbons. The whole of it keepsakes that her girls might one day open. And perhaps they will be reminded of their mother.

Charles Cady and Charlie Stone, holding one girl each, struggle to arrange the children and the bundle of gifts. Frances walks on her own, looking ahead for God. Tamzene Donner watches her three daughters disappear toward the lake. She returns to her husband. She sits. She holds his good hand. Then she opens the burned book of poetry that Baptiste had rescued from the fire.

"I am a part of all that I have met," she begins. "Yet all experience is an arch . . ." George Donner falls asleep.

Three miles after leaving Alder Creek, Cady and Stone sit the three Donner girls on a snowbank and step off a ways.

"Don't worry," Frances tells her sisters. "If they leave us here, I can find our way back to Ma and Pa by our tracks in the snow."

The men come back. They pick up the girls, and they all move on. They promise the girls sweets if they do not cry. They stop to rest a hundred times. They stop three times for the girls to pee.

At sundown, Cady and Stone and the three little girls finally arrive at the lake camp, exhausted. They find Keseberg up and alert, tending the fire. He is drying strips of human flesh over the flames.

"Do you have food?" Keseberg asks.

Mrs. Murphy sits up, slowly, like a ghoul, all skeleton and skin. She says, "Hello, girls. And how is your mother?"

BAPTISTE TRUDEAU —◆— *The Orphan*
At Alder Creek camp

H-U-N-T-I-N spells hunting.
I am back from hunting with Nicholas Clark.
I shot me a rabbit with Uncle George's gun.
I gutted it and dressed the meat to make stew for Mrs. D.
I skinned it and scraped the hide to make mittens for the Littles.

But the Littles are gone!
And Mrs. D just let them go, without a thought for *me*.
I should have expected it.
I had me a mother and she up and left.
I had me a father and he got himself killed.

> *I stab the snow here.*
> *I stab the snow there.*

I know they ain't my real sisters but it still makes me mad.
One day they're here and then next day they're gone.
Just like ol' Buck and Bright covered up by snow,
and you hunt and you hunt for something that ain't even there.

> *I lift the hook looking*
> *for blood, hide, or hair.*

Back in the Murphy cabin at Truckee Lake, two-year-old Georgie Foster stands in his crib wailing. The toddler steps on three-year-old Jimmy Eddy curled up at his feet. Eight-year-old Simon Murphy stands in the corner rocking from foot to foot, staring at nothing.

"She's gone," says Simon Murphy. "That little angel girl done left with her daddy."

Cady and Stone arrange a pallet and feather bed for the girls by the doorway. Frances Donner falls to sleep only after her sisters do.

In the morning, Charles Cady and Charlie Stone gather up their provisions and the Donner girls' bundle of keepsakes and dainties. They crawl, careful as cats, over the threshold. In silence they slip up the frozen stairs. They stand together in the chilly air. They get their bearings by way of the great peak at the north end of the lake. And without saying another word, they walk away. And they leave Tamzene Donner's three daughters behind.

Ludwig Keseberg —◆— *The Madman*
At Truckee Lake camp, the Murphy cabin

Now Cady and Stone have left me with even *more* mouths to feed!
The cowards. *Feiglinge.* Low-life rodents. I would kill them if I could.
I would kill them and chop them up for my stew!
Three more pups in the wolf den to feed. I gather wood.
I go about my day. I have the hatchet. The rest is up to me.
I chop and I chop at the limbs of the trees.
But I'm weak. And I miss. And the hatchet blade slips.
And it plunges into the heel of my newly healed foot.

I howl like an animal. I am wracked with rage and pain.
Blood gushes out from my wound and onto the snow.
And I know that the scent will give me away.
And I think. How absurd to be maimed once again.
As if God had decreed I must walk with a limp
and wear Old Hardcoop like a curse around my neck!
Shhh. Shhh. Shhh.
I drag my damnable foot across the snow.

After abandoning the three little Donner girls at the Murphy cabin, Charles Cady and Charlie Stone make camp at the north end of the lake. They quickly build a lean-to large enough to accommodate themselves and the bundle of heirlooms they had sworn to deliver with Tamzene Donner's daughters.

The storm that had blanketed the camps at Alder Creek and Truckee Lake had become a perfect hurricane on the California side of the mountains. Just over the pass to the west, the Reed, Graves, and Breen families have been pinned down in a place called Summit Valley. For two days they have suffered the abuses of the worst snowstorm yet. But at least for now the hurricane winds have subsided enough for James Reed and the second rescue party to assess their situation.

The robust fire has now sunken down a good ten feet with no sign of reaching the earth. Reed shovels to the surface, cutting steps as he goes. Close behind, Hiram Miller lifts little Isaac Donner's lifeless body out of the pit and lays it on the snow. For Reed's part, he wants to move on while the storm has subsided. Hiram Miller and Bill McCutchen concur. But to their astonishment, the others refuse to go.

"We're too worn out and sick," says Mr. Breen. "And look at us, Reed—at least ten of these children will have to be carried. The snow is too deep and soft. It would be suicide."

"But it's suicide to stay," says Reed.

"We'd rather die warm by this fire than cold out in the open," says Mrs. Breen.

"There's no guarantee that another relief will bring food anytime soon," argues Reed. "Any rescue parties will be caught in the same storms as us."

"Mr. Reed," says Mrs. Breen, standing up now with her hands on her hips. "We followed you across the Hastings Cutoff and you nearly got us kilt. We were in bad straits back at the lake, but now you've come and made it worse! Jayzus, Mr. Reed, you best stop now before you rescue every one of us to death!"

Mr. and Mrs. Breen will not be convinced to move on. And the once-robust Mrs. Graves is now too feeble even to stand up, let alone help her four children along. Seven-year-old Mary Donner has burned her foot in the fire and cannot walk. But fourteen-year-old Solomon Hook will not be left behind.

So McCutchen, Reed, Hiram Miller, and young Solomon gather up what they figure to be two days' firewood. They take care to place the pile within easy reach of the pit. Then they set off. Hiram Miller, bigger and stronger even than Bill McCutchen, carries Tommy. James Reed and McCutchen take turns carrying Patty. Solomon Hook is left to walk on his own. The three other men in Reed's rescue party—Britt Greenwood, Joe Verrot, and Patrick Dunn—have no desire to stay behind and starve. Nor are they inclined to risk their own lives to rescue a group of perfect strangers who refuse to be saved.

About a day and a half later, breaking the silence in the Breen family's deepening pit of snow, it is seven-year-old Mary Donner who first suggests they eat the dead. Without a trace of irony, little Mary declares, "My mama cooked Sam Shoemaker's arm, Mrs. Breen. And I don't think it hurt him one bit."

Mr. and Mrs. Breen, up until now, had been the luckiest of the Donner Party. They had eaten their share of hides. But their meat hadn't run out until the very end. Now, of course, their luck has changed.

The body of Isaac Donner, who had died during the last storm, is first to be eaten. Mrs. Elizabeth Graves, from feebleness or fear, refuses to partake of the loathsome food. Her five-year-old son, Franklin Jr., follows her example. Within a day, both mother and son are dead.

Then mother and son become food themselves. You see how this goes.

Mr. and Mrs. Breen do not discuss out loud the morality of what they have chosen to do. Perhaps they do not want to frighten any of the children. Or perhaps they do not want to tell young Nancy Graves that her lifesaving sustenance comes from the mortal clay of her mother and little brother. Or perhaps, for once, the Breens just don't want God to hear.

In the end, Mr. and Mrs. Breen choose to do whatever they must to keep themselves and the children alive. They climb to the surface and harvest the meat. They descend back into the pit. They cook and they eat. But before they eat, they still say grace.

And while they eat. They weep.

◆ SNOW ◆

elizabeth graves

franklin graves jr.

It has been two days since they abandoned the three Donner girls. Charles Cady and Charlie Stone can tell another storm is simmering, so they hurry to cross the pass. Proceeding through Summit Valley, they encounter the deep pit in the snow, smoke rising from it like a mouth of hell.

Around the perimeter of the pit are the butchered corpses of two boys and a woman. They recognize the dead woman as Mrs. Graves, who earlier had instructed Cady and Stone to take apart her wagon and look for hidden silver. They don't recognize the bodies of Isaac Donner and Franklin Graves Jr. There are too many children to keep track of them all.

Charles Cady and Charlie Stone peer cautiously into the pit and discover the Breen family and about a half dozen others, all of them children. Scattered around the smoky fire, some look to be sleeping; some look to be dead.

Charles Cady whispers to Charlie Stone, "Them's the ones that James Reed and Big Bill took out just before we left. Must've got caught in that last blizzard."

Down in the pit, the only soul awake at the time is nine-year-old Nancy Graves. Nancy is holding her baby sister, dropping water from her finger into the infant's mouth. Nancy clearly hears the two men overhead, but she cannot see.

"Hello?" she says. "Is someone there?"

Charles Cady and Charlie Stone stop suddenly, still as trees. Then they quietly turn away without a word, resuming their march. Their heroism has come to an end.

"Is someone there?" Nancy Graves repeats. But by then, no one is.

One day later, in order to lighten their load and make better time, Charles Cady and Charlie Stone drop Tamzene Donner's carefully tied-up bundle of keepsakes and dainties. And they leave it.

They have no other choice. Tamzene Donner's burden has become too heavy. They still have many grueling miles to go. They have run out of food. They are moving too slow. And worst of all, more snow is on the way.

Ludwig Keseberg —◆— *The Madman*
At Truckee Lake camp, the Murphy cabin

More snow comes down for nearly a week
with occasional breaks when the sun cuts through.
The wolves show me what to do to survive.
I dig where they dig.
And I eat as they eat, from the carrion at hand—
albeit with the help of a cookfire and kettle. Ha, ha.
Mrs. Murphy will not partake of the food I offer.
But all of the children eat it well enough—

William Eddy's son, Jimmy, has become listless and limp.
Simon Murphy is springy and spry, but gone in the head.
The Donner girls are headstrong and spoiled.
Whenever I'm in the cabin, I make them stay in bed.
I cannot tolerate children constantly underfoot!
As for Foster's boy, Georgie, I am afraid it is too late.
I take him to bed as I would my own children
whenever they suffer bad dreams or a chill.
But he never wakes up.

Old Hardcoop has a hand in this. But how?
Shhhh. Shhhh. I hear him scraping a knife in my head
as I hang Georgie Foster's body from a peg on the wall.
Nausea overcomes me. I feel I might be sick.
Hardcoop hones the shadows of my brain to a razor's edge.
Shhh. Shhh. Shhh.

◆ SNOW ◆

*georgie
foster*

Patty Reed —•— *The Angel*
With the second rescue party, west of the pass toward California

Dear God,
Pa sings. So soft and sweet I bet even *you* can't hear.
I tried, for a while, to walk on my own.
I stumbled and Pa reached down and scooped me up.
Pa sings so soft and sweet in my ear. Can you hear?
He bundled me onto his back with a blanket.
See him now as he walks hands-free? Can you see?
See him fall to one knee? See Mr. Miller help us up.
And Pa sings so soft and sweet I bet even *you* can't hear.
So soft and sweet and . . . I'm falling asleep . . . see . . .
and sweet and soft . . . I can't rightly breathe . . . I can't see
. . . and we're walking to heaven and sweetly singing . . .
so close . . . can't you see . . . Pa sings to me on the way . . .
hands free . . . and ain't it sweet . . . to not feel nothin' but
Pa's sweet singing . . . singing singing . . . sweetly . . .
singing . . . sweet . . .

For the third time, James Frazier Reed descends from the mountains. With young Patty strapped to his back, he finally leaves the snow behind. Bare dirt is now beneath his bloody, bursting feet. He knows how close he is. He knows with just another day's travel he and his companions will be within view of Midshipman Woodworth's base camp in Bear Valley. There will be warm fires blazing. There will be bread and biscuits. And freshly cooked beef marbled with fat. There will be sleep and whiskey. The thought of it keeps Reed from collapsing altogether.

He has come close to dying many times by now and has learned to recognize the signs of his own waning life the way you experience a dying fire. He knows the minimum that's needed to keep the blaze alive, even down to the last fading coal, before feeding it a twig and fanning it into flame.

So he knows with certainty the meaning of the sudden limpness of the little girl who rides on his back. He knows the meaning of her soft babbling and raving declarations. Hiram Miller notices it, too, and calls out to Reed. But Reed is already stopping to sit, his legs crossed beneath him, his daughter cradled in his lap. He rocks her and speaks to her.

"Patty! It's Pa! You come on back to us now." Reed speaks loudly, as if calling to a man on the opposite bank of a river. And in a way, I suppose, he is.

All the men stand still. Silent. Helpless.

"Patty! We're almost there, Patty! You come on back to us."

Reed removes his mittens and rubs Patty's face and arms and legs. He rocks her. He gently slaps her cheeks. But the child does not speak. She does not move. Reed holds a hand up to her small nose to see if he can detect a wisp of breath.

Nothing.

Reed holds her small body tightly. And he openly weeps. Buries his face into the nape of her neck.

For all her little prayers to God, Reed thinks bitterly, *when did God ever listen?* He hugs his daughter more tightly. And as Reed increases the intensity of his embrace, his hand rises to his face—just beneath his nose. And somehow through the tears and the grief, James Reed's nose catches the scent of meat. The wonderful aroma is coming from his thumb.

His thumb!

Of course! The portion of meat from the Breens' empty sack. He had placed it there before setting off from Truckee Lake. Of course! Of course!

James Reed reaches for his mitten, quickly turning it inside out. And there at the very tip of the thumb, clinging to the fur, is a frozen ball of dried beef, no larger than a grape.

"Patty! It's Pa. I've got something for you to eat."

Reed places the frozen bit into his mouth to warm. And OH—the taste! Does the thought of keeping it for himself enter his mind? Yes. But there are forces much stronger than hunger at work.

After softening the food, Reed removes it from his mouth. And with exquisite care and tenderness, he reaches his rough fingers toward his daughter's cold lips. And he gently places the food on her tongue.

"Patty! It's Pa."

And the men all around them watch.

"Patty! It's food."

And they wait.

"Patty! It's good. Now EAT!"

And—

The girl's cheeks twitch.

And the girl's lips move.

And she chews.

Patty Reed —◆— *The Angel*

. . .

Patty! It's Pa.

. . .

Patty! It's food.

. . .

Patty! It's good. Now EAT!

. . .

And Pa is singing.
So soft and sweet.
I bet even *you* can't hear.
And who would have thought
that a little dry meat
could taste so good.
And Pa is singing.
So soft and sweet.
Can you hear it?

Can you hear?

Amen

BAPTISTE TRUDEAU —•— *The Orphan*
At Alder Creek camp

W-I-S-P-E-R spells whisper.
"Old man Donner is nearly dead already," whispers Nicholas Clark.
"Ain't no way he'll leave these mountains alive.
Your precious Mrs. D is healthy enough
but the other Mrs. Donner is on death's door herself.
Her kid, Sammie, is as good as dead, too."
Clark is trying to talk me into leaving the camp
so we can save our own hides before another big snow hits.
Clark says, "The Donners ain't nothing to you.
Your real family is all dead and buried.
Your real father and mother wouldn't have sent the girls away
without telling you. As if you was just a hired boy.
No reason at all for you to stay behind. I'm leaving at first light."
But when first light comes, Clark sets out on his own.
"You go on ahead," I say. "I'll just set up a bit of firewood
to tide the camp over for a day or two. I'll catch up."

But I don't catch up. I chop wood and empty chamber pots.
And I help Mrs. D bury Aunt Betsy in the snow.
And I help Mrs. D bury little Sammie right beside Aunt Betsy.
Then I feed the fire in Mr. and Mrs. D's tent.
Then I roll out my father's blanket along the hearth.
And then I sit for an hour by pinecone light
listening to a woman who ain't my mother reading poetry
to a man who ain't my father. So maybe Clark's right;
maybe the Donners ain't nothing to me.
But for now, I reckon they're more than enough.

◆ SNOW ◆

elizabeth
donner

sammie
donner

In case you've forgotten, dear reader, a naval officer, Midshipman Woodworth, had promised—and failed—to meet James Reed with a supply ship on the great Sacramento River. When Midshipman Woodworth finally arrived, he said a speech and manfully disembarked with about ten of his men. After a brief harangue at Johnson's Ranch, Woodworth's rescue party moved on only as far as Bear Valley before declaring it too dangerous to proceed.

Midshipman Woodworth is not a risk taker. For all his talk of saving lives, he seems more interested in setting up a comfortable camp.

He tells William Eddy, "I'm here to establish a base camp, not go mountain climbing. I've been assigned to make minimal food and warmth available to whatever emigrants stumble out of the mountains on their own. Nothing more." Meanwhile, he and his men eat all the best food. And drink all the whiskey.

William Eddy and William Foster, the only two men to survive the snowshoe expedition, are here at Woodworth's Bear Valley camp, resting, recovering, and helping to establish a way station for the various relief parties. Charles Cady and Charlie Stone have arrived here, too, attempting to drink away the memory of the pit.

Finally, James Reed, Big Bill McCutchen, and the second relief party stumble from the mountains into camp. Both rescuers and rescued are fed. Reed explains how the Breen family and a few others are still stranded in the pit somewhere west of the pass. How a second group is starving on Alder Creek. And yet a third group is starving at Mrs. Murphy's lakeside cabin.

James Reed tells Mr. Eddy and Mr. Foster how he saw both their sons—weak, but alive and freshly clothed. And hasn't Reed himself defied the odds and the snow to save his own little daughter and son?

Now Eddy and Foster hope to do the same. William Foster, you may recall, is the man who accidentally shot his brother-in-law to death, and later murdered Luis and Salvador, the Miwok vaqueros. William Foster has swaddled his conscience in layers of rationalization.

For now, Foster is intent only on reaching his family. If he hurries, perhaps he can save his boy, Georgie, not to mention his mother-in-law, Mrs. Murphy, and his nephew, Simon Murphy. At that very moment, though, young Georgie Foster's corpse is hanging awkwardly from a peg in that sad little cabin at the lake. Soon Ludwig Keseberg will set to work and make a meal of it. Hunger doesn't judge. I must leave it up to you, dear reader, to determine if this disturbing occurrence is proper restitution for William Foster's treatment of Luis and Salvador.

Like Foster, William Eddy is hoping to find his *own* son, Jimmy, yet alive. And a call goes out among the men in camp for volunteers. And at first there are no takers, not even Woodworth himself, who is ostensibly in charge of the entire rescue effort.

"It is folly," Woodworth coughs, "to attempt the trip without a proper guide."

"But both Foster and I have made the trip ourselves," Eddy protests. "And the trail is clearly marked by burnt-up trees and bloody footprints in the snow!" Still Woodworth will not be convinced, although he *is* eventually persuaded to offer an incentive of three dollars per day, plus a fifty-dollar bonus for every emigrant brought safely into camp. That monetary enticement inspires the formation of what will be a third rescue party, made up of seven men. Mr. Eddy and Mr. Foster will lead. The superhuman Hiram Miller will join. And three new volunteers—Howard Oakley, William Thompson, and John Stark. And to round out the ranks, the guilt-ridden Charlie Stone, who had refused to answer the call of the suffering child Nancy Graves:

Hello? Is someone there?

Charlie Stone downs his cup of liquor and yells, "Oh, all right then! I'll do it. Else I'll hear the child asking for the rest of my life!" Perhaps not the most honorable motivation. But one can't be choosy in trying times.

TAMZENE DONNER ⟶✦⟵ *The Scholar*
At Alder Creek camp

Only three of us are left alive here at Alder Creek.
The silence is strangely soothing, a kind of opiate that helps me forget.
Then Nicholas Clark arrives in camp, shouting me back to reality.
"Mrs. Donner," he says, out of breath from the hike,
"your three little girls are still at the lake."
"How can that be?" I say. "Mr. Cady and Mr. Stone—"
"Cady and Stone nothing!" Mr. Clark interrupts.
"They left the girls with Keseberg and Mrs. Murphy."
"Left my children?" I shout. "With Keseberg!"
"The little girls looked fine," says Mr. Clark.
"But . . . there were bodies . . . and blood. On the snow.
So I came right here to tell you."

In our tent I tell George my plan to go check on the girls.
He whispers, *Take care when you cross the creek.*
It might look solid enough, but you might fall through.
I say, "I'll be careful, husband." And pat his good hand.
George grabs my wrist and says, *Promise me, Tamzene,*
that you'll take Baptiste with you, and get the girls,
and don't come back. Promise me you'll leave me behind.
I kiss him on his fevered forehead, then I step outside the tent.

"Baptiste," I say. "You will stay with Mr. Donner until I return."
"Mr. Clark," I say. "You will please come with me."
"B-but—" stammers Baptiste. "B-b-but—" stammers Mr. Clark.
Then without another word I set off walking to the lake,
with Mr. Clark doing his best to keep up.

"Hello? Is someone there?" What had at first been a hopeful shout was now barely a whimper. The girl, Nancy Graves, had been asking the question for hours now to no one in particular.

The indomitable Mrs. Breen has been listening. Her nostrils sting from the stink of the latrine set aside in one area of the pit. By now the fire has burned its way through the snow to solid ground. At least the wind cannot reach them here. As her husband slowly gives up, Mrs. Breen passes many hours looking upward. The world at the bottom of a well is a world of truncated days. Looking at a circle of sky, Mrs. Breen can see a horizon in every direction without even turning her head, as if looking through the wrong end of a telescope.

It had been left up to Mrs. Breen to feed the many souls held prisoner in this terrible pit of snow. It was Mrs. Breen who would climb twenty feet to the surface by way of a branch positioned specifically for this purpose. Once there, she would gather firewood by tediously crawling, snakelike, from tree to tree across the snow on her belly, her little hatchet in hand. She would throw the gathered branches before her as she slithered her way back to the pit.

Or she would climb to the surface to look for help. Or climb to the surface to cut more flesh from the corpse of Mrs. Graves, or Isaac Donner, or little Franklin Graves. She recalled Mrs. Graves's final words before she died: "Quick. Take the baby," just before handing her infant to her daughter Nancy, who was barely nine herself. Mrs. Breen remembered speaking harshly to Franklin Graves, who was crying incessantly for his dead mother.

"Your ma is sleepin', lad. Now quiet down an' let her rest!" Or something of that nature. Within half an hour the boy had breathed his last.

Now here she is, the mother of six boys and a nursing baby girl, and she is collecting the meat from the tiny limbs of a child. And while out of earshot of her husband and the children, she mutters, "You *owe* me, Lord. You and Jayzus and the Virgin Mary. You *all* owe me for what you've required these hands to do."

Mrs. Breen's husband, weak and defeated, is barely more than his breath. When his young son James begins to show signs of death, Patrick Breen says, "Let the boy die, mother. He'll be better off."

"You may give up on yerse'f, you old coot," spits Mrs. Breen. "But you'll not be givin' up on your own children. You best snap out of it fast, or I'll kill you m'self and feed you to the wee ones! You'd be better use to them that way."

Mrs. Breen will never forget what her husband said that day. *Let the boy die, mother.* Eventually she will forgive it, but she'll never forget. A few years from now, if God wills it, Mrs. Breen will advise her only daughter regarding her opinion of men: "You have to forgive in order to live; but if you forget, you're a fool."

Eventually Mrs. Breen will forgive herself as well. But she will never forget the things she has seen. She will never forget the things she has done.

BAPTISTE TRUDEAU —•— *The Orphan*
At Alder Creek camp

Tap, tap. Tap, tap, tap.

I run the chalk against the little slate.
I am practicing my letters while Uncle George sleeps.
With Clark and Mrs. D now gone, the tent is silent as the grave.
In fact the whole camp is quieter now than it's ever been.

Tap, tap. Tap, tap.

Then Uncle George speaks without opening his eyes.
Why are you still here, Baptiste?
His weak, ghostly voice scares me at first.

"I didn't know you were awake," I say.

How can I sleep with you tapping like a woodpecker!
Uncle George laughs. Then gasps. Then coughs.

"Are you okay?" I say. "Do you need anything?"

Yes, he whispers. *I need for you to leave me.*
You've done your duty, boy. Now git!
And when you see Mrs. Donner, take her away with you.
I demand it. Toss her in a sack if you must.
She weighs but ninety pounds.

After a minute's silence, he inhales to speak again.
You be careful when you cross the creek.
The snow may look solid, but you could fall through.
He coughs. And gasps. And falls asleep.
He begins to mumble. Something about frost on the crops.

Something about linsey-woolsey. His teeth chatter.
I cover him from chin to toe with my father's blanket.
The shivers stop. The chattering becomes a soft snore.

"That'll keep you," I say. "You need that blanket more than me."
Uncle George sleeps on.
I prop up my slate on the little stool by Mr. Donner's bed.
Something for him to see . . . if he ever wakes up.

F-A-T-H-R spells Father.

Then I leave Alder Creek behind,
my snowshoes crunching against the snow.
Somewhere hidden beneath my feet
lie the bodies of Buck and Bright.
Maybe. If they were ever there at all.

"Well, there is Mrs. Breen, alive yet, anyhow," comes a voice from above. Mrs. Breen tries to speak, but no sound will come. So little Nancy Graves, still holding her baby sister, says loud and clear, "Hello? Is someone there?"

And this time Charlie Stone says, "Yes! I'm here. We're *all* right here. Let's get you out of there."

Only three of the members of this third relief party stay behind to rescue the sufferers in the pit. Howard Oakley carries seven-year-old Mary Donner with her burned foot. Charlie Stone reaches to pick up little Nancy Graves, but she pushes him away, saying, "Thank you kindly. I think I can walk on my own. But would you *please* hold my baby sister. Her name's Elizabeth. And she weighs an awful lot."

"Little girl," answers Charlie Stone. "Your wish is my command."

Rescuer John Stark is big enough and strong enough to carry two children at once. He carries each pair a hundred feet or so, sets them down on the snow, and goes back for two more. In this way he leapfrogs his way back to Woodworth's base camp in Bear Valley.

Later, around the safety of the base camp's fire, Mrs. Breen overhears Midshipman Woodworth take the credit for saving the eleven souls brought down from the nightmarish pit. Mrs. Breen remains seated as she speaks clear and loud across the fire, for all to hear.

"Mr. Woodworth! Sir, you are too flaming scuppered on rum to mount a horse, let alone mount a rescue. I thank nobody but God and John Stark and the Virgin Mary. In that order!"

Even devout Patrick Breen agrees with his wife's assessment. Nor does he take issue with Mrs. Breen placing the heroic John Stark above the Holy Virgin herself. "We *prayed* to Mary," Mr. Breen would say later over a whiskey, "but 'twas Mrs. Breen and John Stark who did the heavy lifting!"

The numerous comings and goings of the past few weeks have marred the smooth surfaces of the Sierra Nevada snow. The rescuers. The rescued. The living. The dead. The villains. The heroes. The where, the when, the how, the who. To follow precisely our story's overlapping and fluctuating rescue attempts would be like separating the tangled canes of a blackberry thicket.

With this in mind, I advise that we keep an eye on the heart of the thicket, the intersection where all canes meet. And the heart of this particular thicket is the Murphy cabin. At this very moment, the Murphy cabin at Truckee Lake is the destination of Tamzene Donner, hiking west to check on her daughters. It is also the destination of the two Williams, Eddy and Foster, with the other members of the third relief coming from the west. Even Baptiste, the orphan, is now on his way toward the Murphy cabin, having left George Donner sound asleep. And of course, the Murphy cabin is now home to anyone at the lake who is somehow still alive.

Imagine, if you will, the confusion within the Murphy cabin. Tamzene Donner, thinking her daughters have gone to safety, has found them here instead. The girls chatter with urgent joy to see their mother. They are full of tales. How Mr. Keseberg hung up Georgie Foster's body like a Christmas ham. How Mr. Keseberg took Jimmy Eddy to bed and devoured the child during the night, bones and skin and eyeballs and toes. How Mr. Keseberg talks with a German accent and limps like a monster. And, worst of all, how he made the girls stay in bed all the time to "keep us from gettin' underfoot!"

For his part, Keseberg's heart had quickened at the sight of Mrs. Donner coming to his door.

The third relief arrives. More confusion. William Eddy and William Foster rush into the rank-smelling cabin fully expecting to find their sons alive. They ask, "Where are the boys? Jimmy and Georgie? Where are our sons?" Followed now by awkward silence.

Until finally, from Frances Donner: "Mr. Keseberg killed them and ate them both!"

"What is this nonsense?" asks William Eddy.

"Your boy is dead, Eddy," says Keseberg gruffly. "And also yours, Foster. I'm sorry to say that. But it is the way."

"What happened?" asks Eddy.

"How did they die?" asks Foster.

"We were all starving," says Keseberg. "I had nothing to do with it. This is Hardcoop's doing. The old man."

"Hardcoop?" says Eddy. "I want to see the bodies."

Silence follows.

"Where is my son?" asks Foster.

Silence.

"Where is my son?" asks Eddy.

Silence.

"It wasn't me alone," says Keseberg. "We all ate of the bodies. We would otherwise be dead."

"I should kill you myself," says Eddy.

"This is Hardcoop's doing. He has cursed me," says Keseberg.

"What does Old Hardcoop have to do with this?" says Foster. "Have you lost your mind?"

"I left Hardcoop behind and now he haunts me," says Keseberg.

"You *have* gone simple," says Eddy.

At just that moment Baptiste Trudeau enters the Murphy cabin, cold and winded from his eight-mile hike from Alder Creek. More confusion.

"Baptiste!" the three Donner girls scream as one. And they clamor to the boy, assaulting him with hugs, climbing him like a tree.

"Baptiste!" echoes Tamzene Donner, not happy at all to see the boy. "You were supposed to stay with Mr. Donner."

"He made me leave," Baptiste protests. "You knew he would."

Mrs. Donner frowns. "You left him alone?"

At just sixteen years old, Baptiste cannot understand how the anger Mrs. D directs toward him is born of her own self-loathing and shame. Mrs. Donner knows she has expected too much of this boy. And *of course* George would make Baptiste leave. She should have made the boy leave herself.

Tamzene offers Foster, Eddy, Miller, and Thompson fifteen hundred dollars if they will take her three girls to safety. They refuse the money, but each agrees to take the children across the mountains. They demand, though, that they leave at once. This third ragged rescue party does not have supplies enough to survive another blizzard. And the stench and gore and stomach-churning reality of the Murphy cabin lets them know without a doubt what their fate would be were they to stay.

Mrs. Murphy's eight-year-old son, Simon, rocks back and forth and makes ready to go, saying, "Gone like the angel. She's gone. That little angel done gone, gone, gone!"

William Eddy gives Mrs. Murphy six finger-thick slivers of dried beef. She whispers, "Have all the children got out?"

William Eddy says, "Yes, ma'am. That's the last of 'em."

Without another word Mrs. Murphy turns her face to the wall.

Keseberg is to stay behind as well. Although his previous foot injury has finally mended, his recently infected heel will not allow him to walk for any useful distance. And at over six feet tall, he is impossible to carry.

Tamzene Donner hugs her precious Littles goodbye.

Then Mr. Eddy takes her aside and says, "We can't wait no more, Mrs. Donner. Baptiste told me how sick Mr. Donner is. He may be dead already. You face a full day's walk there and back. You'll never be able to catch up to us. So I ask you again, will you *please* just come on along with us now?"

Tamzene looks up into the eyes of Mr. Eddy. Then she looks over at her daughters, each one already clinging to a different man's back.

Eddy talks on. "Mrs. Donner, I've walked across these damned mountains twice and both times I've nearly died. And I've done things that'll give me nightmares for the rest of my days.

"My wife was the light of my life, and now she's dead. My daughter is dead. Now I've come all this way just to find out my son is dead, too. I've got nothin', Mrs. Donner. But you've got these three little girls. And you've got two more waiting on the other side of the mountain. Don't give that up."

Mr. Eddy stops talking as a tear escapes the corner of Tamzene Donner's eye. She opens her mouth as if to speak, but swallows whatever words she intended.

"Please, Mrs. Donner," Mr. Eddy says one final time. "Will you come with us?"

Tamzene Donner spins on her heel, turning her back to Mr. Eddy and the others. She pauses as if preparing to approach the blackboard to share an elegant mathematical equation. She runs it over in her head, balancing the values. Then she takes one step. And then another. And walks away toward Alder Creek. And she doesn't say another word. And she never looks back.

TAMZENE DONNER —◆— *The Scholar*
From Lake Truckee to Alder Creek

As Mr. Eddy spoke to me so eloquently of his loss,
I felt a warm tear slipping down my frostbit cheek.
And what's more, I felt my heart beginning to break.
Not just breaking, but breaking *open.*
An unfamiliar sense of calm rushed in,
while years of tired fears went rushing out.

And with every step I took away from the lake
and toward my dying husband, my clarity grew.
It is much easier to love a dead husband than a live one.
The dead ones will never disappoint you.
George Donner is anything but perfect, but he's mine.
What haunts my heart the most is how Tully died *alone.*
He had called my name. Reached out his hand.
But . . . I . . . was . . . not . . . there.

I will not make the same mistake a second time.
And that is why I walk the eight miles back to Alder Creek.
And why I enter our sad snow-covered tent with a smile.
And why I kiss my imperfect husband as he sleeps.
On the slate by the bed, Baptiste has written *F-A-T-H-R.*
For once I don't correct it. It is perfect as it is.
I see George's chest rise and fall beneath Baptiste's blanket.
I'm not too late. He lives.
I hug the slate to my chest as I sit on the stool.
And I watch my husband as he lives.
"I love you, George Donner. I didn't say that enough," I say.

George wakes up at the sound of my voice.
His eyes are wide. *Tamzene?* he asks in a whisper.

"I woke you up," I say. Then, "I'm *glad* I woke you up."

You've come back? he says. *What about the girls?*

"They are safe," I say.

And then George begins to cry. And he smiles.
I can tell he's embarrassed, so I stand and put my hand to his cheek.

I say, "What is it, my love? What can I do?"

No, no. It's nothing. It's silly, he says.
It's just that . . . I thought you had left me.
I thought I was alone.

"Are you glad I've come back?" I ask.

Would it matter if I said no? he says.

"Of course not," I laugh. "We're linsey-woolsey, you and I.
I am the linen warp and you are the woolen weft.
I'm afraid there is no unraveling us."

LUDWIG KESEBERG ⭢✦⭠ *The Madman*
At Truckee Lake camp, the Murphy cabin

After Foster and Eddy left with all the children,
after Mrs. Donner left to be with her husband,
and after the last voice had faded away across the lake,
the cabin was enveloped in a deafening silence.
Like a wind inside my head, the silence roared.
I would sit for hours and watch Mrs. Murphy's back.
I would sit for hours and listen to her breathe.

I have eaten the dried meat that Mr. Eddy left for me.
I have eaten the dried meat he left for Mrs. Murphy.
I have eaten everything I possibly can.
I try to keep myself from eating. I try to starve.
The days go by. And the more hungry I become,
the less I am burdened by the worries of this world.
My raving turns to laughter. My worry becomes wonder.
I sleep. And I wake.
And I sleep within my sleep. And dreams and reality are the same.
And I wake. And I watch. And I listen.
And finally Mrs. Murphy shudders and sighs . . . then dies.
Did you hear it? *Shhhhhhhh.* Did you hear her soul ascend?
I am weak. Too weak to drag the body to the surface.
All the better to do it right here away from the hungry wolves.
Collect the blood while the body is still warm.
Shhhh, shhhh, shhhh.

BAPTISTE TRUDEAU —◆— *The Orphan*
With the third rescue party, west of the pass going toward California

With the help of Mr. Eddy and the other men, we make good time.
My Donner girls cry and complain a little.
They complain a little more. Then they complain a lot.
Hiram Miller finally loses his patience
and gives them all the spanking of their lives!
It is not the type of lesson Mrs. D had ever taught them.
But it seems effective, for the girls seem much reformed.
As bad as I feel about leaving Mr. and Mrs. Donner behind,
I also feel happy to be leaving the mountains.
I have had enough snow to last me a lifetime.
I'll never again take for granted a warm bed and a full belly.
Not sure what I'll do with myself once I get where I'm going.
Maybe I'll settle nearby the Littles and watch 'em grow up.
Maybe get my own ranch and raise a herd of Bucks and Brights.

We happen upon scattered silk skirts and hand-embroidered caps.
And Frances declares, "Them there belong to our ma!"
So I make them each a pretty new dress as best I can.
We all laugh at the sight of their homegrown gowns.
The girls act like three queens for the rest of the trip—
three well-behaved queens, with sore bottoms.

LUDWIG KESEBERG —◆— *The Madman*
At Truckee Lake camp, the Murphy cabin

Shhh, shhh, shhh.
I hear the wolves above. Digging at the snow.
Shhh, shhh, shhh.
I hear Hardcoop walking circles in my head.
Shhh, shhh, shhh.
Mrs. Murphy whispers, *Sleep, Ludwig, sleep.*
Shhh, shhh, shhh.
Hardcoop plays the blade and whetstone.
Shhh, shhh, shhh.
The little girl makes her angels in the snow.
Shhh, shhh, shhh.
The wolves sniff in the doorway.
They smell the blood. They smell the meat.
They're hungry. And they need to eat.
Shhh, shhh, shhh.
I pour the grains of powder into the breech.
I set the cap. I ram the bullet home.
Old Hardcoop whispers, *Let them in. Let them eat.*

Tamzene Donner ––◆–– *The Scholar*
Final day at Alder Creek camp

On March 26, not long after the sky turns light,
the love of my life, George Donner, dies.
He does not call my name and ask if I am there.
But he knows I am there just the same.
He does not reach out for my hand.
For my hand is already resting on his heart.
I feel its cadence grow fainter and fainter,
as if he is marching over some distant hill,
a "margin fading forever and forever as he moves."
I wash his body thoroughly. I shave his whiskers clean.
I dress him in a Sunday suit from the wagon.
I place Baptiste's slate on George's chest
and fold his good hand across the unsteady letters:
F-A-T-H-R it will say to whoever happens upon the scene.
And they will know who George Donner was.
For if nothing else, he was a father first, before anything.
And he was my husband, my lover, and my friend.
He was the woolen weft to my linen warp.
He was a man who collected orphans, and consumptives, and hangers-on.
He rarely said no to anyone in need.
And he was captain of the Donner Party.

◆ SNOW ◆

george
donner

LUDWIG KESEBERG —◆— *The Madman*
At Truckee Lake camp

The wolves are gone for now.
And my mind is clear. And Hardcoop is gone.
And the sun is out and shining down into the cabin
like a shaft of light sent straight from heaven.
And *shhh, shhh, shhh.* I am bathed in light.
And I am warm and my injured heel is nearly healed.
And little Georgie is singing in the crib with little Jimmy.
The boys play at pat-a-cake, slapping hands and laughing.
But the flesh is gone from their arms.
Their small white arm bones gleam in the sunlight.
And Mrs. Murphy is at the hearth, stirring the kettle,
and *shhh, shhh, shhh* stirring a kettle of blood.
And she asks, "Are you hungry, Mr. Keseberg?"
And I say, "Yes." *Shhh, shhh, shhh.* And she turns
and her body has been harvested of heart, liver, and lungs.
I can see her spine clearly as she smiles and speaks.
"I know you must be hungry. You've been sleeping so long."
Then the wolves begin to howl, and Mrs. Murphy is gone.
And *shhh, shhh, shhh.* Wolves are digging at the snow.
Sniffing at the doorway above. I see their shadows moving
in the shaft of light from heaven. *Shhh, shhh, shhh.*
The faces of Philippine and Ada fade before me.
And I ready the loaded pistol in my hand.
I am completely alone.
And Hardcoop holds the puppet strings.
And I raise the loaded pistol.
I put the muzzle in my mouth.
No angels for me, I think.
Let Old Hardcoop have his way.
Let the hungry wolves have their feast.

Then—

"Hallooooo! Are you there? Is anyone there?"

A voice.

A woman's voice saying, "Mrs. Murphy?"

A woman's voice. Coming down the stairs.

Saying, "Mrs. Murphy? Mr. Keseberg? Is anyone alive?"

Tamzene Donner —◆— *The Scholar*
From Alder Creek to Truckee Lake

I finish laying George out by late afternoon.
And within the hour I set out for Truckee Lake.
I know that my girls are well ahead,
but maybe with luck and a good night's rest,
I can catch up to them by following their tracks.

I received a classical education in Newburyport as a girl.
By the time I was thirteen I was teaching school myself.
I traveled unescorted, by steamer, from Massachusetts
to the Carolina coast to take charge of my own school there.
I can recite the presidents and calculate the hypotenuse of a triangle.
I can identify most flora and fauna (including genus and species).
And I can do all of this while knitting a pair of socks.
I am a regular contributor to the *Sangamo Journal*,
including essays, letters, field reporting, and poetry.
I have a banker's knowledge of finance and budgeting.
I am well read in philosophy and literature.
I have personally read the travelogues of Mr. Hastings
and Colonel Frémont, Washington Irving, and a host of others.
Tamzene Donner is *not* a stupid woman.

And so, how did I not take care crossing the snow-covered creek?
It looked solid enough. It did. It looked like solid ground.

But it wasn't.

LUDWIG KESEBERG ⟶⬥⟵ *The Madman*
At Truckee Lake camp

Seeing Mrs. Donner—her pleasing figure,
her proper posture, her handsome face,
her grace like a dancer, her musical voice—
seeing her now in the midst of this lonely nightmare
has shocked me back to myself, my mind perfectly intact.
Seeing her here has kindled my soul's last tinder of hope.
I revive. I am alive. And I find my voice.

"Please come in, Mrs. Donner. You are soaked to the bone!"

"I'm af-f-raid I've fallen into the c-creek, Mr. Keseberg.
The s-s-snow seemed s-s-so solid, and yet I fell through," she says.
"M-m-my husband. He warned me a thousand t-t-imes."

Her clothing has frozen solid. Her lips are blue.
Her teeth chatter out of control. Her whole body is shaking.

"Warm yourself by the fire," I say.
"If you like, you can wear Mrs. Murphy's dress."

"Where *is* Mrs. M-Murphy?"

"I'm afraid she's gone."

"I have to s-s-see my children," she says.
"But first I sh-sh-should sleep. By the fire."

And she lies down on Mrs. Murphy's bed.
And she turns to the wall the way that Mrs. Murphy did.

"No!" I say. "You mustn't go to sleep. You won't wake up."

And I shake her, but she shrugs me off.
"I must catch up to my children," she says.

"They've been gone now three weeks or more," I say.
"Please wait. When my foot has healed fully, we'll go together.
You must get warm. You must eat. But do not go to sleep."

"I must see my children," she says.
"I sh-sh-should get some sleep," she says.
"I *shhh, shhh, shhh*ould sleep."
Over and over. *Shhh, shhh, shhh.*
She falls to sleep, just as Mrs. Murphy had.
She closes her eyes. She turns to the wall. She lets go.
So I cover her quaking body with my warmest counterpane.
And she stops shaking. Her breathing becomes shallow.

I sit. And I stare. I watch her sharp-edged
shoulder bones rise and fall like butterfly wings.
And finally Mrs. Donner shudders and sighs . . .
and then she dies. *Shhhhh.* Her soul ascending.
All of her intelligence, gone. Just like *that*!
The memories she made. The languages learned.
Imagine the volumes of books she had read!
How can it all be gone so fast? *Kaput!*
As if her life story was written in snow.

I am still too weak to move the body to the surface.
I stand and check her breath with the back of my hand.
I stroke her hair, her forehead is still warm from the fever.
I feel the tiny flame of hope in me go out.
And *shhh, shhh, shhh.* That sound in my head.
Shhh, shhh, shhh. Like teardrops on hot coals.
And I hold Mrs. Donner's listless hand.
And I speak *shhh, shhh*, as softly as I can.

"Sleep now, Mrs. Donner. Sleep.
I'll be here when you wake. We'll take a walk.
We'll wait for our saviors together, you and I.
We'll wait and pass the time at chess or cards.
Do you play whist? I'll teach you if you like.
When you wake we will talk about literature and botany.
You can be my Beatrice and show me the way
through this many-leveled hell when you awake.
We will practice our French and walk through the snow
along the Champs-Élysées on our way to this little café I know.
We will talk of poetry and philosophy and art.
We will make a new start in a shining city full of hope.
The coffee will be bitter and the waiters will be rude.
But, ah, the food. Ah, the delicious, delectable food.
Shhh, shhh, shhh.
Oh, Mrs. Donner. Where shall we begin?"

◆ SNOW ◆

*tamzene
donner*

*george
donner*

I know you will forgive Ludwig Keseberg if he has gone a little mad. Odds are *you* would, too, if you were in his snowy shoes. Life has tested him in harsh and singular ways. A broken wagon tongue back on the Big Blue. Hobbling his foot on a willow spike back on Mary's River. And again with an ax to the heel later on. The unbearable loss of baby Lewis. And of Ada's twin sister before that. And now the death of three-year-old Ada herself (although he doesn't yet know).

But none of that is our immediate concern. Ludwig Keseberg may wax poetically regarding bad luck, loss, and sorrows of the heart, but the more pressing reality at this moment is the fact that he is starving. Allow me to articulate the mundane specifics.

Once the food has completely run out, hunger first turns its attention to Keseberg's flesh. His body begins to search its own landscape for little cached pockets of fat. Next, his body feeds upon the muscle masses, which wither away into the blood. Next are the tissues and organs themselves. Hunger wisely begins with those organs least vital to life. Only then do I turn my attention to the liver and kidneys, which both cease to function as a result. Then the all-important brain goes into hibernation. The diaphragm forgets to breathe. The heart forgets to beat.

Keseberg begins to literally devour himself from the inside out. Apathy sets in. Along with a desire to withdraw. And a listlessness that is mystical and holy. Keseberg begins to transcend the temporal world into a state of blissful nothingness.

Just imagine Keseberg's profound disappointment when he finally begins to eat the flesh of the dead in order to survive. His body sadly revives. His organs hum back to life. His diaphragm rises up and down like a bellows. His brain regains its rightful place upon the throne. And Keseberg returns to his dungeon of worry, want, discomfort, and boundless, maddening, insatiable needs.

Better that I should have starved myself, Keseberg thinks. Or perhaps he is speaking out loud. *For what's the use of being alive when you live a life of nightmarish suffering?*

The more Keseberg eats human flesh, the more he resuscitates. But the more his body recovers, the more his soul decays. So mortified is he by the monster he has become that he forgets he has ever been human. So long has he communed with the dead that he forgets he has anything to live for.

And as for food, even corpses are a finite source. Corpses disappear just as any stores from the pantry, cellar, or icehouse. There is only so much meat. The snow remains deep. Keseberg loses hope of ever seeing his family again. He begins to believe that his wife and daughter are better off without him. He loses hope that anyone cares enough to come and guide him home. He loses hope that anyone even believes he is still alive. Keseberg mostly stares into the flames of the cookfire. Old Hardcoop has long since moved out of Keseberg's head. Keseberg's soul is now the lone resident walking the vacant halls of a rotting palace. His soul walks. And waits.

Remember, the body will starve in the absence of food. But the *soul* will starve in the absence of *hope*.

Hope. Kesberg hears the ring of it like a church bell in the distance.

Hope. Keseberg recalls the warmth of little Patty Reed's hand. Her enthusiasm. Her willingness, in fact desire, to be his friend.

Where is she now? he wonders. *By now my angel is happily eating sweet corn back at Sutter's Fort, not giving me a second thought.*

And what has become of the angel's father, who tended to my wounds and washed my feet?

The joyful memory of them is nearly nourishment enough to revive Ludwig Keseberg—at least for another breath or two.

JAMES REED —◆— *The Aristocrat*
At Sutter's Fort, Alta California

I don't take a single breath for granted. The air is pure heaven.
Everywhere here at Sutter's Fort we see signs of the coming spring.
No healthier place can be found—no fever, no ague, no sickness.
All culinary vegetables can be raised in great abundance.
The finest pumpkins I ever saw are here.
And watermelons, I'm told, can be kept for a long period.
Cabbage and lettuce are in perfection the first of May.
Potatoes, corn, and beans by June. Onions grow very large and fine.
Hens lay and hatch the year round without any care.
In short, we will *never* suffer another day without food!

Today the sun shines bright and the children are free to explore.
Patty instructs Tommy how to make mud pies.
Virginia and the Breen boy are off riding horses.
Captain Sutter gladly lent them two mounts.
I realize I owe my family's lives to Sutter's generosity.
But I see now how his kindness is a calculated move.
His quest for power has taken a toll on his humanity.

As for me . . .
I have descended into savagery and paid the toll.
I have driven my knife into a good man's heart.
I did, no doubt, what Captain Sutter would have done.
And yet, at that moment, it all fell apart.
I still believe had I not been banished,
I could have led us all safe to California.

But for now I'll hold my tongue.

LUDWIG KESEBERG —◆— *The Madman*
At Truckee Lake camp, the Breen cabin

Today the wolves leave me in peace.
It has now been three weeks
since Mrs. Donner died.
For three weeks the corpses
have been my only company.
So I have taken up residence in the Breen cabin,
to escape the stink of the dead.
Wherever I go, there is nothing in my head.
Even Old Hardcoop has abandoned me.
I can feel the cold blood of the dead in my veins.
We share the same body and the same vacant soul.
If this is the price of being alive, I know I am better off dead.
No angels for me.
I am alone on this mountain.
Alone in this inhospitable wilderness.
The snows are receding. But what does that matter now?
The wolves have moved on. But I know they'll come back.
My bad foot has healed now. But where would I go?
I eat my last piece of detestable flesh.
I put on a clean waistcoat.
I put on my good Sunday jacket.
I wash my face. I step outside. Into the dark.
I lie back against the freezing snow.
I close my eyes. And wait to die.

VIRGINIA REED —◆— *The Princess*
At Sutter's Fort, Alta California

Edward and I are riding slow and lazy, side by side,
on the trail that leads to Sutter's Fort.
I close my eyes and I think of poor Billy,
abandoned in the desert.
I can still see him in my mind, mired in the mud.
Then I think on how all of us Reeds have survived.
And then I don't feel so bad about Billy.

"Open your eyes, Virginia," Edward teases,
"or you'll step in a gopher hole."
I confess to Edward my solemn promise to God,
that if my family survived, I would become a Catholic.

"I like bein' Catholic," Edward says. "I like the holy sacraments.
It's hard to fall asleep when they're flingin' water at you.
Or when you're eating wafers and wine.
Or singing," he adds. "I sure do like the singing."

"Do you believe the wafer is really the body of Jesus?" I ask.
"And wine is really His blood?"

"Sure I do," Edward says.

"But you *know* that isn't so," I say. "You *know* it's only bread and wine."

"Knowing something is easy," he says.
"Having faith is the hard part.
Faith is when you believe something
even if it don't make no sense.
Like when Miss Virginia Reed has faith
that her old swayback bag-o'-bones nag

can beat Eddie Breen's fleet-footed charger
in an all-out race from here to Sutter's Fort."

"Or like when Mr. Edward Breen has faith," I say,
"that his hobble-hooved cross-eyed hack
can beat Miss Virginia Reed's sleek-winged steed
after you count one-two-three-go?"

Then, without even countin', Edward Breen kicks his horse
and goes flyin' in a dust cloud toward the fort.

"No fair!" I yell after him. "*You* cheated before *I* could!"

I lean down over my horse's neck
and I let out like a crack o' lightning.
My knees feel weak and my head is a little bit dizzy—
either on account o' nearly dying, or on account o' being alive;
I can't tell which one.

The cool air stings my cheeks.
And I'm breathing harder than the horse.
And my bonnet goes flying off my head,
but this time it lands in California!
And I'm catching up to Eddie Breen's broad back.
And the world is a beautiful blur.

PATTY REED —◆— *The Angel*
At Sutter's Fort, Alta California

Dear God,
On the way to Sutter's Fort one of the rescue men, Mr. Pyle,
proposed marriage to Virginia, and she laughed and hurt his feelings.
But then Mr. Pyle asked Mary Ann Graves, and she said yes.
Me and Tommy have been eating real good, but we've both swelled up
as if we've been stung all over by bees, and it itches the same way, too.
Ma says our bodies are trying to remember how to eat.
When we got here Ma hugged us so hard it hurt.
And I admitted how I hid my doll, Angel, in my dress.
I told her it was Angel who had kept us all safe.
And Ma cried and cried and cried. But she didn't get a sick headache
on account of the healthful and invigorating California air.
Just one last thing, God, before I Amen this prayer to a close:
I've propped Angel up on the mantel over the fire,
so maybe Mr. Keseberg might feel a little warmness.
Mr. Keseberg is still out in the snow. Cold and hungry and sad.
I know you're busy, but he'll be needing some hope.
Just a thimbleful will do, like them crumbs in the thumb of Pa's mitten.
So give him some hope, and also let him know
that Mrs. Keseberg is here, safe and sound, and she wants him to come
   home.
Oh, and I almost forgot, God.
      Tell him to look in his pocket.

Amen, Amen, and Amen

Ludwig Keseberg ─◆─ *The Madman*
At Truckee Lake camp

I lie back against the freezing snow.
My body numb from head to toe.
But light blushes the sky. *I'm still alive.*
The darkness lifts. The sun comes up.
Please God why am I still alive?
I hear the wolves circling round,
curious to see if I'm living or dead.
I'm determined to lie still.
A bold wolf comes closer to get a smell.
I wonder, Is this how Hardcoop had it? *Yes.*
Abandoned? *Yes.* Forgotten? *Yes.* Left behind? *Oh yes.*
Devoured by the hungry wilderness? *Yes.*
Another wolf. Hunger has made them bold.
Then a snarl and a *NIP.* Sharp teeth tear at my jacket.
Another snout sniffs at my bleeding heel.
Then a snarl and a *RIP.* More teeth tear my sleeve.
And I'm tugged by the arm, and I open my eyes.
It's alive! the wolves say.
And they run.
The sun is up. The wolves are gone.
Dear God, it's just so hard to die. *Why?*
A torn-off sleeve . . . a ruined pocket . . .
and . . . a piece of folded paper?
That girl. My angel. A note.

I shudder with cold. I cough. I sigh.

Without warning, now, I feel my arm move.
My other arm moves. I prop myself on an elbow.
Stiff from hours of lying still.

And now I move my hip.
My leg. My foot. My hand.
And I reach across the snow.
And with clumsy frozen fingers.
I pick up the note.
I open it. And I read.

THE PROPER WAY TO MAKE A SNOW ANGEL
for Mr. Keseberg, the German man

by
Martha Jane Reed,
"Patty" to her friends

A new patch of snow is best, very smooth.
Tread light into position, with yer back to the patch.
Don't leave no footprints.
Clench feet and legs tight together. Count three <u>OUT LOUD</u>.
On three, close eyes. Fall back with spred out arms.
Trust.
The snow will catch you.
Keep still a spell. Look up at sky.
Move straight legs. Apart. Together. Apart.
Flap straight arms. Down. Up. Down. Up.
Close yer eyes. Reach pointyest finger over head.
Draw haylo with pointyest finger in snow over yer head.
Stand up carful.   Dont leave no mark.
Leep away as   carful as you can.
Turn. Look down.   Put hands on hips.

Behold yer angel!

Ludwig Keseberg had come so close.

A bold wolf rips off Keseberg's pocket. A folded note falls out onto the snow. And Keseberg's curiosity alone is enough to show the wolves he is yet alive.

What's this? he wonders. And he reaches out.

And lifts it up.

He wonders. He wonders. He wonders.

Wonder, itself, is a lot like hope. And suddenly he knows. It's a note from the girl.

His freezing fingers tremble to open the small square of paper. He lingers over the childlike handwriting. And oh how the memories of his family flood in. Memories of love, and pride, and purpose, and belonging. The memories lift Keseberg to his feet.

Suddenly Ludwig Keseberg is his ten-year-old self. He is in Berleburg, where he grew up. His left cheek is still warm from the kiss he just got from the Zimmermann girl.

He reads out loud, "On three, close eyes. Fall back with spread out arms."

And he counts out, *"Eins! Zwei! Drei!"* And he launches himself with dizzy glee backward onto the snow.

I am hunger. And I am everywhere and in everything.

I linger above the lake camp now as a cloud might linger, looking down on all below.

From my vantage point above, I hear Keseberg read from Patty Reed's letter. I watch him as he tussles in the snow, his arms making wings, his legs making a wide gossamer robe.

Now his eyes are closed. And he wears a grin that hints at an inward paradise. He is visited by Philippine. His children. James Reed. Even Old Hardcoop, the cutler. Ghosts bent on salvation.

Then he opens his eyes, looking at the soft white flakes that have begun to fall. As he lies on his back, he feels like he is flying, with exhilarating speed, upward to heaven, the snowflakes hurtling against his face. Almost as if he has wings of his own.

Ludwig Keseberg begins to laugh, loud and deep.

From high in the sky, I can see the whole camp. The cabin rooftops rising from the whiteness. The single chimney expelling smoke. The blemishes of blood. The silent scattered corpses. The lurking wolves weaving through the rough-hewn stumps. The sad abandoned tents at Alder Creek. The bloated bodies of Buck and Bright emerging from the melting snow. And finally, to the north, Truckee Lake, gleaming like a single magnificent ice-covered eye.

And there. Descending the long and treacherous slope of the pass, I see seven slowly moving figures make their way toward Truckee Lake. Their packs are mostly empty. They have come to see what treasures can be salvaged. They move across the lake at a leisurely pace. By now there's little hope of finding anyone alive. It would take a miracle. The intervention of angels.

◆ SNOW ◆

william
hook

augustus
spitzer

isaac
donner

snow

john
denton

margaret
eddy

snow

luis

milt
elliott

landrum
murphy

lemuel
murphy

snow

snow

charles
stanton

snow

harriet
mccutchen

sam
shoemaker

baylis
williams

patrick
dolan

luke
halloran

snow

james
smith

tamzene
donner

snow

elizabeth
graves

snow

ada
keseberg

snow

salvador

catherine
pike

dutch
charley
burger

ludwig
keseberg
jr.

eleanor
eddy

jay
fosdick

franklin
graves

antonio

snow

william
pike

old
hardcoop

john
snyder

joseph
reinhardt

jacob
donner

sarah
keyes

To Mary C. Keyes
Springfield, Illinois

From Virginia E. B. Reed
Napa Vallie California
May 16, 1847

My Dear Couzin,

I am a going to write to you about our trubles in getting to Callifornia. We had good luck til we come to Big Sandy. Thare we lost our best yoak of oxen, Balley & George. The people at Bridges Fort persuaded us to take Haistings cut off over the salt plain.

It was a raining then in the Vallies and snowing on the montains. We could not go over & we had to go back & build cabins & stay thare all Winter without Pa. The cattel was so poor thay could not hardly git up when thay laid down. What we had to eat I can't hardly tell you & we had Mr. Staton & 2 Indians to feed too.

I froze one of my feet verry bad. We had nothing to eat then but ox hides. O Mary I would cry and wish I had what you all wasted. We had to kill littel Cash the dog. We lived on litle cash a week.

We went over great hye mountains as steap as stair steps in snow up to our knees. Litle James walk the hole way in snow up to his waist. He said every step he took he was a gitting nigher Pa and somthing to eat.

We have left everything but I don't cair for that. We have got through with our lives. Don't let this letter disharten anybody. Never take no cutoffs. And hury along as fast as you can. You are for ever my affectionate couzen,

Virginia Elizabeth B. Reed

NOTES

Author's Note: Narrative Pointillism

Poor George Donner. Modern maps are crowded with place names that honor the successes of great explorers and pioneers of the past. But George Donner is so honored because of a catastrophic failure! Dying ninety slight miles away from his final destination, Donner would never cross the mountain pass that bears his name. Nor would he ever gaze upon Donner Lake. Or Donner Creek. Or the Tahoe Donner Campground where "campers enjoy flush toilets, laundry facilities, hot showers . . . plus free WiFi access for those who still want to stay connected to the outside world."

Each progressive generation revises history much like new tenants taking up residence in a grand old house. They redecorate and remodel to suit their own taste and the latest fashion. Restoration, on the other hand, requires us to go backward in time. Historians must strip away layer after layer of well-intended "improvements" to reveal the original truth that lies beneath. Strip away the name Donner Lake, for example, and you will find Truckee Lake, named by white people in honor of Chief Truckee, the Northern Paiute leader who guided travelers safely through these mountains for years. Strip away the name Truckee Lake, and you will find *awegia behzing*, the lake's Washoe name, meaning Little Watchful Eye. This is the name I like the best. Not only because the Washoe people have lived here for six thousand years, but also because the pretty lake really *does* look, for all the world, like an eye.

Donner Lake, the "little watchful eye," no doubt saw exactly what happened to all the suffering souls trapped in the Sierra Nevada mountains. But Donner Lake isn't talking. Only by combining the stories of every player can we fully understand what took place. This is the essence of narrative pointillism—creating a picture or a story one point at a time. Each point has its own unique perspective. And only by stepping back to consider all the points together will the picture or story become complete.

Although it is historical *fiction*, this novel is a great jumping-off place for anyone interested in the Donner Party. As usual, I have learned as much as possible about what "really happened" before allowing my imagination to run rampant within the confines of the facts. The facts—the numbers, names, dates, and details—are the bones of historical fiction. It is up to the poets to fill in the gaps and dress the bones in flesh.

I have tried not to judge the Donner Party too harshly. These were not professional trappers and mountain men. The wagons of the Donner Party (like most pioneer wagons) held the belongings of farmers and families. More than half of the members of the Donner Party were children. After crossing the South Pass in what is now southwestern Wyoming, the Donners began following trails that were only two years old and in constant flux. There were no rest areas, gas stations, or fast-food restaurants. No mile markers, road signs, or cell phone towers. In most cases, if you wanted to travel down a different road, you had to get out and make one.

I hope, like me, you won't judge the Donner Party too harshly. But I do hope you will judge them, not based solely on their failures but also on their grit, determination, and humanity. And even if you cannot sympathize with them, I hope you will try to empathize with them. I hope you will try placing yourself in their trail-worn shoes. You may find something in common with them all, the heroes, the villains, and the somewhere-in-betweens.

Select Character Biographies

Virginia Reed
(June 28, 1833–February 14, 1921)

Virginia Elizabeth Reed, who was thirteen years old when trapped in the Sierra Nevada, was a baby when her biological father died. She went by the last name of her stepfather, James Reed, who raised her as his own. The letters and descriptions she wrote soon after the Donner Party's overland ordeal provide a valuable contemporary account. She really did have a pony named Billy that she sadly abandoned along the way. And by all accounts, she was a skilled equestrian all her life.

Her prairie romance with thirteen-year-old Edward Breen is my own creation, although it serves as a nod to many such actual romances recorded at the time. Apparently, Virginia really did receive an offer of marriage from one of her rescuers, Edward Pyle Jr., just as Patty relates in this book. (Virginia shrewdly turned the offer down, and Pyle soon married Mary Ann Graves instead.) Three years later, however, at the age of sixteen, Virginia married a Mr. John Murphy, member of the earlier pioneer group who had coincidentally built the cabin that the Breen family would find and occupy two years later.

Reportedly, James Reed did not approve of the match, so young Virginia and her beau eloped. The couple had nine children and a successful insurance business that Virginia ran after her husband's death. Virginia Reed Murphy died on Valentine's Day at age eighty-seven.

James Frazier Reed
(November 14, 1800–June 24, 1874)

Was Reed a hero or a rascal? A loving father or a violent murderer? A wise leader or an arrogant braggart? By most accounts, it seems he was all of these things.

Reed himself was born in Ireland, though his family (originally named Reednoski) was descended from Polish nobility. After his father died, Reed moved with his mother to the state of Virginia. He was smart, industrious, and prosperous. His writings reveal a man of great confidence, and it seems he had the competence to back it up. He moved to Springfield, Illinois, where he owned many businesses and where he served as a soldier with Abraham Lincoln and the man who would eventually warn him against taking the Hastings Cutoff, James Clyman.

He really did adopt Virginia when she was three years old. And he really did marry Margret Keyes (Virginia's mother) while she had taken to bed due to one of her epic "sic headaches" (likely chronic migraines). According to Virginia, it was her stepfather who first had the idea to move west. The Donner families, also of Springfield, later joined forces with the Reeds.

James Reed killed teamster John Snyder and was banished for the deed pretty much as I've described in my story, but the details and nuances of how the events truly unraveled are lost to history. By the time the snows finally melted, most of the witnesses were dead, so Reed's actions were considered self-defense and the matter was dropped. Reed never even mentioned it in later writings.

Although Reed had lost nearly everything on the trip west, he settled in nearby San Jose, where he did very well in mining and real estate. Margret, who had apparently lost a child not long before they set out, successfully gave birth to two more children in their new home. She suffered from no more headaches, but she died in 1861, aged only forty-seven years. Thirteen years later, James Reed, who had survived so much for so long, passed away at the age of seventy-three.

Tamzene Eustis Dozier Donner
(November 1, 1801– ca. March 31, 1847)

Much has been written about Tamzene Donner, and for good reason. She was intelligent, hardworking, courageous, well educated, and accomplished. Born and raised in Newburyport, Massachusetts, she traveled unaccompanied to Elizabeth City, North Carolina, to take up a teaching position. By all accounts, she seemed to thrive in the role. Although she stood barely five feet tall and weighed less than a hundred pounds, she reportedly kept strict order among even the rowdiest of her young pupils.

In *Impatient with Desire: The Lost Diary of Tamsen Donner*, novelist Gabrielle Burton imagines what this intellectual and observant woman might have recorded on her fateful journey west. While it is certainly possible that Tamzene kept a journal, none has ever been found. She *did* leave behind many letters that give us a glimpse into her history and her personality. Much of what Tamzene says in *The Snow Fell Three Graves Deep* I have lifted from her written correspondence full of emotion and keen observation.

At the then late age of twenty-eight, Tamzene married Tully B. Dozier, the Elizabeth City postmaster. They had two children, a daughter and a son, and were very happy until the winter of 1831 when both children and her husband all died within three short months. The heartbroken widow later moved to Sangamon County, Illinois, to help raise her brother's children. She began teaching again, and while on a botanizing field trip with her pupils, she reportedly met a tall, dark-eyed widower with silver streaks through his hair. George Donner, a well-respected farmer known to family and friends as "Uncle George," was raising two girls alone. Tamzene soon became George Donner's third wife.

C. F. McGlashan's well-researched *History of the Donner Party*, based on interviews and correspondence with many living survivors, devotes six full pages to this amazing woman's life story. Author Eliza Farnham, in 1851's *California, In-Doors and Out*, effusively depicts Tamzene as the embodiment of womanly honor, self-sacrifice, and purity. Donner Party lore would have us believe that Tamzene became the camp's lone beacon of light. And, considering how every adult male in camp was either dead or incapacitated, this claim may not be an exaggeration.

From our twenty-first-century vantage point, you may consider Tamzene's determination to remain with her dying husband to be curiously dated. Was her fatal decision to stay a symbol of love, devotion, and courage? Or was it a pointless waste of life? Let the debate begin. However we may judge it, Tamzene Donner's choice was steadfast and clear.

According to Ludwig Keseberg, after Tamzene's husband died she made the eight-mile hike to the lake camp, falling into a creek along the way. She lay down, delirious with cold and fatigue, repeatedly saying that she wished to go be with her children. Keseberg covered the shivering woman with a blanket. By the morning she was dead.

All of Tamzene Donner's five daughters arrived safely in California. The eldest, Elitha, soon got married at age fourteen to a man who turned out to be a drunkard and was eventually dragged to death by his own horse. Elitha's second husband, however, was a keeper. Leanna, Tamzene's second-eldest daughter, lived with Elitha and her new husband until Leanna got married herself. Frances, oldest of the three "Littles," lived at first with the Reed family, but later joined Elitha, eventually marrying Elitha's husband's brother. This made Elitha and Frances half sisters *and* sisters-in-law. The two youngest daughters, Georgia and Eliza, were raised by an older German couple until eventually going to live with Elitha like their sisters before them. They, too, got married and started families of their own. The youngest, Eliza, helped C. F. McGlashan write the above-mentioned *History of the Donner Party* and then went on to write her own book, titled *The Expedition of the Donner Party and Its Tragic Fate*.

As a bittersweet coda to her story, Tamzene Donner's desire to establish a school was realized, in a way, with the opening of Donner Springs Elementary School in

1996 in Reno, Nevada. The school was built on the site of Truckee Meadows, where this hopeful, indomitable woman had passed one hundred fifty years earlier with a wagon full of schoolbooks and a heart full of dreams.

Jean Baptiste Trudeau
(ca. 1830–October 9, 1910)

Jean Baptiste Trudeau was born in Utah Territory to a French Canadian father and a Mexican mother. It is unclear what became of his mother, but his father was reportedly killed in a skirmish with Native Americans. Although I have placed his meeting with George Donner at Bridger's Fort, it is not clear how and when he actually joined the group. But by July 31, 1846, Baptiste was on hand when they started out on Hastings Cutoff. His name is sometimes listed as John, or John Baptiste, or, according to one newspaper article, simply "Baptiste, as everybody calls him." I have chosen to use the latter name, in part because of this news article posted in the *San Francisco Chronicle*, September 5, 1897.

In the Patty Reed Lewis Collection at Sutter's Fort are notes for goods-on-credit written by the pioneers at Alder Creek, just as I have depicted in this story. Milt Elliott, intent on hiking over the pass, was going to deliver these to John Sutter, but neither Milt nor the notes ever made the trip. On the back of Jacob Donner's note is a second note, only partially legible, that reads ". . . but a poor orphan . . . with nothing . . . dians killed my father . . . I will give my rifle for a pony or a mule to ride. John Trudeau." But the note appears to be in the handwriting of Jacob Donner. Historian Kristin Johnson and others suggest that Trudeau was illiterate, dictating the contents of his note while Jacob Donner wrote. This gave birth to my depiction of Baptiste learning how to read from Tamzene Donner, who was, after all, a professional schoolteacher.

Some have accused Baptiste of abandoning the Alder Creek camp, though it seems to me that he simply decided it was time to leave. And this he did only toward the very last. Tamzene Donner, often praised for staying by her husband's side to the bitter end, is rarely chastised for allowing (perhaps even expecting) this sixteen-year-old boy to do the same.

Young Baptiste was often the only able-bodied male in camp. He probed the snow with a long stick looking for cattle beneath the drifts. He played with the three youngest Donner girls by rolling them up in a blanket that Eliza Donner quaintly calls "Old Navajo." But Eliza's older sister, Elitha, claimed in 1911 that Baptiste had to be cajoled into clearing snow from the tents, evidence that he may not have been the most energetic hand about camp. Elitha's disdain for Baptiste may also suggest that the Donners saw this illiterate mixed-race boy as more of a paid servant than an equal.

Jean Baptiste Trudeau settled in Marin County, California, where he picked crops and fished in Tomales Bay. In 1855 he married a woman named Lupe De Massano, with whom he had six children, the first named Baptiste. He paid occasional visits to the Donner girls, once to borrow money from Elitha, who thought he was not to be trusted. In a well-documented visit to Eliza in 1884, Baptiste swore that neither Eliza nor any of the Donners had ever eaten human flesh. And while this was precisely what Eliza wanted to hear, it was most certainly a lie. He died in 1910.

Ludwig Keseberg
(May 22, 1814–September 3, 1895)
In the mythological saga of the Donner Party, Ludwig Keseberg has become scapegoat, whipping boy, and villain. And yet Keseberg endured every unspeakable hardship and more. And unlike James Reed (or William Foster), he did it all without murdering anyone.

Beginning with news reports of the day and continuing on through the years in book after book, Keseberg has been portrayed as a troublesome, bitter "German" who turned into a mad, flesh-hungry savage in order to stay alive.

My portrayal of him may err toward nuance and sympathy, but for good reason. As I researched early newspaper accounts, published narratives, and survivor interviews, I detected in them a provincial prejudice (sometimes subtle, sometimes overt) due to Keseberg's being a foreigner. His ideas, experiences, mannerisms and thick accent, everything about him, may have seemed abrasive and strange (and slightly suspect).

In 1844, at nearly thirty years old, Johann Ludwig Christian Keseberg immigrated to the United States with his wife, Elisabeth "Philippine" Keseberg (née Zimmermann) and their one-year-old twin daughters. Just two years later, one of the twins had died, Philippine was expecting a third child, and the Kesebergs were on their way west with what would eventually become the Donner Party.

Ludwig Keseberg's debilitating foot injuries, his overturned wagon, and the birth and death of his infant son are all taken from contemporary accounts. Keseberg was also the last member of the Donner Party to be rescued, after having survived alone for weeks by harvesting the flesh from the corpses of his dead companions.

The fourth and final rescue party that we see approaching the Truckee Lake camps at the close of this telling had been sent mostly in order to retrieve any goods or money that might be salvaged to support the newly orphaned children living around Sutter's Fort. Most of these "rescuers" were inspired largely by the fact that they would be allowed to keep a portion of what they were able to bring back.

Keseberg, at first overjoyed to be rescued, soon found he was accused of murdering Mrs. Donner and stealing her money. The men put a rope around Keseberg's neck and threatened to hang him. One of the men, Reason Tucker, who had been leader of the first rescue, intervened to protect Keseberg, who had already endured so much. But Keseberg's nightmare was far from over.

A few days into his final escape out of the mountains, Keseberg noticed a bit of calico protruding from the melting snow. And this is how he discovered the body of his three-year-old daughter, Ada, whom he thought had escaped to safety months earlier. Fantastic rumors swirled around Keseberg from the very start and followed him wherever he went. He was portrayed as a crazed cannibal who had killed infants for their flesh and kept their blood simmering in a kettle. Poor Keseberg even sued one of his "rescuers," Ned Coffeemeyer, for defamation of character. Keseberg won the judgment but was awarded only one dollar.

Keseberg and Philippine would go on to have eight more children. He worked for John Sutter for a while and later established a hotel business (that burned down). And then a profitable brewing business (destroyed in a flood). Author Charles F. McGlashan devotes two chapters of his iconic history of the Donner tragedy to an evenhanded, sympathetic treatment of Keseberg. McGlashan includes an extensive and articulate statement from Keseberg himself, from which I have based much of the character you meet in *Three Graves Deep*.

McGlashan was instantly convinced that Keseberg had been wronged. But by then the myths and misinformation had taken on mean-spirited lives of their own. Historian H. H. Bancroft concurs with McGlashan, writing that "Louis Keseberg is entitled to a verdict of not guilty. He has been merely the unfortunate object about which has crystallized all the popular horror excited by the cannibalism of the Donner party."

In the spring of 1879 (more than thirty years after the events depicted in this book), Keseberg would claim that he "was born under an evil star." He would eventually outlive Philippine and all but one of their eleven children. "I often think," he relayed to McGlashan, "that the Almighty has singled me out, among all the men on the face of the earth, in order to see how much hardship, suffering, and misery a human being can bear!"

Luis and Salvador

(1827?–January 1847) and (1818?–January 1847)

Speaking of the two Miwok vaqueros who lost their lives so that the Donner Party might live, Mary Stuckey, in "The Donner Party and the Rhetoric of Western Expansion," says, "These American Indians were robbed of their names, replaced with those of their conqueror's choosing. In addition, they were never given a voice. Even in the fictionalized versions of the story, they are rendered mute." Whether or not, as a privileged white person, I have the right to speak for them at all is a question that haunted every stroke of my keyboard. In the end, my intention was to give these two brave human beings the names and voices that history has denied them.

Little is known with certainty about Luis and Salvador, "Stanton's Indians" who were killed and devoured by the starving members of the Donner snowshoe party. I have based my fictional representation on an article by Joseph King, who suggests they were both "neophytes" (Catholic converts) from the nearby Mission San José. Examining the mission's baptismal records, King highlights the following entries:

> *December 1, 1834–Entry #7188:*
> *"child Eema Ochehamne, about 7 years of age,*
> *son of Chisen and Topchi, given the name Luis Antonio."*

> *May 3, 1836–Entry #7474:*
> *"QuéYuen Cosumne, about 18 years of age,*
> *and given the name Salvador."*

Ochehamne and Consumne are two tribelets of the Miwok. This record would indicate that Luis Antonio (aka Eema) would have been about nineteen years old during his attempted rescue of the Donner Party. The ironically named Salvador (aka QuéYuen) would have been about twenty-eight years old.

There is little doubt that the real Luis and Salvador were "employed" at Sutter's Fort as vaqueros, or cowboys. As such, they would have looked after the fort's huge herds of livestock and working animals, but their duties would likely fluctuate based on whatever needed doing. Obviously, Captain Sutter trusted Luis and Salvador enough to send them into the mountains with Charles Stanton and half a dozen valuable mules. Luis and Salvador may have been two of a handful of indigenous people who held positions of nominal privilege at Sutter's Fort, but hundreds more (indentured servants, peons, and outright slaves) toiled under inhumane conditions. It is impossible to claim with certainty the true nature of Luis and Salvador's "employment," but given what we know about Captain Sutter and the history of Native American slavery in Alta California, it is a good bet that some sort of coercion was involved.

Martha Jane "Patty" Reed
(February 26, 1838–July 4, 1923)

Only two miles into the first relief's escape from the mountains, eight-year-old Patty and three-year-old Tommy Reed were too exhausted to go on. Just as I have depicted in this story, the rescuers made the decision to take the children back to camp. Patty reportedly comforted her distraught mother by saying, "Well, Ma, if you never see me again, do the best you can." Depending on the source, the exact wording changes slightly, but the little girl's preternatural composure is constant. It was this and similar stories of Martha "Patty" Reed that gave birth to the character in *Three Graves Deep*.

It is easy to forget that of the eighty-one pioneers trapped in the mountains, more than half of them were children. In her own unassuming way, the courageous and hopeful voice of Patty Reed speaks for all of them.

Among Donner Party enthusiasts, the story of Patty's doll, barely four inches tall with simple painted eyes and hair, has become a symbol of innocence, hope, and survival. Most of Patty's story within these pages is based on recorded facts: her special connection to her youngest brother, Tommy; eating the hearth rug; sitting atop the roof of the cabin with her feet reaching the snow; and being revived by a vigorous foot rub and a morsel of meat hidden within the thumb of her father's mitten. Regarding the latter event, Patty, probably suffering from extreme hypothermia, had become delusional and claimed she was seeing angels.

When Sarah Handley Keyes died and was buried along the trail, Patty reportedly prayed, "Dear God, watch over and protect dear Grandmother, and don't let the Indians dig her up." Grandma Keyes had told Patty and Virginia many ominous stories about "dangerous" Native Americans that the girls found to be mostly untrue. Seen through my own poetic lens, Patty Reed is the embodiment of grace, love, and forgiveness. While her sympathetic relationship with Ludwig Keseberg is my own fiction, it is certainly within the realm of the possible.

As a grown woman, Patty Reed married a man named Frank Lewis, who died twenty years later, leaving her with seven children whom she supported by opening a boardinghouse. On June 6, 1918, eighty-year-old Patty Reed Lewis was on hand for the dedication of a Donner Party memorial statue placed on the location of the Breen cabin. She was joined by two of Tamzene Donner's three youngest daughters, Eliza Donner Houghton and Frances Donner Wilder. The statue's base is over twenty feet tall to represent the depth of the snow that had fallen more than seventy years earlier. The monument had cost upward of $35,000 ($743,822 in modern dollars), funded in part by selling small glass vials containing shards of wood from the Murphy cabin at one dollar each.

If you visit Sutter's Fort today, you can find many Donner-related documents and artifacts that remained in Patty Reed's possession until she passed away at the age of eighty-five. The most popular artifact of all is the small, unassuming doll that had kept an eight-year-old girl company during one very hard winter.

Mary Ann Graves
(November 1, 1826–March 9, 1891)
Born in Dearborn County, Indiana, the real Mary Ann Graves was reportedly tall, attractive, strong, and outspoken. Mary Ann provided the saga of the Donner Party with a memorable sidenote by marrying Edward Pyle Jr., who had been turned down earlier by Virginia Reed. Mary Ann and Pyle were married in May 1847 at Sutter's Fort, within three months of surviving her ordeal as a member of the snowshoe party. The marriage was cut short when Pyle was murdered. The story goes that Mary Ann would visit the jail with food to be sure her husband's murderer lived long enough to be hanged (which he was). She remarried and had seven children.

Edward Breen
(September 1833–August 30, 1890)
Around August 3, 1846, barely three days along the Hastings Cutoff, thirteen-year-old Eddie Breen was riding with Virginia Reed when he was thrown from his horse. He was knocked unconscious. A broken bone stuck out between his knee and ankle. The event spun out as I've depicted it here, with Eddie's parents sending back to Fort Bridger for help. Eddie refused to allow Fort Bridger's ersatz EMT to amputate, so the badly broken leg was mended as well as possible. In the time it took the Donner Party to complete the ill-advised cutoff, Eddie and his leg had both fully recovered. The romance between Eddie Breen and Virginia is my own invention,

though it certainly is possible. The real Edward Breen went on to marry twice and have six kids. Like most of his brothers, he became a prominent landowner and farmer. Also like his brothers, he was tall, handsome, and an excellent rider.

Patrick Breen
(1795–December 21, 1868)

Patrick Breen was born in Ireland before immigrating to Canada and then Iowa. Historian Kristin Johnson has found evidence that the Breens may have moved west to escape anti-Catholic sentiment. Patrick Breen's journal is the only real-time record of the day-to-day events at snowbound Truckee Lake and, in part, Alder Creek.

Because Patrick Breen was often ill during the ordeal, his wife, Margaret, played a prominent role in ensuring her family's survival. The Breens began their winter imprisonment of 1846 with more to eat than most of the other families, yet Mrs. Breen had many children to feed. Early publications of Donner history paint her as a miserly shrew, but author Eliza Farnham revised Mrs. Breen's image as a saintly Mother Teresa. Of course, the truth lies somewhere in the middle.

One truth is certain: every member of the Breen family survived, even one-year-old Isabella. Mr. and Mrs. Breen's oldest son, John, became wildly rich during the gold rush when he was still but sixteen years old. The Breens became wealthy landowning farmers in the area of California that would eventually become San Benito County. Patrick Breen died there, aged seventy-three years. Just over five years later, in 1874, Margaret Breen passed away at age sixty-eight.

Old Hardcoop
(?–October 1846)

The Old Hardcoop depicted in *Three Graves Deep* is based on a mysterious Donner Party member referred to by last name only, usually Mr. Hardcoop, Old Hardcoop, or simply Hardcoop. In 1849, author Jesse Thornton wrote:

> He was from Antwerp, in Belgium—was a cutler by trade, and had a son and daughter in his native city. He had come to the United States for the purpose of seeing the country. He owned a farm near Cincinnati, Ohio, and intended, after visiting California, to go back to Ohio, sell his farm, and return to Antwerp, for the purpose of spending with his children the evening of his days.

Most sources say, or imply, that he was "old," perhaps in his sixties. He seems to have been traveling with the Kesebergs (also from Ohio) and was likely the driver of one of the two Keseberg wagons. Keseberg, our favorite scapegoat, is typically blamed for "leaving Hardcoop behind to die." But a more nuanced look at the situation places Hardcoop's death in the same category as the deaths of the exhausted Charles Stanton or John Denton, who were also "left behind to die." To blame Keseberg alone is to ignore the fact that no one else would risk a rescue either.

Captain John Augustus Sutter
(February 23, 1803–June 18, 1880)

Born Johann August Suter in Germany and raised in Switzerland, the self-titled Captain John Sutter seemed to be in the right place at the right time. Arriving in Alta California in 1839 with an entourage of Hawaiian servants and his own private militia, Sutter befriended local native tribes (mostly Maidu and Miwok people) and began using a mixture of political manipulation, calculated benevolence, and brute force to build what amounted to an agricultural and economic empire. When the Donner Party finally arrived at Sutter's Fort in 1847, Captain Sutter had reached the zenith of his power.

Although Sutter had declared his allegiance to Mexico, he welcomed the steady trickle of emigrants from the United States as potential allies, employees, and customers. Because of this, he had a reputation among whites for being a gracious and altruistic host, even as he treated the surrounding indigenous people (who outnumbered the whites ten to one) as little more than a resource to be exploited.

While the abuse and enslavement of Native Americans by Europeans had been thriving for about four hundred years, the pioneers arriving overland from the United States were often taken aback at its extent. In 1846, the American James Clyman (who had warned James Reed not to take the Hastings Cutoff) famously wrote how Sutter "keeps 600 to 800 Indians in a complete state of Slavery." Clyman went on to describe how field hands were kept locked up in inhumane conditions and fed gruel in long troughs, as I have depicted in this book. Lansford Hastings himself, in his infamous *Emigrants' Guide*, writes matter-of-factly that "the natives . . . are in a state of absolute vassalage, even more degrading, and more oppressive than that of our slaves in the south."

Barely more than a year after the Donner Party saga, gold was discovered on Sutter's land. The resulting gold rush of 1849 attracted thousands of prospectors from the East who ruined crops, killed cattle, and took control of land. Sutter's empire was abandoned and quickly fell into ruin. Eventually, today's city of Sacramento would rise up in its place. Sutter moved to Pennsylvania, where he died after years of attempting, without success, to convince the United States government to reimburse him for financial losses caused by the gold rush.

Charles Stone

(?–October, 1849?)

Hero or villain? Sound familiar?

In my story, Charles (Charlie) Stone is a very minor character. Yet I felt it necessary to include a word about him here. James Reed mentions Stone many times, as he does Charles Cady, in journal entries depicting what has come to be known as the "second relief." As I have depicted here, Stone and Cady acted heroically *until* their decision to leave behind the three Donner girls and to bypass the suffering Breen family. Then Charles Stone seemed to regain his heroic (albeit mercenary) status by returning with the "third relief." This intrigued me, for when it comes down to it, are we not *all* varying mixtures of heroes and cowards? So I made the choice to shine a little heroic light upon Charlie Stone, although in real life he may not have deserved it.

Little to nothing is known with certainty about the Charles Stone who helped rescue the Donners in 1847. But at least one historian, H. H. Bancroft, believes this Charles Stone may have been the same Charles Stone who would later be killed by the Pomo at Clear Lake in 1849. The Charles Stone killed at Clear Lake was anything *but* a hero. In fact, reports of Charles Stone's torture, rape, murder, and enslavement of the Clear Lake Pomos suggest he was even more abusive than Captain John Sutter himself. It was this unbridled cruelty that led a group of Pomo to retaliate and bring a "permanent end" to Stone's abuse. United States soldiers retaliated against the assassination of Charles Stone (and his business partner, Andrew Kelsey) by killing hundreds of innocent Pomos in what came to be known as the Bloody Island Massacre.

Lansford Hastings

(1819–1870)

Lansford Hastings, born in Ohio, was a lawyer by trade. After emigrating west in the early 1840s, Hastings reportedly hoped to establish Alta California as a state, independent of Mexico. In 1845 he published *The Emigrants' Guide to Oregon and California*, in part to entice more whites from the United States to populate the area.

Contrary to popular myth, *The Emigrants' Guide* was not written with the intention to persuade pioneers to travel the Hastings Cutoff. In fact, this untried route is given only a passing mention embedded within a single paragraph. Hastings had not actually traveled the entire route himself.

In 1846, when Lansford Hastings began actively urging emigrants to take the untried shortcut with himself as a guide, he clearly underestimated the difficulties of Weber Canyon, the Wasatch Range, and the Great Salt Lake Desert. But it is not clear that Hastings was knowingly attempting to deceive anyone. And lest we forget, the pioneer train headed by Hastings *did* successfully complete the cutoff and make it over the mountains safely to California. I don't mean to absolve Hastings of all responsibility in the disaster that ultimately befell the Donner Party, but neither were Hastings's actions necessarily malicious or even unusual.

After he eventually married and started a family, Hastings left California for Arizona. He was still living there during the Civil War, when he plotted (without success) to win California for the Confederacy. After the war, he wrote another book, titled *The Emigrants' Guide to Brazil*. He organized a group of disgruntled Southerners who set sail for Brazil (where slavery was still legal) to start a new colony and a new life. One can imagine Hastings leaning against the ship rail, excited with anticipation, when he begins to feel the first signs of the fever that will eventually kill him before he reaches his destination. He fell ill, probably with yellow fever, and died along the way.

NATIVE AMERICANS AND THE DONNER PARTY

Just like the Lewis and Clark expedition had done forty years before, the Donner Party was trespassing through lands populated by a network of diverse societies that had established residency there for nearly ten thousand years. These were a patchwork of distinct nations, each with its own history, language, and social and political structure. Some practiced sophisticated agriculture and animal husbandry. Many lived in thriving towns and cities. Others were nomadic, moving according to season and resources.

By 1846 the Oregon Trail cut through the lands of the Fox, Sauk, Shawnee, Potawatomi, Pawnee, Arapaho, Cheyenne, and Sioux. Farther west were the homelands of the Shoshone, Kiowa, Crow, Ute, and Paiute. Travelers taking the more southerly route to California crossed the Sierra Nevada mountains through the backyards of the Washoe, Miwok, and Maidu. Members of the Donner Party reported encountering Sioux at Fort Laramie, Shoshone near the Ruby Mountains, and Paiutes along Mary's (Humboldt) River.

Near Truckee Meadows, William Eddy claims to have shot a young man who had been firing arrows at the cattle. This was most likely one of the *wel mel ti*, or Washoe people. In fact, Truckee Meadows, *wel ga nuk* to the Washoe, was located well inside the core *wel mel ti* territory that included no less than eight Washoe settlements. Washoe narratives about the Donner Party include attempts to reach out to the suffering white pioneers, as recorded in Patrick Breen's diary when a lone man appeared out of nowhere offering roots to eat. This was likely the quamash root called *sésmi* by the Washoe. By this time, the kindly man would have heard the reports of cannibalism that may explain both his wary approach and his hasty exit.

Finally, we must not forget the vital role that the Miwok played in helping the remaining members of the snowshoe party (the so-called "Forlorn Hope") reach Johnson's Ranch alive. Had William Eddy not been helped those last few miles of his journey, the rest of the Forlorn Hope would have perished. Nor would news of the remainder of the party still suffering in the mountains ever have reached Fort Sutter. James Reed knew that Charles Stanton, Luis, and Salvador had returned to the mountains with supplies. But Reed had no idea that the wagon train had lost so many cattle. In addition to saving the lives of the Forlorn Hope, these helpful Miwok likely saved the lives of many still trapped at Truckee Lake and Alder Creek.

The Donner Party by the Numbers: A Miscellany

The overall number of Donner Party members listed below includes Luis and Salvador (the Miwok men sent from Sutter's Fort). I have *not* counted Sarah Keyes (who died before the Donner Party formed) nor Hiram Miller (who left before the Donner Party formed). Although I include baby Elizabeth Graves and her seven-year-old brother, Jonathan Graves, among the survivors, both of these orphaned children were dead within a year, likely due to complications of their winter entrapment. I have defined children as those under the age of eighteen. Start date indicates when the Donners and Reeds set out from Illinois. Finish date indicates the day the last survivor, Ludwig Keseberg, arrived at Sutter's Fort.

Dates: April 14, 1846 to April 29, 1847

Total overall members: 89
Number who died: 41
Number who survived: 48 (53.9%)

Number of females: 34
Number of females who died: 9
Number of females who survived: 25 (73.5%)

Number of males: 55
Number of males who died: 32
Number of males who survived: 23 (41.8%)

Number of children: 45
Number of children who died: 14
Number of children who survived: 31 (68.9%)

Number of infants (two years old or younger): 7
Number of infants who survived: 2 (28.5%)

Number who traveled ahead before getting caught in the mountains: 4

Number who died before getting caught in the mountains: 5

Trapped in the mountains
> Overall number trapped: 81
> Number of adults trapped: 36
> Number of children trapped: 45

Trapped at Alder Creek camp
> Number trapped at Alder Creek: 22
> Number who died at Alder Creek: 8

Trapped at Truckee Lake camp
> Number trapped at the lake: 59
> Number who died at the lake: 14

Number who died trying to hike out: 14

The snowshoe party (aka the Forlorn Hope)
> Total number: 15 (10 men, 5 women)
> Number who died: 8 (8 men, 0 women)
> Number who survived: 7 (2 men, 5 women)

Number of homicides: 6
> **Note:** Includes John Snyder, William Pike, Mr. Wolfinger (see p. 388), Luis and Salvador, and an unnamed Washoe (*wel mel ti*) man reportedly shot in the back by William Eddy near Truckee Meadows. Does not include Mr. Hardcoop or Luke Halloran.

Number of people eaten: 19 or 20

Number of people who starved to death before survivors began eating the pet dogs: 14

Dogs by family:
> Donner: Uno
> Breen: Towser
> Reed: Cash, Tyler, Tracker, Trailer, and Barney

Number of wagons they started with: 22

Number of wagons that reached California: 0

Number of people living in San Francisco in 1846: about 200
    Note: Until 1847 San Francisco was called Yerba Buena.

Number of years of pioneer emigration: 25 (ca. 1844 to 1869)

Total number of emigrant pioneers over twenty-five years: Around 400,000

Total number of emigrants who traveled west in 1846: 2,700

Number of emigrants killed by Native Americans in 1846: 4

Number of Native Americans killed by emigrants in 1846: 20

Average traveling speed of a covered wagon: 3 mph

Number of oxen typically pulling a wagon: 6

Total length of the California Trail: 3,000 miles

Miles left to travel when the Donner Party got stuck: 90

Age of last living survivor: 90
    Note: Isabella Breen was only one year old during the winter of 1846–1847.
    Her death in 1935 at the age of ninety was reported in *Newsweek* magazine.

TIME LINE
1846

April 14/15: The Donners and Reeds set out from Springfield, Illinois.

May 10: They reach Independence, Missouri.

May 19: They join the William Russell Party.

May 29: Sarah Keyes dies at Alcove Spring.

June 9: The emigrants begin a monthlong leg along the Platte River.

June 18: The William Russell Party becomes the William Boggs Party.

July 11: The Boggs Party reaches Independence Rock.

July 19: The Donner Party forms. It includes seventy-one members of the Donner, Reed, Breen, Eddy, Murphy, Foster, Pike, Keseberg, and Wolfinger families, plus servants, teamsters, and a few others.

July 28–31: At Fort Bridger, the McCutchen family and Jean Baptiste Trudeau join, bringing the total to seventy-five members.

August 1: The Donner Party begins Hastings Cutoff.

August 3: Edward Breen, thirteen, breaks his leg.

August 10?: At the Wasatch Mountains, the eleven members of the Graves family and John Snyder join, bringing the total to eighty-seven.

August 11–22: The Donner Party cuts a road through the Wasatch Mountains to the Great Salt Lake Desert.

August 25: Luke Halloran dies of tuberculosis. The total is now eighty-six.

September 4–9: The emigrants cross the Great Salt Lake Desert.

September 9: Stanton and McCutchen go ahead, reducing the total to eighty-four.

September 10–25: The Donner Party circumnavigates the Ruby Mountains.

September 26: They complete Hastings Cutoff and rejoin the California Trail.

October 5: Reed kills Snyder. Reed is banished, reducing the total to eighty-two.

October 6?: Herron goes ahead with Reed, reducing the total to eighty-one.

September 26–October 13: The Donner Party follows Mary's (the Humboldt) River.

October 6–13: Hardcoop is left behind, reducing the total to eighty.

October 6–13: Wolfinger is killed by Joseph Reinhardt (and maybe Augustus Spitzer), reducing the total to seventy-nine.

October 15–30: Charles Stanton, now with Luis and Salvador, rejoins the rest, increasing the total to eighty-two.

October 15–30: William Pike is accidentally killed by William Foster, reducing the total to eighty-one.

October 15–30: The Donner wagon's axle breaks. George Donner injures his hand.

October 28: In California, the banished James Reed reaches Sutter's Fort.

October 30–Nov. 4: The Donner Party becomes snowbound.

December 16: The snowshoe party (later called the Forlorn Hope) sets out with fifteen members. Sixty-six members are left in the Donner Party camps.

December 25–29: The snowshoe party is trapped by a blizzard at what's later called the Camp of Death. The first reported instance of cannibalism occurs.

1847

January 17: William Eddy arrives at Johnson's Ranch. The remaining members of the snowshoe party arrive over the next couple of days (seven of the original fifteen survive).

February 18: The first relief arrives and rescues twenty-three members.

March 1: The second relief arrives and rescues eleven members.

March 5–7: The second relief is trapped by a blizzard at what's later called Starved Camp.

March 12: The third relief rescues Breen and Graves survivors from Starved Camp.

March 13: The third relief arrives at Truckee Lake.

April 17: The fourth relief arrives. Ludwig Keseberg is the sole survivor.

April 29: Ludwig Keseberg arrives safely at Sutter's Fort.

Donner Party Members by Family

SURVIVED. PERISHED.

✗ = member of the snowshoe party (aka the Forlorn Hope)

Note on ages: All ages are either correct or very close approximations. Use of a ? indicates that little to no evidence exists. I refer you to Kristin Johnson's excellent "roster" in *Unfortunate Emigrants*, pages 294–298, if you want more specificity. Following Johnson, all ages are as of July 19, 1846, the date the Donner Party was officially formed.

Breen
Patrick Breen (51) and wife Margaret Bulger Breen (40)
> John (14), Edward (13), Patrick Jr. (9), Simon (8), James (5), Peter (3), and Margaret "Isabella" (1)

Donner
George Donner (62) and wife Tamzene Eustis Dozier Donner (44)
> Elitha (13), Leanna (11), Frances (6), Georgia (4), and Eliza (3)

Jacob Donner (65) and wife Elizabeth "Betsy" Blue Hook Donner (45)
> Solomon Hook (14), William Hook (12), George (9), Mary (7), Isaac (5), Samuel (4), and Lewis (3)

Eddy
✗William Eddy (28) and wife Eleanor Eddy (25)
> James (3) and Margaret (1)

Graves / Fosdick
✗Franklin Graves (57) and wife Elizabeth Cooper Graves (45)
> ✗Sarah Graves Fosdick (21) and husband ✗Jay Fosdick (23), ✗Mary Ann (19), William (17), Eleanor "Ellen" (14), Lovina (12), Nancy (9), Jonathan (7), Franklin Jr. (5), and Elizabeth (1)

Keseberg

Johann Ludwig "Lewis" Keseberg (32) and wife Elisabeth "Philippine" Zimmermann Keseberg (23)

> Juliane "Ada" (3) and Ludwig "Lewis" Jr. (1)

McCutchen

William McCutchen (30) and wife ×Amanda Henderson McCutchen (25)

> Harriet (1)

Murphy / Foster / Pike

Levinah Jackson Murphy (36)

> ×Sarah Murphy Foster (19) and husband ×William Foster (30)
>> Jeremiah George "Georgie" (1)
> ×Harriet Murphy Pike (18) and husband William Pike (32?)
>> Naomi (2) and Catherine (1)
> John "Landrum" (16), Meriam "Mary" (14), ×Lemuel (12), William (10), and Simon (8)

Reed / Keyes

Sarah Handley Keyes (70)

> James Reed (45) and wife Margret Keyes Backenstoe Reed (32)
>> Virginia "Puss" (13), Martha "Patty" (8), James Jr. (6), and Thomas "Tommy" (3)

Williams

Eliza Williams (31) and brother Baylis Williams (25)

Wolfinger

——— Wolfinger (?) and wife Dorothea "Doris" Wolfinger (20)

Unattached

×Antonio (23), Charles "Dutch Charley" Burger (30), John Denton (28), ×Patrick Dolan (35), Milford "Milt" Elliott (28), ×Luis (19?), Luke Halloran (25), ——— Hardcoop (60?), Walter Herron (27), Noah James (16), Joseph Reinhardt (30), ×Salvador (28?), Samuel Shoemaker (25), James "Jim" Smith (25), John Snyder (25), Augustus Spitzer (30), ×Charles Stanton (35), and Jean Baptiste Trudeau (16)

Note: Hiram Miller (28) started with the Donners and Reeds from Springfield but is not listed here since he left the Donners' employ on July 2, 1846, to travel by mule with the Bryant-Russell Party via Hastings Cutoff. Miller had been keeping a journal that Reed continued. He reached California safely but returned as a member of both the second and third relief parties. Miller was guardian to George Donner's orphaned daughters for a while. Toward the end of his life, he lived with the Reeds.

The Rescuers and the Rescued

First Relief: Arrives February 18, 1847

Rescuers

Adolph Bruheim, Edward "Ned" Coffeemeyer, Aquilla Glover, Riley Septimus Moutrey, Daniel Rhoads, John Pierce Rhoads, Reason P. Tucker

Rescued

Edward Breen (13), Simon Breen (8), Elitha Donner (13), Leanna Donner (11), George Donner Jr. (9), ∞William Hook (12), William Graves (17), Eleanor "Ellen" Graves (14), Lovina Graves (12), Elisabeth "Philippine" Keseberg (23), ×Ada Keseberg (3), Meriam "Mary" Murphy (14), William Murphy (10), Naomi Pike (2), Margret Reed (32), Virginia Reed (13), James Reed Jr. (6), Doris Wolfinger (20), ×John Denton (28), Noah James (16), Eliza Williams (31)

× = dies en route

∞ = dies after rescue

Second Relief: Arrives March 1, 1847

Rescuers

Charles Cady, Nicholas Clark, Matthew Dofar, Patrick Dunn, Joseph Gendreau, Brittain Greenwood, William McCutchen, Hiram Miller, James Reed, Charles Stone, John Turner, Joseph Verrot, Selim Woodworth

Rescued

*Patrick Breen (51), *Margaret Breen (40), *John Breen (14), *Patrick Breen Jr. (9), *James Breen (5), *Peter Breen (3), *Margaret "Isabella" Breen (1), *Mary Donner (7), *×Isaac Donner (5), Solomon Hook (14), *×Elizabeth Graves (45), *Nancy Graves (9), *∞Jonathan Graves (7), *×Franklin Graves Jr. (5), *∞Elizabeth Graves (1), Martha "Patty" Reed (8), Thomas "Tommy" Reed (3)

* = left behind at Starved Camp, rescued later by third relief

*∞ = left behind at Starved Camp, rescued by third relief, dies after rescue

*× = left behind at Starved Camp, died and cannibalized

Third Relief: Arrives at Starved Camp, March 12, 1847

Rescuers
John Stark, Charles Stone, William Thompson

Rescued
Patrick Breen (51), Margaret Breen (40), John Breen (14), Patrick Breen Jr. (9), James Breen (5), Peter Breen (3), Margaret "Isabella" Breen (1), Mary Donner (7), Nancy Graves (9), *∞Jonathan Graves (7), *∞Elizabeth Graves (1)

*∞ = dies after rescue

Third Relief: Arrives at Truckee Lake camp, March 13, 1847

Rescuers
William Eddy, William Foster, Hiram Miller, Howard Oakley

Rescued
Frances Donner (6), Georgia Donner (4), Eliza Donner (3), Simon Murphy (8), Jean Baptiste Trudeau (16)

Fourth Relief: Arrives at Truckee Lake camp April 17, 1847

Rescuers
Edward "Ned" Coffeemeyer, William O. Fallon, William Foster, Sebastian Keyser, John Pierce Rhoads, Joseph Sels, Reason P. Tucker

Rescued
Ludwig "Lewis" Keseberg (32)

Other names associated with rescue efforts:

Rescue stations and supplies: William Johnson (Johnson's Ranch), John Sinclair (Sinclair home), John Augustus Sutter (Sutter's Fort)
Paymaster: Edward Meyer Kern
Auxiliary support: William Coon, Caleb Greenwood, Perry McCoon, Edward Gantt Pyle, Edward Gantt Pyle Jr., Matthew Dill Ritchie, William Dill Ritchie, George W. Tucker

DONNER PARTY DEATHS

Name (age), date, cause, location

* = died before the party became trapped in the mountains
∞ = died after rescue

Ages are at time of death and are as accurate as possible.

*Sarah Keyes (70), May 29, 1846, tuberculosis, along Big Blue River, Kansas
*Luke Halloran (25), August 25, 1846, tuberculosis, near Great Salt Lake
*John Snyder (25), October 5, 1846, murdered, along the Humboldt River
*——Hardcoop (60?), around October 8, 1846, disappeared, along the Humboldt River
*——Wolfinger (?) around October 15, 1846, murdered? along the Humboldt River
*William Pike (32?), late October, 1846, accidentally shot, near Truckee Meadows
Baylis Williams (25), December 14, 1846, starvation?, Reed cabin
> Jacob Donner (56), before December 20, 1846, starvation?, Alder Creek
> Joseph Reinhardt (30), before December 20, 1846, starvation?, Alder Creek
> Samuel Shoemaker (25), before December 20, 1846, starvation?, Alder Creek
> James Smith (25), before December 20, 1846, starvation?, Alder Creek
> *It appears that these four Alder Creek campmates died in rapid succession.*
Charles Stanton (36), December 22 or 23, 1846, starvation/exposure, Forlorn Hope
> Franklin Graves (57), December 25, 1846, starvation/exposure, Forlorn Hope
> Antonio (23), December 25, 1846, starvation/exposure, Forlorn Hope
> Patrick Dolan (35), December 27 or 25, 1846, starvation/exposure, Forlorn Hope
> Lemuel Murphy (13), December 28 or 26, 1846, starvation/exposure, Forlorn Hope
> *Sources conflict about who dies first at the camp later dubbed Camp of Death. But it seems certain that Franklin Graves, Lemuel Murphy, Patrick Dolan, and Antonio all died (probably in this order, but maybe not) within a seventy-two-hour period. All but Lemuel were eaten.*
Charles "Dutch Charley" Burger (30), starvation, December 29, 1846, Keseberg cabin
Jay Fosdick (23), before January 17, 1847, starvation/exposure, Forlorn Hope
Luis (19?), before January 17, 1847, murdered, Forlorn Hope
Salvador (28?), before January 17, 1847, murdered, Forlorn Hope
Lewis Keseberg Jr. (1), January 24, 1847, starvation, Keseberg cabin
John Murphy (16), January 31, 1847, starvation, Murphy cabin

Harriet McCutchen (1), February 2, 1847, starvation, Graves cabin

Margaret Eddy (1), February 4, 1847, starvation, Murphy cabin

Eleanor Eddy (25), February 7, 1847, starvation, Murphy cabin

Augustus Spitzer (30), February 7 or 8, 1847, starvation, Breen cabin

Milford "Milt" Elliott (28), February 9, 1847, starvation, Murphy cabin

Catherine Pike (1), February 20, 1847, starvation, Murphy cabin

Ada Keseberg (3), February 23 or 24, 1847, starvation/exposure, en route with first relief

John Denton (28), February 24, 1847, starvation/exposure, en route with first relief

∞William Hook (12), February 29, 1847, overeating, with first relief in Bear Valley

Isaac Donner (5), March 1847, starvation/exposure, Starved Camp

> *Reportedly, Elizabeth Graves refused to eat human flesh at Starved Camp and so her son Franklin Graves Jr. refused as well. Since only three died at Starved Camp, the flesh offered must have been that of Isaac Donner by process of elimination. Thus Isaac died before Elizabeth or Franklin Jr.*

Elizabeth Graves (46), March 1847, starvation/exposure, Starved Camp

Franklin Graves Jr. (5), March 1847, starvation/exposure, Starved Camp

James Eddy (3), March (between 1–13), 1847, starvation, Murphy cabin

George Foster (2), March (between 1–13), 1847, starvation, Murphy cabin

> *Both James Eddy and Jeremiah "George" or "Georgie" Foster were both reported alive and crying together in a filthy bed in the Murphy cabin when James Reed of the second relief arrived around March 1. But both boys were dead (and at least George had been cannibalized) by the time William Eddy and William Foster arrived with the third relief in mid-March.*

Lewis Donner (3), around March 9, 1847, starvation, Alder Creek

Elizabeth Donner (45), (after Lewis) before March 12, 1847, starvation, Alder Creek

Levinah Murphy (36), soon after March 12, 1847, starvation, Murphy cabin

Samuel Donner (4), around March 12, 1847, starvation, Alder Creek

> *It's not clear if Sammie was dead before the third relief arrived (March 12) or sometime after. There are conflicting reports. My date is a well-educated fabrication, but it seems pretty certain that Sammie was dead before George.*

George Donner (61), around March 29, 1847, infection, Alder Creek

Tamzene Donner (45), around March 31, 1847, exposure/starvation, Breen cabin

> *Historian Kristin Johnson says Tamzene died in the Breen cabin where Keseberg seems to have moved, probably after Mrs. Murphy died.*

∞Elizabeth Graves (1), summer 1847, complications of starvation/exposure

∞Jonathan Graves (7), summer 1847, complications of starvation/exposure

Both Elizabeth and Jonathan were alive on March 22, 1847 (according to a statement made on that day by Mary Ann Graves), but both apparently died not long after, during the summer of 1847, while the family lived near Sutter's Fort along the American River. Many years later, William Graves claimed the two had died as a result of complications from the ordeal. Lovina Graves, also many years later, reported that they had both died the following summer of what she called "mountain fever."

Reality Checks

Many of the scenes depicted in this book are based on the written words left behind by the people who lived through it. But even the contemporary accounts of those who were there are sometimes accidentally flawed, coyly incomplete, or deliberately falsified. Written accounts by James Reed, for example, always leave out the part where he stuck a knife in John Snyder and killed him dead. And although Eliza Donner Houghton, the youngest of the three "Littles," wrote an entire book on her family's ordeal, she went to her grave insisting that cannibalism had never occurred at Alder Creek camp. Even books by "official historians" sometimes propagate false-hoods, promote stereotypes, and reflect the authors' personal prejudices. As for my own work of fictionalized facts, I humbly offer the following disclosures.

I have no idea if Tamzene Donner ever read Tennyson's poem "Ulysses." ♦ Although young Jean Baptiste Trudeau apparently *did* have a favorite blanket, he did *not* have two favorite oxen named Buck and Bright. ♦ It was actually Milt Elliott, not Eddie Breen, who went with Virginia to deliver guns and ammunition to the banished James Reed. ♦ Although I use the names Alder Creek and Alder Creek camp freely, to the best of my knowledge the Donners would not have known it by that name at the time. ♦ The watercourse that members of the Donner Party called Mary's River is now known as the Humboldt River. ♦ The "beautiful spring at the base of Pilot Peak" is now called Donner Springs. ♦ Truckee Lake is now called Donner Lake. ♦ The Donners' biweekly Springfield newspaper, the *Sangamo Journal*, is now called the *State Journal-Register*. ♦ To compress the story's action, I have combined events of Fort Bernard and Fort Laramie at the end of June 1846. ♦ I depict Keseberg as living in his lean-to attached to the Breen cabin much longer than he really did. ♦ Tamzene Donner did *not* really call her three youngest daughters "the Littles."

Murder and the Mysterious Mr. Wolfinger

The Wolfingers were a childless couple from Germany traveling with a single wagon. We don't even know Mr. Wolfinger's first name, but Mrs. Wolfinger was apparently named Dorothy or Doris. In October 1846, like many of the others forced to continue on foot, Mr. Wolfinger left the Humboldt River to cache his possessions. He was allegedly being assisted by two other Germans, Joseph Reinhardt and Augustus Spitzer. Mr. Wolfinger was never seen again. One version of the story has Reinhardt and Spitzer returning to say that Wolfinger had been killed by Native Americans.

The widowed Mrs. Wolfinger lived with the Donners at Alder Creek until the first relief rescued her in February 1847. Jesse Thornton's 1849 book claims that, just before Reinhardt died at the Alder Creek camp, he confessed to murdering Wolfinger. Thirty years later, Leanna Donner (who was eleven years old while trapped at Alder Creek) affirmed, "Joseph Rhinehart [sic] was taken sick in our tent, when death was approaching and he knew there was no escape, then he made a confession in the presence of Mrs. Wolfinger that he shot her husband; what the object was I do not know."

In an enigmatic diary entry dated December 30, 1846, Patrick Breen writes, "Keysburg [sic] has Wolfinger's rifle gun." Breen also documents how Keseberg and Spitzer take possession of money, clothing, and other items when Charley Burger (another German) dies. Were Keseberg, Spitzer, and Reinhardt all up to no good? Hints of such a conspiracy are (at best) based on circumstantial evidence and (at worst) fueled by xenophobia. In part because of this, and in part to simplify an already complex chain of events, I chose to leave out the Wolfinger episode altogether.

About the Documents

Note about the letters: All letters, if real to begin with, have been altered in some way. The notes below give a bit more explanation for each and refer the reader to the location of the original text that gave birth to my fabrications.

Edwin Bryant to Reed and Donner, July 18, 1847: I fabricated this one. Bryant claims to have left letters warning (or at least advising) travelers to avoid Hastings Cutoff. Bryant describes these letters' contents in his 1848 memoir, *What I Saw in California*. But to my knowledge, the actual letters have never been found.

James Reed to Gersham Keyes, July 31, 1846: This is greatly excerpted and slightly edited from the letter named "James Frazier Reed to [James or Gersham Keyes?]" that I found in *Overland in 1846: Diaries and Letters of the California-Oregon Trail, Vol. 1,* pages 279–280. I have added occasional connective words for continuity. The letter originally appeared in the *Sangamo Journal*, November 5, 1846, according to the book's editor, Dale Lowell Morgan.

James Reed to Gersham Keyes, July 2, 1847: This is greatly excerpted and slightly edited from the letter named "James Frazier Reed to Gersham Keyes," which I also found in *Overland in 1846*, pages 301–305. The letter originally appeared, according to Morgan's note, in Springfield's *Illinois Journal*, December 23, 1847.

Virginia Reed to Mary Keyes, May 16, 1847: This is greatly excerpted and slightly edited from the letter named "Virginia E. B. Reed to Mary C. Keyes," which I also found in *Overland in 1846*, pages 281–288. Morgan's version is from the original draft of this very quaint letter along with her father's "corrections" and amendments. I have kept much of the original's spelling, syntax, and grammar, as I think it allows the best idea of Virginia Reed's authentic voice. The final version of this letter, with James Reed's edits, first appeared, according to Morgan's note, in the *Illinois Journal*, December 16, 1847. Finally, I have pulled Virginia's spelling of *cousin* as *couzin* and *couzen* from an earlier letter from Virginia to Mary dated July 12, 1846, from Independence Rock, found on page 278 of the same Morgan volume. I also lifted from this particular letter the final signoff phrase "You are for ever my affectionate couzen."

Note about the newspaper article: *Three Graves Deep* includes my own edited version of the original article that appeared in the February 13, 1847, issue of the *California Star*. I made slight changes for clarity, continuity, and brevity. "Capt Johnson's" became "Johnson's Ranch," "Fort Sacramento" became "Sutter's Fort," etc.

Note about George Donner's "Westward, Ho!" advertisement: This is the word-for-word advertisement that appeared in the Springfield, Illinois, biweekly newspaper, the *Sangamo Journal*. Although George Donner had dated it March 18, 1846, it actually ran in the March 26 and April 2 issues. Again, my source is Dale Morgan's *Overland in 1846*, page 491.

SPECIAL TERMS FROM THIS STORY

Buck and Bright: a traditional name for a pair of oxen

gee and haw: right and left; morphed into *yee-haw*

linsey-woolsey: a rough cloth, durable and cheap

mission: a Catholic church and settlement established by Spain

neophyte: a recent convert to Catholicism

ranchería: a small village often occupied by mission laborers

span, yoke: a pair of draft animals that work as one

vaquero: a ranch hand or cowboy; morphed into the English *buckaroo*

German Words from This Story

die Zukunft: the future

Dummkopf: idiot

Feiglinge: cowards

kaput: done, broken

mein Engel: my angel

Read More About the Donner Party

What follows is a selection of books and articles that gave birth to *Three Graves Deep*. Each one adds something unique to the Donner canon, but titles marked with an asterisk are particularly accessible and factually accurate if you are looking for a place to start.

Bancroft, H. H. *California Pioneer Register and Index, 1542–1848*. Baltimore, MD: Regional Publishing, 1964. Specifically, page 344, regarding Charles Stone's possible identity, and pages 346–348 for a blistering biography of John Sutter.

Bancroft, H. H. *History of California*. Vol. 5, 1846–1848, from *The Works of Hubert Howe Bancroft*. Vol. 22. San Francisco: History Company, 1886. Especially chapter 20, about many of the earliest pioneers, and specifically pages 529–544, about the Donner Party.

Breen, Patrick. Manuscript Diary. November 20, 1846–March 1, 1847, Banc MSS C-E 176, Bancroft Library, University of California, Berkeley. The only known journal kept during the winter of entrapment. Transcribed and published in many later works. Read the amazing handwritten original online: https://calisphere.org/item/ark:/28722/bk0004b217j.

*Brown, Daniel James. *The Indifferent Stars Above: The Harrowing Saga of a Donner Party Bride*. New York: William Morrow, 2009. Despite the melodramatic title, this is quite a good book and quite accurate.

Bryant, Edwin. *What I Saw in California*. Lincoln: University of Nebraska Press, 1985. First published 1848. Probably the most literate of the firsthand accounts of the 1846 migration.

Burton, Gabrielle. *Impatient with Desire: The Lost Journal of Tamsen Donner*. New York: Hyperion, 2010. A fictional account that imagines the contents of the fabled Tamzene Donner journal, which has never been found.

Burton, Gabrielle. *Searching for Tamsen Donner*. Lincoln: University of Nebraska

Press, 2009. Part memoir, part history. Includes an appendix with ALL seventeen extant letters written by Tamzene herself!

DeVoto, Bernard. *The Year of Decision: 1846*. New York: St. Martin's Press, 2000. First published in 1942.

Dixon, Kelly J., Julie M. Schablitsky, and Shannon A. Novak, eds. *An Archaeology of Desperation: Exploring the Donner Party's Alder Creek Camp*. Norman: University of Oklahoma Press, 2011. A unique and all-inclusive look at the events of Alder Creek.

Farnham, Eliza. "Narrative of the Emigration of the Donner Party to California, in 1846." In *California, In-doors and Out*. New York: Dix, Edwards, 1856. An early published account of the Donner tragedy, based on interviews with the Breen family. Republished in Kristin Johnson's *Unfortunate Emigrants* and available online at the Library of Congress, www.loc.gov/item/rc01000780.

Hall, Carroll D., ed. *Donner Miscellany: 41 Diaries and Documents*. San Francisco: Book Club of California, 1947. Includes a transcript of the Miller-Reed diary and the various documents found in it. The existence of this diary was not known for one hundred years.

Hawkins, Bruce R., and David B. Madsen. *Excavation of the Donner-Reed Wagons: Historic Archaeology Along the Hastings Cutoff*. Salt Lake City: University of Utah Press, 1990. Archaeological analysis of alleged remnants of the Reed and Donner wagons, with information about the trail near the Great Salt Lake.

Hardesty, Donald. *The Archaeology of the Donner Party*. Reno, NV: University of Nevada Press, 2005. Details the 1984 excavation of the Murphy cabin site and the several 1980s excavations at Alder Creek.

Hastings, Lansford. *The Emigrants' Guide to Oregon and California*. Bedford, MA: Applewood Books, 1994. Originally published in 1845. Available online at the University of Virginia's American Studies hypertext collection, www.xroads .virginia.edu/~HYPER/hypertex.html.

Houghton, Eliza Donner. *The Expedition of the Donner Party and Its Tragic Fate.* Lincoln: University of Nebraska Press, 1997. Originally published in 1911. Available online at the Library of Congress, www.loc.gov/item/11035962.

*Johnson, Kristin. "Donner Party Cannibalism: Did They or Didn't They?" *Wild West*, December 2013. The very final word on cannibalism and a very concise overview of the entire ordeal. Highly recommended.

Johnson, Kristin. "The Pioneer Palace Car: Adventures in Western Mythmaking." *Crossroads*, no. 5 (Summer 1994), pages 5–8.

*Johnson, Kristin, ed. *Unfortunate Emigrants: Narratives of the Donner Party.* Logan: Utah State University Press, 1996. Accounts by James Reed, Virginia Reed, Bill McCutchen, William Graves, and more, all annotated by Johnson.

King, Joseph A. *Winter of Entrapment: A New Look at the Donner Party*, 3rd ed., Lafayette, CA: K&K Publications, 1998. An earlier edition was the basis for the 1993 Ric Burns documentary *The Donner Party* for the PBS series *American Experience.* The program is available on DVD from www.shop.pbs.org.

King, Joseph, ed. "William G. Murphy's Lecture and Two Letters to Mrs. Houghton," and with Jack Steed, "Newly-Discovered Documents on the Donner Party: The Donner Girls Tell Their Story." *Dogtown Territorial Quarterly*, no. 26 (Summer 1996). Text of an 1896 lecture by William Murphy, and Eliza Donner Houghton's notebook, discovered in 1994.

Korns, J. Roderic, and Dale L. Morgan, eds. *West from Fort Bridger: The Pioneering of Immigrant Trails Across Utah, 1846–1850*, revised and updated by Will Bagley and Harold Schindler. Logan: Utah State University Press, 1994. Originally published in 1943.

Lienhard, Heinrich. *From St. Louis to Sutter's Fort, 1846*, translated and edited by Erwin G. and Elisabeth K. Gudde. Norman: University of Oklahoma Press, 1961. Manuscript prepared by one of the five German boys who followed Hastings across the cutoff just ahead of the Donner Party.

McGlashan, C. F. *History of the Donner Party: A Tragedy of the Sierra*. New York: Barnes and Noble, 2004. Originally published in 1880. A classic. The first comprehensive history, based on previously published letters and journals, and on interviews and correspondence with twenty-four survivors. Also available online at Project Gutenberg, www.gutenberg.org/ebooks/6077.

McLaughlin, Mark. *The Donner Party: Weathering the Storm.* Carnelian Bay, CA: Mic Mac, 2007. Revised 2013. A unique look at the Donner Party story through the weather.

Morgan, Dale L., ed. *Overland in 1846: Diaries and Letters of the California-Oregon Trail*, Vols. 1 and 2. Lincoln: Bison Books/University of Nebraska Press, 1993. Originally published in 1963. A treasure trove of diaries, letters, maps, and commentary regarding the California-Oregon Trail. Another classic.

Mullen, Frank. *The Donner Party Chronicles: A Day-by-Day Account of a Doomed Wagon Train, 1846–1847.* Reno: Nevada Humanities Committee, 1997. A mostly accurate chronology of events, with present-day photographs of the sites.

Murphy, Virginia Reed. "Across the Plains in the Donner Party (1846): A Personal Narrative of the Overland Trip to California" *Century Illustrated*, no. 42 (July 1891), pages 409–426.

Parkman, Francis. *The Oregon Trail.* Mineola, NY: Dover, 2002. Originally published in 1883. A historian chronicles his own 1846 journey west at the age of twenty-three.

*Rarick, Ethan. *Desperate Passage: The Donner Party's Perilous Journey West.* New York: Oxford University Press, 2008.

Stewart, George R. *Ordeal by Hunger: The Story of the Donner Party*. Lincoln: University of Nebraska Press, 1960.

Thornton, J. Quinn. *Oregon and California in 1848*. Vols. 1 and 2. New York: Harper & Bros., 1849. Chapter about the Donner Party published as *Camp of Death* (Outback Books, 1986).

Unruh, John D., Jr. *The Plains Across: The Overland Emigrants and the Trans-Mississippi West, 1840–60.* Urbana: University of Illinois Press, 1979. An excellent, often quoted, comprehensive look at pioneer travel.

*Wallis, Michael. *The Best Land Under Heaven: The Donner Party in the Age of Manifest Destiny.* New York: Liveright, 2017.

Read More About Luis and Salvador
Washoe Narratives, Native American Enslavement, and California Native American History

*Nevers, Jo Ann, and Penny Rucks. "Under Watchful Eyes: Washoe Narratives of the Donner Party." Chap. 9 in Donald Hardesty's *The Archaeology of the Donner Party.* Reno, NV: University of Nevada Press, 2011.

King, Joseph A. "Lewis [*sic*] and Salvador: Unsung Heroes of the Donner Party." *The Californians* 13, no. 2 (1994), pages 20–21.

Lankford, Scott. "Luis and Salvator [*sic*]: The Donner Party Murders." Chap. 5 in *Tahoe Beneath the Surface: The Hidden Stories of America's Largest Mountain Lake.* Berkeley, CA: Heyday and Sierra College Press, 2010.

Powers, Stephen. *Tribes of California.* Berkeley: University of California Press, 1976. Originally published in 1877.

Reséndez, Andrés. *The Other Slavery: The Uncovered Story of Indian Enslavement in America.* Boston: Mariner Books, 2017.

Stuckey, Mary. "The Donner Party and the Rhetoric of Western Expansion." *Communication Faculty Publications* 24 (2011). Available for download at https://scholarworks.gsu.edu/communication_facpub/24.

Books Specifically for Younger Readers

*Brown, Skila. *To Stay Alive: Mary Ann Graves and the Tragic Journey of the Donner Party*. Somerville, MA: Candlewick Press, 2016.

Calabro, Marian. *The Perilous Journey of the Donner Party*. New York: Clarion Books, 1999.

*Hale, Nathan. *Donner Dinner Party*. New York: Amulet, 2013. Excellent middle-grade historical graphic novel by the master of the genre.

Kimball, Violet T. *Stories of Young Pioneers: In Their Own Words*. Missoula, MT: Mountain Press, 2000. First-person accounts of young pioneers.

Laurgaard, Rachel K. *Patty Reed's Doll: The Story of the Donner Party*. Davis, CA: Tomato Enterprises, 1989. Originally published in 1956.

Internet Resources

New Light on the Donner Party: www.user.xmission.com/~octa/DonnerParty
This website, created by Kristin Johnson, contains a wealth of information, including biographies and rosters of all members of the Donner Party, as well as each member of each rescue party. Also includes links to other research, articles, myth busting, FAQ, and more.

The Donner Party Diary: www.donnerpartydiary.com
Daniel M. Rosen's comprehensive day-by-day accounting of what happened (including helpful photos of locations and terrain). Particularly helpful is Rosen's use of parallel texts from many different sources.

Miwok Indian Info Sheet: www.bigorrin.org/miwok_kids.htm
A simple introduction to the Miwok people, with links to information on other Native American tribes.

Thanks and Acknowledgments

Thanks to Kristin Johnson—historian, author, and librarian at Salt Lake Community College in Salt Lake City, Utah—whose extensive research, resources, reasoning, and writing were a constant Pilot Peak guiding me across a literary Salt Lake Desert in search of historical accuracy. And to the amazing and magical Dr. Beth McDonough at Hunter Library, Western Carolina University, who is always able to track down (and obtain) the most obscure articles and documents imaginable.

To the amazing Candlewick Press staff and freelancers who have made me appear much smarter than I really am! Sophie Kittredge for the lovely maps. Lisa Rudden and Sherry Fatla for spot-on interior design. Jackie Houton and Susan VanHecke for copyediting. Emily Quill and Tracey Engel for proofreading. Pam Consolazio for the cover design and Sterling Hundley for the chilling jacket art. Book-whisperer Grace Worcester for writing the discussion guide. Katie Cunningham for line edits, friendship, and wisdom. And special thanks to this book's main editor and trail boss, the legendary Liz Bicknell, for her thoughtful mentorship, brilliant clarity, and friendship.

To Bob Falls for reading early drafts.

To all of my many feline collaborators—Nemo, Karma, Scurvy, Mange, and especially Nikki (RIP), who meowed in German and rearranged my outline notes.

For a place to write: The Walkers (Abby, Austin, Gus, and Norah), Klaus and Susan Spies, Charlie and Julia Akers, Bob Hannah, Michael Platz, and Ramsey Library at UNC Asheville.

For supporting Asheville Writers in the Schools and Community (AWITSC) in my name: Ken Abbott, Cassandra Love, Jennifer Murphy, Beverly West, Elizabeth Wills, and Cindy Trisler and Rodney Bowling at Mudluscious Pottery and Gardens.

West Wolf, ho! One of the biggest takeaways of the Hastings Cutoff fiasco could be stated thus: *Don't risk traveling uncharted trails in the family wagon!* My writing career has been a long series of untried cutoffs, trackless mountains, and barren deserts. There have been unforeseen storms, cracked axles, and broken bones. And perhaps I should have left my family "back east." Perhaps I should have made the journey alone, just me and my gun and a sturdy mule. But through every dry spell, stumble, and mudhole, my family has been there with me. So thanks to Ginger West and our "not-so-Littles," Simon, Ethan, and Jameson Wolf.

Huzzah, y'all.